Native Believer

Native Believer

Ali Eteraz

Published by Akashic Books
©2016 Ali Eteraz

ISBN: 978-1-61775-436-4
Library of Congress Control Number: 2015954060

First printing

Akashic Books
Twitter: @AkashicBooks
Facebook: AkashicBooks
E-mail: info@akashicbooks.com
Website: www.akashicbooks.com

Perhaps home is not a place but simply an irrevocable condition.
—James Baldwin, *Giovanni's Room*

If you can't be free, be a mystery.
—Rita Dove, "Canary"

. . . the boys who settled in America—and they always have this odd tamed look, a bit sheepish . . .
—Daniyal Mueenuddin, "Our Lady of Paris"

CHAPTER ONE

This is the story of an apostate's execution. It begins two years ago, under Mars, when I invited the people of Plutus Communications to our apartment and served prosciutto palmiers, braised ram shanks, and bull-tail stew. The aim of the festivity was to welcome, to bewitch, to charm one George Gabriel, the Philadelphia branch's new boss sent from New York. By appealing to him I hoped to circumvent the hierarchs who had prevented me from getting my own team at work, who had sequestered me in the wrongly named Special Projects.

The deeper I got into my thirties—the decade where choice replaces chance as the Prime Mover of life—the better I became at such supplicatory hosting. I wore charcoal slacks and an off-white cardigan with silver buttons. In America, those who want something have to dress like those who already have everything.

I pulled open the curtain and confirmed the snow outside. The art museum, with green streaks in its fading copper, sat on its stony plinth like an old country dame, once a beautiful golden goddess, now crisscrossed with varicose veins, incapable of getting up. Chipped stairs fell like an aged necklace at her feet. A solitary man trudged up the steps, the gauzy snow-curtain a wedge that perforated around him. It was cold outside, but within me there was warmth.

I made the preparations alone, while Marie-Anne, my wife of nine years, after spending a week at MimirCo's headquarters in Virginia, took the train back from DC. I wondered how she would greet me. Her departure had not been amicable. When I had dropped her off at 30th Street Station I had made the mistake of gesturing toward a pair of toddlers. "Control your uterus," she had retorted. "So tired of your ovulation."

Marie-Anne wasn't expected until eight, around the same time as the guests. But she took the Acela and got into 30th Street Station two hours early. She cabbed it home and burst through the door of our apartment, throwing the luggage near the umbrella rack, shuffling my way with arms extended. She had forgotten the events of a week ago and I was ready to forgive as well. If I was ever going to persuade her to start a family, I had to show her that I was an edifice of patience and absolution, like a father was supposed to be.

"I-can't-analyze-any-more-video," she droned.

"There's my busy buzzard." I always used that phrase, partly because of the consonance and partly because her job involved hovering above others. "How is work?"

"So many feeds. We are in four countries now."

Marie-Anne's job at MimirCo involved taking notes on video collected by unmanned aerial vehicles and writing brief summaries about the hours of footage. Most of what she described were naturalist scenes, with the occasional appearance by human subjects. As a creative writing graduate, Marie-Anne was well suited to writing about topography.

"Well, now it's the weekend. Now you can rest."

"MimirCo doesn't take a day off," she said. "I brought the laptop home. I have a bunch of reports to write."

"I thought you were gonna call them vignettes . . ."

"Yeah, then I can change the locations and submit them to literary journals!"

She grasped me by the waist and pulled. She was a tall, full-figured, plump woman, standing six-foot-one over my five-foot-eight. When she wore heeled riding boots, like now, I had to look up at her even more than usual.

We touched tongues because it was easier than extending our necks. She fluttered hers. When Marie-Anne was in a good mood like this—which had been rare since MimirCo expanded operations to the Middle East and Africa—her light-green eyes kindled warm and she ran her white hands through her titian hair in such a way that there was no one more enthralling.

"You didn't need to catch the early train," I said. "I have everything under control."

"I wanted to work out before the party," she said, tugging at the flesh on her waist. "If I hurry I can still get it done."

"Gotcha. Well, I hung your workout clothes in the bathroom. And your poem is in its usual spot."

She changed, put her music player on her arm, and, because it was difficult for her to bend forward and reach her feet to tug on her sneakers, sat down on the floor.

Three years ago she had put on forty pounds, almost overnight, going from a voluptuous size twelve to a hefty twenty-four. She started working out like a triathlete, but this only served to increase her weight. Twenty more pounds gained. And another ten. The doctors couldn't figure it out. Then it was discovered that it all had to do with cortisol. The hormonal steroid in our bodies that helped our ancestors scurry away from saber-tooth and woolly mammoth; the engine behind the flight mechanism; the stress hormone. Under normal conditions, after peaking during a moment of stress, cortisol was supposed to go back down, to let the body decelerate. But in Marie-Anne, after every stressful incident, cortisol increased.

"I am basically a 'roider," she'd said when they told us that her hormones had a hard time coming to rest. In fact, that was why her initial exercising had worsened her weight: it had come out of panic. The doc-

tor said that she would only be able to lose weight if she attained perfect tranquility. Not only in the day-to-day, by way of better breathing
and mental relaxation, but also by being in a harmonious mental state
when she exercised. I didn't get to learn more about the problem because
Marie-Anne said it made her self-conscious for me to speak with her
doctors and it would be best if I left myself out of future conversations
between "me and my physicians." I had respected her wishes.

As for the exercise and the tranquility, we had come up with a solution on our own. I was to write her a poem before every visit to the
gym, because she said my poems reminded her of our first few months
together, soothed her. Over the past three years I had written close to
six hundred poems. Iambic pentameter. Blank verse. Abecedarians. Son-
nets. It hadn't been easy because I was more a reader than a writer. But
by studying everyone from the Elizabethans to the Germans to the Vic-
torians and Americans, I had managed a steady output. And the tactic
had been effective. Marie-Anne shed thirty pounds. She was not close
to where she wanted to be, but she was on her way, there was progress. I
took delight in the notion that we had united not just our wills, but even
art and exercise, all to push back against the hegemony of disease. It was
the kind of self-sacrificing defense that a couple could only pull off in a
marriage, where the early incendiary crackle of passion turned into the
more sedate but reliable warmth of loyalty, where you could trust the
other person not to bail on you after you had helped them.

But the fight wasn't just about me and Marie-Anne. It was about
children. She told me that the doctors had said that unless she lost the
weight, they would advise us against trying to have children. In fact, they
said that while the child would likely handle birth just fine, because of
the hormonal imbalance the weight caused, labor could be fatal for the
mother. The thought of putting Marie-Anne at risk was obviously unac-
ceptable. But the thought of going without children was unbearable as
well. I was a second-generation American with dead parents. I had no

aunts or uncles or siblings. I had no community. Putting children into the American bloodstream was the only way for me to have a people. I simply could not let that chance slip away. I couldn't be the end, because I hadn't even gotten to begin. My poems, therefore, were not just the soundtrack to weight loss. They were, however badly weighted, spears prodding against oblivion.

Marie-Anne went to the gym downstairs. I imagined the two security guards ignoring her as she walked past. Once she would've been ogled, their eyes peppering her rump, her waist, the palpitation of admiration thrumming through their bodies, cocks. But that Marie-Anne was gone. Now she only had bloated elbows and folded shoulders. I pictured her walking, collapsed into herself, like she was seeking to disappear into some central cavity, calling herself the Michelin Woman, Pillsbury Doughgirl, Big Bertha. Despite her self-pity, I admired her. How could she keep going like that? Making one step follow another, and all with a smile on her face? I, meanwhile, felt broken if someone didn't notice my new cuff links or a new haircut. Marie-Anne had an inner reservoir of survival that I didn't. Where other people might have scattered, she became gathered. She made me wonder if there were two types of people in the world: the lakes and the sands. If so, I was among the latter, the lesser.

I went back to the kitchen and checked on the drinks, placing the bottles of Latour and Papé Clement in line with our egg-shaped bowls with beveled stems. I found a soft cloth and cleaned each glass thrice. Then I arranged the Belgian beers purchased at Monk's near Rittenhouse, and removed every smudge from their surface.

Finally, there was the centerpiece of our wine collection, given to us as a gift by Marie-Anne's father the last (and final) time he had come up from South Carolina: a single bottle of Cheval Blanc '98. I wiped it down and pushed it to a more prominent position. Dr. Quinn had come alone, without his wife, Florence Quinn, who didn't socialize with us.

I made one more sweep of the living room. Found a couple of inkless pens, a limp headband, and an unmarked bottle of pills. Vitamins by the look of them. I put everything on Marie-Anne's desk.

It was cardio day for Marie-Anne. She came back within thirty minutes. Her round moon face, with its thickness across the neck and back of the head, was covered in a watery sheen. The cortisol spike had also made her hairier. The thick sideburns were like red steam shooting from her ears. Her scent had also thickened—a peppery ferocity. Since she started exercising her limbs had thinned out a little, but her middle was still expansive. She resembled a kind of sun-dried brick. But this was better than the ball she used to be before the exercise.

She gave me a peck on the forehead, put the poem in a scrapbook, and went to the shower. A few minutes later she came out wearing the tight purple sweater dress that I had laid out. She had added black stockings to it. She considered putting on a pair of boots and then dismissed the idea "since it's my own house." The dress was an old one, before "the great expansion" as she called it, and it was still a couple of sizes too small. I regretted my error. But I wasn't about to suggest that she should change. I was still in love with her and enjoyed the gratuitous sight of her flesh. More flesh on your beloved was just more beloved flesh.

She stood in the doorway outside the second bedroom, which doubled as our study. I came up to her and touched her hip. She playfully pushed me on the chest. But as I was fading away she grasped me by the wrist and crushed me back into herself. She put her hand on the top of my skull and turned my head toward the room.

"What is that?" She pointed to the desk I had purchased in her absence.

"Don't worry," I said. "It's not a crib."

She ignored my dig. "You got new furniture without checking with me? It looks expensive."

My tone turned into a salesman's. I walked up to the desk and waved my hand up and down its side like a showgirl. "Listen, Marie-Anne, just hear me out. Acquired in the heart of Philadelphia's historic Antique Row, this desk, this tan burr walnut desk, represents a Southern revivalist strain of design. A triple-paneled leather top, and look, just look, at these piecrust edges. And the drawers, would you believe, they have swan handles. The whole thing rests on cabriole legs. Just imagine the history that sits in the soul of this desk. Imagine how much of America it has witnessed."

She walked around it, trailing her finger behind herself like the train on a dress. "I like it."

"Well, that was easy."

"I'm easy when you persuade with Southern jingoism."

"Does that mean that you're about to go down on me?"

"No, Lord Dark Wind, I am not." The nickname had a backstory. In the comics, Lord Dark Wind was the Asian scientist who injected adamantium into Wolverine's body. Marie-Anne called me this whenever I requested fellatio because giving me head created a metallic taste in her mouth.

We headed into the living room and waited for the guests. Marie-Anne put Erik Satie's *Gymnopédies and Gnossiennes* on the stereo and we stood by our tenth-floor window overlooking the southeastern edge of Fairmount Park. She hugged me from behind and we watched the snow spread over Philadelphia. Denuded trees, bereft of their vegetative ornaments, cowered in the wind. One tree, standing in the grove next to a town house, inscribed with a long knotted branch something invisible upon the glass.

I leaned back and let myself feel at peace. Maybe her good mood meant Marie-Anne would be able to impress George Gabriel a little. Maybe the social capital gained could bring an end to my career rut. Maybe a raise would follow. The extra cash would be nice, because for the longest time I had been raving about one of those retro-looking cast-iron stoves, the ones that came fitted with lava rocks, teppanyaki grills, and induction plates. My mouth drooled at the thought of the cooking that could be done on such a range.

Marie-Anne, meanwhile, went back to the bedroom and decided she was more comfortable in a long skirt and a long white dress shirt.

I heard her standing in front of the mirror, referring to herself as a polar bear.

It was the old secretaries of Plutus Communications—Danielle, Beatrice, and Connie—who were first to arrive. They had lived in the city all their lives and took our view toward North Philadelphia as an opportunity to talk about the city's history. They panned their hands along the length of Girard Avenue and talked about when the black neighborhoods were white, before the Great Migration brought Southern blacks into Philadelphia.

"How're y'all liking the food?" I asked.

Beatrice chuckled and fixed her horn-rimmed glasses. "I never got over how you still say that. Even after all these years with us Yankees. How long now?"

"Thirteen years since I left Atlanta," I replied. "But why wouldn't I talk like that? I was born in Alabama. Cow-tipping country."

The laughter caused the briefly formed convergence to pulsate. I looked at Marie-Anne with concern in my eyes because no one else had shown up yet. She sensed my disquiet and squeezed my arm. I checked on the texts and e-mails. There weren't any. Most of the people who I had invited, though familiar with me as a colleague, didn't know me well enough to keep me updated about their arrival. I hadn't even gotten RSVPs.

It took ten more minutes of nervous small talk with Danielle before someone else arrived. It was a group of three. Sam Arrington, Aaron Paul, and Mark Stark. They were associates, about four years my junior. I took their coats. They had heard about the party from one of the secretaries. They didn't recall having met me; but I knew exactly who they were because I had been the one to orient them on their first day at work and I had an uncanny ability to remember the names of people who didn't remember mine. Their coats smelled of dogs.

Carla and Jesse, two of the newest, came in next. They had found parking in a little row called Pig's Alley and we laughed about the eccentric name. They stood and chatted with me until they realized that I was on Special Projects and not on a particular team, and they went off to merge with Sam, Aaron, and Mark.

The three members of my former team—Candace Cooper, Mark Vasquez, and Dinesh Karthik—were the next to arrive. I greeted them with as much effusiveness as I could muster and then let them be. They huddled in their coats and mittens near the door, leaving poodle-shaped puddles at their feet. I was a little surprised that they had come, particularly after Mark had gotten Dinesh to push me out. It hadn't been very pleasant working with them, but I did miss Candace, whom I had hired and then watched as she leapfrogged me. I could tell she wasn't certain if she should come over and chat. In the end she stayed with her team. I could hear her complaining about the effects of the moisture on her hair. She wished she had gotten her mother's hair instead of her father's.

The idling guests rolled their heads around the apartment and made approving comments. They pointed to the Venetian crystal swans, to a Greek vase, and to the Chagall hanging over the fireplace.

"The painting is a knock-off," I said out loud so no one would impute to us wealth of the sort that people like Marie-Anne's parents in South Carolina possessed, the kind of wealth that wouldn't be passed to us because Marie-Anne had married me against their wishes. Dr. Quinn would have been willing to get over his daughter's decision, but Marie-Anne's mother still maintained a healthy distance from us. We expected that she would maintain it all the way to her death. "Mother grew up Catholic," Marie-Anne liked to explain. "She is unable to forgive betrayal."

My eyes went to the Blanc. Our lack of real affluence, the entrenched wealth people called *old money*, was what made the Blanc even more important. Its presence said that despite our apparent mediocrity we were a couple who aspired higher, expected more from the world. It allowed me to imply to the people of Plutus that we would be better than them, even if I didn't always have confidence that we would be.

The bottle served its function well. Draped in its white robe, with the chateau's two seals in baroque gold, and the *1998* written within filigreed vine, it seemed to command enough attention that even though it wasn't open yet I could go and stand next to it and hold a discussion about it. I told everyone the story of how the owner of the legendary chateau once released his attack dogs upon a critic who had given his wine a bad review.

That wasn't all the hype. Translating "Cheval Blanc" as "White Horse," I brought up the tavern of the same name in New York City where the poet Dylan Thomas had taken his last drink. I didn't know a single verse from the guy, but he was among those artists who tended to be feted more for the myth of their persona than for their output, which made it unnecessary to have any familiarity with his work.

The conversation about White Horse Tavern created greater interest in the Cheval Blanc. My approach had been effective. Americans only truly understood the world when it was defined for us in reference to things we already knew. For example, referring to Osama bin Laden with the epithet of Geronimo, or using the sports names Celtics, Mavericks, and Red Wings to refer to military operations in Afghanistan.

We socialized and drank while waiting for the final guest, the new boss, George Gabriel. Soft candles warmed the room. Those that wicked out, Marie-Anne replaced with new flames. I didn't have George's cell phone number so had no way of checking if and when he might come. I also couldn't ask anyone for it in case they turned out to have it. That would confirm to them that they were closer to George than I was.

Marie-Anne went to the stereo and replaced Erik Satie's soft pianistic sprinkles with Enrico Caruso's soaring tenor. The music filled the empty time-space between the guests, producing a sense of greater familiarity. I approached Candace Cooper because she had drifted away from the others. Clinking my drink with hers, I asked her how her acting classes were going.

"You remember?"

"I pay attention."

"It's not Shakespeare or anything."

"The opera we are listening to? It's *Macbeth*. Adapted by Verdi."

Candace's brown eyes flickered. She wiped her hand on her forehead and played with her curls. My eyes turned to the window. An occasional snowflake flitted down the glass and left a web.

I was just about to find someone else to speak to when clutching the seam of her skirt, walking bowlegged, Marie-Anne came over with great concern on her face. She grabbed me by the wrist and waddled with me toward the bathroom. "The flood is here," she said, looking around to make sure no one heard us, "and Noah doesn't have an ark."

"What?"

She raised her eyebrows and gestured between her legs with her chin. "Out of tampons. I can't find the second box. The bleeding."

I pulled her into the bathroom and shut the door. One of the effects of her hormonal imbalance was that her menstruation was extremely heavy. On a good day she went through five tampons. I looked at the toilet paper; it was all gone. I rushed to the cupboard. The second box of tampons was empty. I had forgotten to pick up a replacement.

Marie-Anne sat down on the toilet and sobbed. "It will get on my skirt."

I clenched my fists and knelt down on the cold tile in front of her. I stroked her arms and spoke with resolve, putting a second toilet paper roll in her hand. "I'm going to run to the pharmacy."

"I love you," she said.

"I love you too," I replied. "Just sit tight."

I locked Marie-Anne in, composed myself, and tried to sneak out the front door of the apartment. I had only made it to the kitchen when Candace came to me with her head tilted to the side, trying to whisper into my ear.

"Something's wrong with Marie-Anne."

"You noticed?"

"Just the way she ran out. Is it a woman issue?"

"It is," I said. "But her issues are my issues too."

She opened her purse and walked me back to the bathroom. She had two tampons in her hand. "Don't leave your party."

I blushed. "Thank you so much."

"Consider this good karma for when you got me hired."

With a deep breath I entered the humid bathroom. Marie-Anne was dabbing her eyes with toilet paper and had taken off her shoes. She saw the tampons in my hand.

"My savior."

"Just your average Southern gentleman."

"Southerners aren't average," she said.

She propped her right foot up on her toes and with a bent arm applied the tampon. I observed the rise of the bones in her feet, like piano keys popping. Long lines with gaps of skin in between. The indentations reminded me of a time Marie-Anne had gotten cornrows, back in college, during volleyball season. She hadn't been unwell then. The memory of her healthy and spry, resolute like a tree, without sap leaking out of her, brought tears to my eyes. I took the square she had been using and dabbed my eyes with it.

Marie-Anne got up and smoothed her skirt, joyous that there was no stain. I washed my face. One after another we resumed entertaining our guests. They remained oblivious to the effort we put into their seduction.

* * *

The doorbell rang. Once, twice. I turned on the first toll and nodded at Marie-Anne. I wanted her to be the one George Gabriel saw upon entry.

He was a surprisingly tall man, much taller than Marie-Anne, with big wide shoulders, wearing a bespoke gray suit that no longer fit well on account of his expanding gut. He was bald, head full of treasure-map freckles, bushy blond eyebrows, and clean-shaven, though the shadow on the cheeks suggested he had come straight from work. I noticed his eyes, which looked like insects that had been stamped on his face. His overall appearance made me miss my last boss, Tony Blanchard, who, as the first person of color to run a regional Plutus office, wasn't just the life of the party, but also knew how to dress. Tony had been a legend in every way and had deservedly been promoted to work with the lobbyists in DC where he would never have to worry about turning a profit because in the American capital everyone got paid, especially those like him who helped people get contracts.

Marie-Anne guided George my way. I moved forward and extended my hand. It occurred to me that George had been at work three days already and yet this was the first time I had interacted with him. As we shook hands I angled him into the shade of the Blanc. "A very warm Philadelphia welcome from all of us," I said with a raised voice. "On a very cold Philadelphia night . . ."

The room turned toward us, expecting some kind of response from George, verbal acknowledgment, hell, a smile. But he only waved and turned away, as if they were easily dismissible.

One by one people returned to their conversations. None of them tried to come over. Marie-Anne and I were the only ones with George. He glanced around and dug his thick-knuckled fingers into a bowl, spilling raisins and cashews and macadamia nuts. I touched Marie-Anne on the small of her back to entice George to say something to her. No luck.

He juggled nuts in a palm and popped them into his mouth one at a time. Marie-Anne bit her lower lip and shrugged at me.

"Is this the art museum area?" he asked.

"It is," Marie-Anne said.

"There's a restaurant here I like. It's called Figs. I went there with my wife recently. It's Middle Eastern. But they call themselves Mediterranean. I don't think the countries on the eastern coast of the Mediterranean should use that term. It's misleading. Regardless, the food is exquisite."

I nodded. "We know Figs."

I expected George to say something more; but he had moved on. He pointed to the wall with his middle finger, a nut between forefinger and thumb. "That. Interesting painting. I have seen this one. I do believe I have seen it."

"It's called *The Poet*," Marie-Anne said, running her hand over the image of the upside-down green head taking a cup of tea with a wine bottle near him. "By Chagall."

"Are you aware that Chagall was a Jew?" George looked at me.

"Yes, I believe his first name was Moishe," I said. "Russian. Going with his Jewish name was a big deal. Jewish artists in Russia could either hide their roots or express them. He was one who chose to express them." I said all this in a glib manner, because I was actually insulted by his initial question. There was little about Western cultural history I didn't know. And I was always updating and revising that knowledge. All this technology that came out every few months was developed for people like me. I was a man who ate the West, breakfast, lunch, and dinner.

"And what do you think about that?" George slid next to me. "Which side do you fall on? Hide or express?"

"Do I look Jewish?"

I had meant it as a joke. But the grim look on George's face made me pause. I wondered if I should clarify that I wasn't making a comment about what Jews looked like; rather, I couldn't be expected to second-guess the fear, the pressure, the persecution that Russian Jews of a particular time and age had been creating art against.

Trying to find a way out of Lake Awkward, I found a life preserver on my bookshelf. I reached forward and touched my copies of Ozick, Chabon, and Roth, with near-ritual piety. "But all kidding aside, in answer to your question, today's Jewish artists seemed to have followed the route of expression. Children of Chagall, one might call them."

George Gabriel seemed to find my answer either perfectly adequate or entirely worthless and dropped the line of inquiry. Piqued by the books, he came forward to inspect the bookshelf. The mahogany fixture hung on the wall and had five levels. The bottommost contained a Balinese carnival mask Marie-Anne and I had picked up during our second honeymoon. It was porcelain white and had two faces, one male and one female. The next three levels contained books. And the topmost shelf, far out of casual reach, was empty. George ignored the mask and got lost in reading every last title. Because of his immense height he had to bend and crane in a peculiar way.

Marie-Anne watched George turn away and excused herself to go and open the Blanc. This brought a small cheer from the crowd, and they huddled around the table. George didn't seem fazed by the other guests. He inspected each and every book, trying to read the tiniest inscription, asking me where I had purchased them, even their prices.

I gave him one-word answers, looking to the party with envy. Here I was, stuck with this boorish inquisitor, while the others were enjoying themselves. I became irritated by his presence. With the way he flicked his hands in his pocket and made the nuts rattle, and the way he poked his fingers around like he had three little erections. I was also annoyed that he had come completely empty-handed. I was even annoyed that judging by his dry clothes it could be surmised that he hadn't even suffered the ignominy of a distant parking spot. My mind rushed. What kind of name was George Gabriel? Where was he from? What was up with that Jewish question?

It struck me that I had played this hand badly. Had I presented Marie-Anne too blatantly? Had I been too earnest in my welcome? Was it too obvious that I was trying to appeal to him? Maybe George Gabriel had simply seen through my game and now everything was a kind of taunt.

I began wishing I had invited Richard Konigsberg, the man who had brought me into Plutus and otherwise sponsored me through the gauntlets of the profession. He had what I lacked, and what Marie-Anne, as a woman, couldn't be too blatant about: the authority to command, to instruct, to establish order. "A big swinging dick," as Marie-Anne put it when describing men with standing.

It would be George, ultimately, who saved me from my rampant thoughts.

"I see you like your Goethe and your Nietzsche." He pointed to the complete works of both, taking up the third- and second-highest shelves.

I smiled. Despite the notoriety of the authors, talking about their work was actually the least controversial, least confrontational thing we could do. These two authors were my favorites. They qualified as my intellectual home court. I could talk about them casually, esoterically, academically; probably even make a poem about them. From the start of German romanticism to its end. The earlier antipathy George had inspired seemed to fade. Maybe there was still a way to ingratiate myself to him.

"Gods among men," I said.

"Agreed," he said with his first smile since arrival. "And definitely deserving of the elevated place you've given them." He put his hand up in the air and measured the distance of the books from the floor. "They should hover above us mortals. Hover over all the other books in the world."

George put a hand on my back. It was warm. He kneaded my shoulder. I felt a companionship form between the two of us and the book-shelf. George looked over to a row of idle people leaning against the sofa. He gestured at Mark. "You there. Bring me a glass of the Blanc."

Mark bowed without so much as a pause and returned holding the wineglass with both hands under the base. George throttled it. He was about to dismiss Mark but caught himself. "Get the host a drink as well." I wondered when in his life George had reached that moment when he attained total certitude. Were some people simply born with executive force? As the descendent of a subject race, I always feared that authority had to do with genealogy, a kind of historical grooming that took place unseen, maybe an enriching of one's blood, maybe a kind of spectral psychosexual force field that surrounded you. Whatever it was, I didn't have it and George did.

I did find a great deal of delight in seeing this sort of docility in Mark. When he had first gotten hired to our team he had completely sidelined Candace and me, refusing to answer our e-mails for unreasonable pe-riods, while taking himself straight to Dinesh's office to discuss all our ideas as his own. Dinesh started to think that the new employee was sim-ply more talented than the known quantities he used to work with, and appointed him our supervisor. Before long I ended up getting called into Dinesh's office, where Mark told me the news about the Special Projects assignment. Candace had survived, largely because Mark said that it was good for male morale to have a pretty female to look at.

Mark came back with a bottle of Chimay. He thrust it into my hand and backpedaled. I was disappointed not to get some of the Blanc, but there was nothing I could say.

"Just curious," George said after sloshing and gargling his first sip and letting out a satisfied moan. "What's that? Up on the empty shelf?"

I shrugged. "Nothing?"

"No, there's something. All the way to the back. Can you not see it? It's something on a stand."

I had always thought that was just the dusty shelf in the house, the empty one, the one too far to reach, the one that, when I cleaned, I made a little halfhearted flip of a towel at, and that was that.

I got on my toes and then made a pair of desperate hops. My eyes fell upon something, a small X-shaped wooden stand with something multicolored resting upon it. I waited for George to recognize that I wasn't tall enough to grasp it; but he didn't move until I verbally requested his assistance. "Please?"

"Yes, sure," he said, pretending that he hadn't noticed my struggle.

He took a long sip from his glass. Then, with a casual sweep, he brought the colored object off the wooden stand and handed it to me.

It was a little palm-sized item, wrapped in a glittery pink cloth cover. I put my beer on the shelf and inspected it. The pouch bore my name in green thread. The stitching reminded me of the way my mother used to identify the inside of my golf uniform back in high school in Alabama. I grew nervous. Since she had passed away, this was my first encounter with something that I knew had touched her hands.

George, gleeful at the thought of a new discovery in someone else's home, leaned in and blew at the dusty pouch. There was a book inside.

I assisted him by swiping my hand over the cloth. Then, with a deep breath, I put forefinger and middle finger into the pouch and pulled at the book. I hadn't so much as touched the calligraphic arabesques on the spine when I figured out what it was. And rather than pulling it out, I stuffed it deeper and prepared to launch myself up and put it back on the shelf.

"What is it?" George whispered, lowering his head like a giraffe in search of water.

"Nothing," I said. "Nothing. Just something my mother must have put there the last time she visited."

"How classic. So what is it?"

"Nothing exciting," I said. "Just a miniature Koran in a pouch. She came here for the last time after my dad passed away and before she left us. I guess she had nothing to do but stitch and sew this cover."

I thought that upon being told that both my parents were dead, George would adopt an attitude of condolence, of reluctance, become a little less excited. But he had no such inclination. He thrust his wine glass into my hand and yanked out the Koran. Then, with his mouth still full of the Blanc, he ruffled the pages with a slide of his thumb. He wiped it on his pants, licked his middle finger, and browsed through a few more pages. His fingers seemed to discover the ribbon bookmark and he flipped toward the end of the volume. "Chapter 74," he said out loud. "The Hidden Secret." He looked at me, popped his eyebrows a couple of times, and then went back to skimming. At last he closed the Koran, inspected it, and handed it back. It was in his possession no more than fifteen seconds.

I didn't know what to say. I avoided George's gaze. I took back the Koran, slid it into the pouch, and moved to place it back atop the shelf.

As I got on my toes, I heard George chuckle behind me. "You're putting something higher than Nietzsche?"

"It's just a decoration." I came back down and dusted my hands.

"Are you sure it's not an expression of your residual supremacism?"

I turned into a pillar of salt. "Pardon?"

"I'm just noting," he said, both hands up, but with a smile on his face, "that without thinking, you put the collected works of Muhammad above the collected works of Nietzsche. A theist over an antitheist. The Prophet of Arabia over the Devil of Bavaria. I'm just asking if that was an expression of some residual supremacism on behalf of the Koran."

"I didn't mean anything by putting it where I put it. I just put it."

"That's my point," he persisted. "You did it without even thinking."

"It's just a decoration, George," I said. "And besides, if I was thinking of anything, it was of my late mother."

He became apologetic, returning to the inquisitive and empathetic person he had been earlier, when he had been kneading my shoulder. I felt his firm hands on my back again, this time a little lower than before. "Hey, cheers," he said, offering his glass. "To matriarchs."

He appeared genuine. There was a glimmer of gentle warmth in his eyes. I nodded with a smile and clinked, leading him away from the bookshelf. We briefly discussed what we most missed about our mothers and grandmothers. His mother had left him when he was a teenager and his grandmother had died during the bombing in Dresden. He said she deserved it; she had been an avid Nazi.

As the night went on, people became increasingly drunk, and the frostiness outside kept the party going. In her drunken state, Danielle declared half the firm to be anti-Semitic and revealed that her love of Jews began as a result of a tryst with Woody Allen. We had a good time cross-examining her and revealing the story to be hokum.

As for George, once he was properly drunk, he sidled up to Marie-Anne and asked her probing questions about where she had grown up and what she did for work. She managed to keep him at half an arm's length, and yet he was wound up in her like a comb in her hair.

I moved aside with Candace Cooper. When I put my hand on her waist she downed the wine like a shot. Dabbing her mouth with the back of her wrist she tried to lock eyes with me. But she separated her mouth from the skin too quickly and there was a little runoff of wine down her arm, into her sleeve. She was about to say something when Dinesh appeared and took her away by the arm. I bubbled in anger at the ease with which she was swept away. She always had a tendency to let people strong-arm her.

Marie-Anne saw me standing alone and came over to hold my hand, encouraging me to take in the scene, telling me of a job well done, running her middle finger down the center of my palm to indicate her approval. Whenever we organized a party and it went well, she tended to want to play. It had something to do with having expressed Southern hospitality perfectly, the satisfaction of having done something that would have made her mother happy. I asked her about the bleeding. She said that the success of the party had improved her mood and things were under control.

My eyes stayed on George Gabriel. He walked to Candace and pulled her out of the conversation with Dinesh and led her toward the window. I willed for her to resist him but she did not.

I turned to Marie-Anne and smiled, doing whatever I could to not look at the bookshelf looming behind her. Every time my eyes went toward the top shelf, I redirected my gaze to a picture of Marie-Anne playing volleyball in college. Her youthful beauty was the only thing in the room that could prevent me from spinning into the hole that George Gabriel had opened.

Once the guests were gone, Marie-Anne waited for me to get into bed and then spooned me from behind, reaching around and taking my cock in her hand. Our feet were at the same level; her head was higher than mine. She threw one wide thigh over my hip and planted kisses on the top of my skull. This was the position in which most of our play was inaugurated.

"How tall do you think that girl Candace is?" she whispered.

"She can't be more than five feet tall," I replied, pushing my buttocks into her groin. Marie-Anne had often told me I had a "model ass." Once, during the early days of her weight gain, she even made me wear a pair of her boy-shorts because she said my ass looked better in them than hers.

"Five feet? She might even be shorter than that," she said.

"She's skinny, isn't she?"

Marie-Anne bit into my neck. "Skinnier than any black girl I've seen."

"She's actually a mix."

Marie-Anne bit again. "Crafted like a ballerina. An ice skater."

"I think she used to be a gymnast. Now she wants to be an actress."

"Tell me where I run into her."

I knew where she wanted to go and cleared my throat to take her there. But I was still caught up in my encounter with George. I straightened up a little, stiffened my back, and turned to try to talk about the incident at the bookshelf; but Marie-Anne didn't let me start. She was in that tipsy place. She put a finger on my lip and put her mouth on mine. My protestation became passion. I kissed for a while and pulled my mouth free to give her the bedtime story she wanted.

In it Marie-Anne was a vampire queen, the mistress of a sector of Philadelphia, assigned by the vampire high command to convert pretty little girls to darkness. "You see Candace at the gym," I said. "You are doing the elliptical. She's in the dance area. Glass separates you. She is dressed in stockings and a leotard. Her hair is up in a bun. Her skinny neck is exposed."

"Her clavicle is thin. Breakable." Marie-Anne started sucking on my neck. Then she rolled back and lifted her leg for a moment so I could turn around and face her. She gave me a little kiss and with both of her hands on the top of my head pushed me down until my mouth was latched onto her breasts. She took a pillow and put it between her legs. I suckled and periodically glanced up at her.

"You are sweaty and hot after your workout. You go into the dance studio to stare at her. She is stretching with her leg up on the bar. Suddenly she loses her balance and you rush forward to grasp her. You hold her, you keep her upright. You inhale her scent. She is overwhelmed by your scent."

"My tits . . ."

"Your big tits press against her back. You hold her small body in your arms. You tell her she is safe."

"I tell her she is tiny."

"Yes," I licked her nipple, "you tell her she's tiny. A toy."

"She's a doll."

I licked harder. "You know what to do with dolls."

Marie-Anne nodded and increased her pace. "I know what to do with dolls. They are to be played with."

"Do you play with her?"

"I take her home. I play with her. All the people see me leave with her. All the men. All the men were staring at her. All the black men and all the white men. They all want her. All the big swinging dicks. But I take her."

"Do you play with your doll in your bed?"

Marie-Anne's thighs squeezed harder on the pillow and she rocked faster. "I throw my leg over her like I throw my leg over you and suck on her tongue."

"What else do you suck on?"

"I suck on her neck," she growled. "I suck on her neck. I bite into her neck. She is afraid. She is afraid I will bite into her jugular. I will drink her blood."

"Are you converting her?"

"I am converting her. I'm showing her I'm her boss. I'm showing her she can't show herself off to anyone but me."

"And she will know you are her—"

"Mistress!" Marie-Anne screamed her trigger word. Whenever she uttered it I knew my job was to start licking her nipple even harder, to clamp onto her erogenous point with puckered lips and teasing tongue and not let up until she climaxed. The rest of the Candace story wouldn't take place with words. It would take place inside Marie-Anne's mind. Her eyes closed. Her mouth opened. She was in that imaginary bed with Candace, where Marie-Anne was the owner, where Marie-Anne was the empress. I licked. My mouth grew tired, still I licked. My tongue dried up, still I licked. My jaw hurt, still I licked. It wouldn't be long now. Within her vision Marie-Anne would soon reach her desired apogee.

The moment when her authority over Candace would be so immense that it would make her explode. I just had to keep licking, to do nothing surprising, to let her have a perfect mental encounter. Ballerinas. And dolls. And sluts. College girls who wore yoga pants with dirty words written across the backside. And interns in six-inch heels. And masseuses with tight little bodies. And innocent virgins brought into the realm of vampirism. Marie-Anne consumed them all, in this, our interpretation of sex. Marie-Anne clutched my head to her chest. I felt the tension in her thighs. And then there was no more, only the unreeling of her existence. A shudder. Then a harder shudder. And then she was still. She'd consumed Candace, chewed her up, turned her into wetness.

"Goddamn," she said with a kind of ripple in her voice. "That was so perfect."

"You're perfect."

"Your turn," she said. My face was between her breasts. She considered them necessary and sufficient for me to climax.

I stroked. Because she didn't take birth control for the weight gain it caused, I was expected to stay out of her. Condoms weren't an option because I couldn't stay hard in them. We had tried every kind.

I suckled and pumped. Marie-Anne encouraged with touching and cooing. Before long I was at the threshold. I made sure to angle myself so I spilled on her thighs and not between her legs. An accident like that would have messed up her buzz. The last thing she needed was a reminder of mortality.

Before she fell asleep Marie-Anne said that she liked how I was always willing to channel girls into our bed for her. She said it was my superpower.

I kissed her on her hand and told her *she* was my superpower.

I soon got up to take a shower.

Under the water I was calm because of the orgasm and thought about the party in a new light. I told myself that I had panicked for no reason and recited a couple of quotes by Nietzsche. He and Goethe, along with Wallace Stevens and Emily Dickinson, always had a calming effect on me. The dead poets represented the apex of Western wisdom, a revelation made not of light but of words, one that was approachable, which you could access because it was made by fallible beings instead of dropped down by faultless angels.

When I came out and dried myself, I did so in front of Marie-Anne's volleyball picture. It reminded me of our origin story, and a good origin story, like the kind we had, was the best thing in the world.

I had met her in college, when she played volleyball at Emory and was called Hangtime. The name had to do with her aerial prowess. When she leapt there was a natural double-clutch in her body, a kind of belated twitch in the torso that allowed her to stay airborne far longer than any other player at the net. In volleyball terms this made her ideally suited to play the position of the destructive outside hitter. Just as everyone else would be coming down, her legs would fold a little and she would rise for a brief moment longer—a girl turned hovercraft—as her arm with the force of a trebuchet knocked the ball back into the court, leaving blisters on the hardwood. *"Haaang-time, Haaaang-time,"* the crowd would chant. For three years Marie-Anne led the conference in kills and regularly had as many blocks as Jackie Joao, the star Brazilian middle blocker who had an inch on Marie-Anne and weighed about twenty pounds less. It was rare for a joust—a loose-ball situation at the net—to go against Marie-Anne's squad. Like an alert sentry on a medieval rampart she would push the ball down onto the heads of the opposition. At her best, Marie-Anne's approach and jump were measured at nine foot eight. This would have allowed her to play for Division I powerhouses like Stanford and UCLA and possibly even take a shot at the Olympics. But the strike against her was that she had no high school experience, nor even any exposure to club play, and had not developed the necessary tactical agency to be part of a successful offensive system. Marie-Anne blamed her mother for keeping her "stunted."

Her mother had thought that sports were an inappropriate and un-dignified way for a young lady to order her life. There was the endless travel that inhibited stable family building. The casual dressing that in-dicated a complete disregard for aesthetics and fashion. And there was also the fear of lesbianism. Women couldn't be allowed to turn into men, her mother had consistently preached, and one way this pernicious thing happened was through sports. As a result, Marie-Anne's exceptional collegiate career went entirely unknown to her parents. They didn't find out how good she was. How she could fly. A butterfly of thunder and lightning, adorned in spandex shorts and crew socks, her ponytail like some manic crankshaft, pushing her up and down the escalator that only she could see.

I used to cover women's sports for the *Emory Wheel*. My beat was the tennis and swim teams. But one day at the student center, as I manned a table for a toy drive for tots, I saw Marie-Anne headed toward the gym with her friends, in those spandex shorts. The knee pads around her ankles loose like unwilling manacles; shoelaces undone; nearly a head taller than anyone around her. There was a drawstring bag over her shoulder, clapping against her sculpted thigh. She passed by me without looking my way, and in her lengthy form there was so much presence that I followed. I told myself that I was just going to the gym to write about the volleyball match against NYU. What I ended up writing, how-ever, was a four-page, single-spaced biography of Marie-Anne. Her mon-strous attacking prowess. How her coaches devised offensive schemes around her ability to hit kills crosscourt even if she was fading down the line. Her extraordinary leaping. Her jump serve, the only topspin serve on the team, that had an ace-to-fault ratio higher than former all-American Bernice Darren's. I took particular delight in that serve. What a thing of beauty the toss was. Like she was a waitress passing through a crowd with a tray, she would perch the ball on her palm, way up in the air, taking a moment to look around at her team, at the opposition, at her coaches, at the crowd. With a flick she tossed the ball both forward and high, releasing it as if it was a dragonfly, and then proceeded to run after it like an obsessed entomologist. She leapt over the line, the drawn hand smashed the ball, and the spanked sphere screamed through the air and made a dipping arc over the net. Sometimes the ball dipped so hard and so fast that the opponents didn't even have a chance to move. They would just look at one another after the play was over, as if the ball had traveled faster than communication.

There were other things too. Like the leadership Marie-Anne displayed, hugging, yelling, clapping, gesturing; I speculated that she was an ENTJ on the Myers-Briggs scale. She was intensely protective of the smaller players, especially when the enforcers on the other side tried intimidating them with stare-downs and smack talk. But the high point of the profile was a long paean to her presence, inspired by my course work at the time. How she redefined feminism, because instead of slouching and compressing herself to fit some ideal version of what constituted femininity, she occupied as much room as she desired. How she moved all over the court, confident in her mastery of space, a lioness in the Serengeti—an attitude that she would one day carry out into the world, and from which both men and women could draw lessons for their own lives. Without meaning to, I had taken her biggest sporting shortcoming, namely her freewheeling, and turned it into her asset, her strength. I finished by comparing her double-clutch to Michael Jordan's.

For me the profile hadn't been an attempt to appeal to the real Marie-Anne. It was something akin to worship, an articulation of sentiment that didn't demand affirmation in return. The thought of accessing someone like her—someone who looked like her, who hobnobbed with the fraternity boys, who drank alcohol on a fake ID—had never even entered my mind. I was content with the idealized version of her that

I had put on paper. The tall, glorious athlete. The apex of vitality and unrestrained energy. The superstar. Besides, I was cognizant of the distances between us, particularly related to size. I was short enough to be a jockey. She carried herself like an undomesticated mustang. There couldn't have been communion between us. But then, out of the blue, she had reached out. *You marketed me really well*, she wrote in an e-mail. *Do you want to come to the Tri Delt house and write a follow-up piece? ;-)*

It hadn't been an invitation of the romantic sort. It was exactly what she had written. In the meeting she and her sorority sisters decided that I could be very useful to them in promoting their activities and wanted to know if I was up for it. I agreed to everything, turning into Marie-Anne's personal publicist. Her life became my beat. If her sorority held an event, I wrote about it. If a group of her friends hosted a speaker, I was there in the front row. I helped her publicize her fundraising and I pushed feel-good stories about the volleyball team to various news stations around the city. It was an internship where the only payment was her validation. I never asked her out and she never suggested that there could be a romantic spark between us.

But loyalty became its own seduction. Because I was always around, always observing, always learning, Marie-Anne told me things that she didn't tell others, particularly her secret fondness for writing fiction. Between the volleyball team and the sorority house she never had the requisite solitude to write her stories, the ones about growing up under a suffocating mother, the ones about experimenting with girls at Christian youth camps. So under the guise of taking her away for an interview, or to have her look over my latest write-up about the sorority's activities, I would sneak her into my dorm room and let her write. I, meanwhile, lingered around, listened to Portishead, or printed quotes and plastered them on the wall. Once she finished a story, she left it for me to read when she was away and then tell her what I thought about it. We weren't in a relationship, but we were slowly getting there.

The story that brought us together for the first time was called "The Jock." It was about a muscular athlete named Henry, the star center of his college basketball team, who was regularly humiliated by his teammates because of his chastity. He pretended that it didn't bother him; but it hurt him that his love of the church, his immersion into the essence of Christ, didn't eliminate from the world the taunt of the peer, the sarcasm of other youths. The bullying became so bad that Henry killed himself, dramatically hanging himself in the nylon nets of a basketball hoop in the practice gym. The morbid story gave rise to our first conversation about sexuality. It allowed me to reveal to Marie-Anne that I was still a virgin. She shocked me and said she was too, and that she intended to remain that way until marriage, because she didn't trust anyone except her future husband, who was bound to her by something more meaningful than the accomplishment that was intercourse. "That's what I want too," I said. "To wait till marriage." I had exulted in response, because my parents had told me to 'stay a virgin until marriage, and because following their diktat had been easy given my anxiety with women. Within a few hours, in the sanctuary of the dorm room, surrounded by Marie-Anne's stories, I was in her arms, writhing and wrapping myself around her river of a body, lapping insistently, letting her tongue into my mouth. Oral penetration had been enough for us.

For a little while it had been unbelievable to me that, given the disparity in our sizes, Marie-Anne would want to be with me. When I pressed her about this she told me that she actually wanted to be with a man smaller and thinner than her. It was because of her only high school boyfriend. His name had been Emmit Thomas. A varsity football player whom she dated precisely because she thought she was meant to be with a bigger man. He had six inches and a hundred pounds on her. He forced himself on her in the car. He hadn't gotten as far as he wanted. But neither had she been able to stop him from overpowering her and getting some fingers into her before she managed to escape. It had been a watershed moment for her in terms of love. She would never again let herself be attracted to a bigger man; she feared the physical violence a male might inflict upon her more than the social consequences of flouting the aesthetics of gender relations. "It's not strangers that scare me," she had said. "I am scared of being scared of the ones closest to me." My smallness, in other words, imparted security. It had made sense to me, the way a doorstopper could hold an entire door.

Now here we were. More than a decade later, I was still propping her up. I put the picture down, smiled, and came to bed, the sleet outside slicing at the window. Marie-Anne was facing the other way in bed. I tucked myself into the depression around her body, wedging my nose and eyes between the bed and her fleshy back. I liked having my face covered. It kept nightmares from getting into the mouth.

CHAPTER TWO

P lutus was a full-service public relations company. We made and then kept things famous. We did this for our clients because they believed that fame translated into sales. Although this wasn't empirically true, or even verifiable, we didn't challenge their belief. Marketing was a religion that paid well and we would have been foolish to cast doubt upon our deity. Once a client sat down in our conference room overlooking the newly refurbished city hall—gleaming white from having been cleansed of its ashen scales—we promised them that their brands, their art, their accomplishments, their whatever, would make its way down to every lobbyist, governmental figure, reporter, blogger, product reviewer, critic, radio personality, local TV producer, bar, club, lounge, restaurant, and even the self-styled celebrities. "Your name will be known," we promised everyone. Communicators. That's what we were.

When I first got into the job, the snappy press release had been our most important tool. We would send the press release out and then go around to conventions, industry events, trade journals, business parties, and approach people of influence and hold conversations that were prefabricated and premeditated in every way. Using psychological cues, we would drill the name of the chosen product into the target's psyche.

The Internet changed the course of our work. Every mastodon on the street started thinking she could stamp around on the virtual highways and swing her tusks and pin people down long enough to tell them about a product or two. And for a while, yes, the firm teetered and tottered. In fact, that was when Richard Konigsberg had gotten pushed out. Ultimately we recovered, however, because in the end the Internet became too crowded, too chaotic, and there was a need for nodes, for guardians, gatekeepers. With our long list of contacts and friends we were perfectly poised to take that role. Individuals couldn't compete against an institution. We brought order to the savage web. It was like taming the Wild West, an act of enlightened imperialism.

I had gotten my start in boring industries. My first clients were a group of small wood-laminates manufacturers. They taught me about resin and bonding and adhesive and how school desks were made. Most of the big hitters in their industry had been based in the Deep South and looked at me funny when we first met. But after I told them my backstory and invoked SEC football and mentioned Marie-Anne, they seemed to open up.

Later I worked with the milk industry; horseshoe manufacturers; and a woman who built wood blocks for children. All these people were afflicted with the perennial inability to translate desire into persuasion. I bridged that gap for them.

Plutus used to have a good bit of competition in Philadelphia; but the other companies couldn't keep up with us. Yet recently we were confronted by a guerrilla marketer by the name of Ken Lulu who used to work for the conceptual artist Jenny Holzer, but had decided to branch out and bring art into marketing. He had moved to Philadelphia from Montreal, where he already had an operation going. His approach to marketing was very different from our institutional sort. He bypassed everyone and went straight to the consumer, using the walls, roofs, cupolas of public places and buildings. His most recent caper had been to have the sad logo of a bicycle manufacturer appear on the Comcast Tower, with the bicycle taking a trip up the building to the sound of "Clair de

Lune" by Debussy. I wasn't very fond of the anarchy that Ken Lulu represented. He was like a fish in a pond, whispering and nipping at the other
guppies. To me, the only ones worthy of respect were those who swooped
down from on high, like eagles. Still, I liked to keep tabs on him and did
that through Candace who had some mutual friends with Ken.

Over time I moved on from industrial work and came to the department headed by Dinesh. This was the most sought-after team because
of the mix of work it did, involving museums, local celebrities such as
columnists and politicians, leading law firms, insurance companies, ca-
ble companies, and the foundations. There was always an event to go
to, and nearly every event had glamorous or ostentatious presentation,
food, and the associated gravitas. I had been into the homes and offices
of all those who lorded over this stretch of the Atlantic. Not quite the
rapacious lords of finance in New York and not quite the lords of war
produced by Washington, DC. Ours had a less aggressive view toward
the world. Where New York and Washington conquered, the lords of
Philadelphia went to explore and categorize, to discuss in magazines related to crafts, to show off in museums, to have academic symposiums
about, and all under the cover of the Quaker liberalism that allowed
Philadelphia to sustain a posture of purity, of innocence. New York and
Washington were Zeus and Hades, the dominant and the destructive.
Philadelphia was Poseidon, the beautiful moderate. It was no surprise
that his statue sat in one of the ovals near Center City.

My progress came to an end when I got shoved into Special Projects. I was atomized. Any team that had a project they didn't want to
do pushed it toward me. My first order of business had been to create a
database of all the wholesale perfume sellers in the Mid-Atlantic. I had
to follow this with creating a database for the entirety of North America.
It was a lot of sitting around with industry newsletters.

I probably would have continued on the database forever had it not
been for a contract that came in via Tony Blanchard and the wife of a

general who sat in the Pentagon. The job required taking military wives and their children, and finding positive stories among them and blasting these to media. It involved getting military wives onto TV shows to get makeovers, both personal and for their houses. It involved finding home footage that cast soldiers in a positive light. A dog greeting his owner after he came back from Iraq. A family surprising a mom after she came back from Germany. The feather in the cap was that wife or mother whose husband or son had gotten killed in combat but who, rather than giving in to stultifying depression, had transmogrified her misery into doing positive things for society, whether it involved sending care packages to others, or providing for abandoned pets.

Even though it was just a contract, I hoped to do good work and potentially turn it into my niche. Perhaps one day I could find a military wife, ideally with children, who upon learning of her husband's death would announce that she was going to join the military as a form of revenge against the enemies of America. Her I would make huge. I wouldn't just get her on every major TV show; for her I could get big-time agents, a movie, a book, a national campaign. She just needed to be found.

I came to work on Tuesday. I had taken the Monday off to spend a little time with Marie-Anne. The atmosphere at the firm felt like the inner sanctum of some criminal conspiracy. Those who had been invited to my party walked past each other evading me and giving sideways smiles. It was quite something to have entertained in my home, fed and intoxicated, lurched from laughter and hilarity with all these people who otherwise were strangers to me, with many who otherwise thought me subservient. Now we had a quiet equality. I was sure of it.

I arrived early, took the spiral staircase down to the storage room that had been converted into my office, and after a couple of hours went to get lunch. I brought it back to my desk and ate it while reading an article on my phone. I had just leaned back with a drink in hand when I was startled by Candace. She stood waiting for me by the coat rack. She wore her peacoat because she tended to get cold easily. She always said it was on account of her minimal body fat.

"You scared me," I said.

"I'm sorry."

"What can we do for you in the Underdark?"

"In the what?"

"It's what Mark calls this area."

"That's weird. Anyway, I just came in to tell you that George stopped by my cube asking where you were. He told me to bring you to him when you got back."

"George Gabriel?"

"The one and only."

I tossed my food in the trash and headed up. Candace came up behind me and grabbed my bag from the desk.

"He said you should bring your stuff."

I wondered what George wanted. Did he want to go somewhere for lunch? Put me in a different office? Was there a meeting at the Sheraton, perhaps? For a brief moment I let myself imagine that my party had engendered such goodwill in him that he had a new team for me.

I made my way toward George Gabriel's office. It required passing through the firm's vast central area, where the cubicles were spread about in the shape of a chessboard. I remembered when Richard Konigsberg and I had come up with the idea, back when I had been an essential part of Plutus. Some of the workers had said that the design likened them to pawns. Richard had replied that for every pawn there were multiple bishops, queens, knights, and kings. "And you can be that one day, if you want to be." It had made the chessboard much more palatable. We were even able to get Ingrid Glass, the architecture critic from the *Philadelphia Inquirer*, to come and write about our unique offices.

Maybe it was the way people looked at me, or the vibrations in the air, but with each additional step toward George there was an upwell of something hard and edgy in my throat. It filled my larynx. I slowed. A part of me wanted to ignore this invite, to just go back to my office and pretend I hadn't heard.

I turned to Candace to take my mind off this meeting. "Any word on what the guerrilla guy is up to?"

"Ken Lulu?"

"Yeah."

"Why are you asking me?"

"Didn't you say you knew the guy?"

"Well, yeah."

"So what is he up to?"

"Nothing. Not since he came back from doing the thing with the Grand Mosque in Abu Dhabi."

"So this can't be about Ken then . . ."

I reached George's office and slid past the secretary. George was at his desk, a pencil in hand, but without a pad or paper, as if he was just trying to appear busy.

He wasn't alone. Two women, one from legal and the other from human resources, both in pinstripe suits and wearing dour maquillage, stood on either side of him, like mummified cats around a pharaoh.

I knew I had trouble when it wasn't George who spoke. The tall white brunette to his right, with a sunken chest and wide hips, cleared her throat and started saying things that were all legalese and sophistry. She went on for a while. George remained expressionless the whole time, his arms on the desk, still, except for an occasional lifting of his palms from the surface. Sweat made the skin squeak.

"So I am being let go?" I asked the woman when she was finished. The statement was more for effect than confirmation. My eyes were focused on George. I wanted to make him speak.

"Yes," he said.

"I didn't hear a reason in there."

He was about to say something when the women put their hands on his shoulders. He sawed at the table with the edge of his palms and grew quiet.

"Business decision," said the brunette.

"This is all very mysterious," I said. "Just tell me the reason."

The brunette wasn't having it. "Thank you," she said, and gestured toward the door with her neck. George remained still and silent. I wondered what part he had to play in this. Was he the messenger? Was he the instigator? Had he been aware that I was going to be fired when he'd come to my house? This last possibility frightened me the most. Had he thought that I was a kiss-ass? Had I not kissed his ass enough? Did it have anything to do with Marie-Anne?

"I have been with this firm for a long time," I said. "I deserve to be told the specific reason why I am getting laid off."

The brunette ignored my request. She simply repeated how I should go about filing for unemployment benefits and how long my health insurance would remain in effect. I kept observing George, but for some reason his stony and severe face only added to my helplessness.

"Can I give you a little unsolicited advice?" he said at last, ignoring the cautionary looks given to him by the women.

"Yes."

"I've been in this business a long time," he said. "Seen a lot of changes."

I nodded.

"And you know what I found, at the end of the day, that a person needs for success? Mind you, I am not suggesting you haven't had success. I have read your reports. You have done some good things in your time . . ."

"Thank you."

"But, as I was saying, the thing that really puts a person over the

top, that gives them longevity, is being an advocate for your clients."
He raised his hand to squash my immediate protestation. "I know what
you're going to say—that you are an advocate. Yes, you probably are, but
having gone over all the work you did for the past few years, you are not
an advocate to the degree I want." He paused and ran his hand over his
head. "It's almost like you are restrained in your advocacy; like you keep
a part of you close to your chest . . ."

"Like, afraid?"

"Like, concealed," he said. "Dormant. Latent. Mysterious."

"What am I keeping dormant?"

"I don't know," he said. "Just that I have a different vision for the
kind of culture I want to incubate here. A more collaborative relationship between client and advocate. Democratic. And a freer exchange
between all the coworkers too. Where your associates don't have to be
careful around you, to be cautious about your inclinations. This is purely
a business-culture decision, as you can see."

"You are entitled to your opinion," I said, still sitting.

George received a nod from the women and stood to extend his
hand. I looked at it and back at him. I didn't want to shake it. He had
taken something from me. I wanted to take something from him in return. Deny him closure. Deny him my acceptance. But that was not
what I did. Hammurabian acts—deny for a deny—required a certain
hardness that I didn't possess. I was too much a man of this age. When I
was declared unwanted, I accepted it.

I gave the handshake and left the office, bag in hand, head hanging, toward the elevator. The people around me, still working, had no
idea what had happened. Life went on within the chessboard. I had always thought that upon the playing surface of Plutus, I was a back-row
power, perhaps even a grandmaster who got to move the pieces. But if I
had been once, I wasn't anymore. That was the violence at the heart of
chess. Anyone could be overturned at any moment.

I couldn't get out with my dignity. Candace was standing at the elevator, trying to appear casual. She was actually whistling with her hands in her pockets and rocking on the balls of her feet. But her face showed even more worry than before.

I told her point-blank what had happened.

"That's so shocking," she said, reaching forward to keep the elevator door open.

"Imagine how I feel."

"Isn't this coming out of nowhere?"

"You tell me," I said. "You talked to him last. This morning and also at my party . . ."

"Nothing this morning," she said, and got into the elevator because it had started to beep. "Just summoned you. That asshole."

"And at the party?"

She shook her head and bit her nails. "He was really drunk."

"What did you talk about? Was it Marie-Anne? Look, if it was Marie-Anne, I hope you will tell me."

"Not at all," she said. "He was all intellectual. Bored the fuck out of me. Totally killed my buzz. He was going on about history. I should've known he was an asshole. Historians are the worst people in the world."

"Anything else?"

"Nothing," she said. "I promise you it wasn't Marie-Anne."

"Well, that's it, then," I said, and patted her on the head. "Good luck, you. And thank you." For a brief moment I wanted to kiss the top of her head. To muffle my mouth in her dark hair. To clutch her to me and be pained together. Then I put that thought out.

The elevator pinged on each floor like it was carrying on a xylophonic recitation.

We reached the ground floor and I stepped out. I didn't even bother to turn around and wave a symbolic goodbye. You spun your arms during a drowning, not after.

* * *

The bars in Center City weren't open yet. The reliable one near Shula's Steakhouse, toward Fairmount, which tended to open earlier, couldn't serve me today, because the bartender would have to call her manager to get his login information and he was currently indisposed. I cursed, wound my bag around my body, and headed toward Ben Franklin Parkway, gazing at its Parisian sweep. On a regular day I would evaluate the architecture, its Gothic cathedrals, the neoclassical fountains in their ovals, the honeycomb condos straight out of the Soviet avant-garde, and compare it to the places I had traveled to, trying to create a narrative about the history they were suffused with. Today I was indifferent. My hand stayed in my pocket, touching and releasing the cell phone like Lenny with his mouse. I wanted to call Richard Konigsberg. He was the man for moments like this. He was the one person I knew who not only understood the intricacies of this American life, but also knew how to explain them.

It took awhile to dial. I lost reception the first time and tried again. He picked up on the fourth ring.

"Hello."

"Are you in town?"

"Yup."

"I thought you would be in Chicago."

"Still here, buddy."

"Let's meet up, then," I said. "Right now—"

"But I'm at a strip club . . ."

"What kind of strip club opens this early?"

"The kind that stays open all night."

"Don't they run out of girls?"

"They have seventy-two every night."

"Please. Come to the art museum café. It's important."

"How important?"

"Plutus let me go. I'm too angry to talk on the phone."

"Shit." I heard shock in his voice. "All right, see you soon. And don't do anything stupid."

I hung up and looked around. I was at St. Peter's Cathedral, a good distance from the art museum, but despite the cold I decided to walk it. Philadelphia was America's only major walkable city. You could go from the Delaware River to the Schuylkill River in a light, easy stroll. You could go from Geno's and Pat's in the south to King Fried Chicken near Temple Hospital in the north. Most locals were comfortable walking around Philadelphia, especially in Center City, where the chances of running into a familiar face were very high, and each encounter was heightened by the joy that came with being on foot. How had Philadelphia resisted the otherwise inexorable domination of the car and the highway? It must have been an act of collective resistance of some kind. But who had resisted? When? No doubt the fateful encounter between the peripatetic and the vehicular took place long before my time, as was the case with most things in America. But I hadn't gotten to see it. I was among those who came of age after the end of history.

I passed the Rodin Museum. The statue of the Thinker was up front, sitting hunkered in the snow, rendered white-skinned by the powder. I thought about going to sit at his feet and doing a little wail and whine, but he seemed too stentorian, too analytical, too lacking in melancholy. I recalled that the poet Rilke used to be Rodin's assistant. And even though Rilke had been quite the sentimentalist, none of that tenderness seemed to have made its way into the Thinker. Looking at the statue, unforgiving and aloof, a philosopher with his eye on some prize beyond this world, beyond time, colder than the icicle beard on him right now, darker than the gray skies above, I could understand why Rilke had gone toward softness, love. Rilke as a reaction to Rodin. It was a good thought to have. I would have to use it at some party I might hold in the future, assuming I was ever worth visiting again.

Inside, they charged me for a ticket. When I first arrived in Philadel-phia, years ago, you weren't obligated to pay. There was a box you could drop dollars into if you wanted. But as Philadelphia became more corpo-rate, welcomed more people coming down from New York and coming up from DC, it changed. Now the guards played another game. If they thought you could afford it, they scuttled you into a line and made you pay. A kind of class-based profiling. And that was not even the worst thing about it. By taking away the voluntariness of the contribution they changed the way a person came to art. Now you didn't come like a lover, making an offering. You came like a debtor. You didn't enjoy for the sake of enjoyment; you enjoyed because you had paid.

It had been a good idea to walk. The distance gave me an opportu-nity to calm down and replay what had happened. I paid the entry and went to the café located on the second floor. I ordered a vanilla cappuccino and reserved a latte for my guest.

When Richard Konigsberg arrived, half an hour later, he came in through the back entrance, where he had parked. I rose up with a smile. It was very taxing.

He was a tall, thin man, who wore loose-fitting suits and wide-brimmed black hats that would make him appear like some Orthodox rabbi, were it not for the fact that he was clean-shaven and every third sentence from his mouth was either laced with profanity or merged na-ture and women in some vulgar fashion. And these comments tended to come out in the most inappropriate moments. "Do you think that girl's bush is deciduous or coniferous?" he had asked about an acquaintance for whom Marie-Anne had been maid of honor. "Do you think that girl would make me cum cumulus or cirrus?" was what he asked about a secretary he once hired. The more convoluted his metaphor, the more likely he was to sleep with the girl. He had never said anything about Marie-Anne.

Richard was a self-made millionaire. His family was among the few that hadn't left for the Main Line when the urbanites turned sub. His architect father never really kept a good job, and the family had mostly come up on his mother's income as a corner-shop psychic. Richard had decided that the way out of the lower-middle-class morass was by way of politics. And swinging from far-right to far-left and settling in the middle, he had made his way into city hall as an advisor, and from there to Plutus, where we had met. After a few years there, he had gone off to practice law with a corporate firm that he had pulled out of bankruptcy. Last we'd talked, he was going to buy out a smaller firm in New York. They represented private plaintiffs defrauded by the big investment banks.

"So, buddy, what a fucking emergency this is. I was taking a nice happy stroll in cleavage canyon, and now here I am." He put his hat down and brushed snowflakes from its brim.

"What's her name?" I asked, trying to seem casual.

"I'm not too good with names," he said. "Especially not strippers."

"With the amount you've given away to strippers you could've gotten married to a very high-maintenance princess."

"I'm too much of a redistributionist," he said.

"Perfect excuse for promiscuity."

The bit of banter lifted none of the darkness from the meeting.

"So they let you go," he doubled back. "Tell me what happened."

There was a silence. I felt reluctant at having elevated my anxiety and panic to such a degree that I had dragged him away from his brief moment of fun and pleasure. I could see that he had come in carrying a good deal of strain on his face. I should have thought more before calling. He had always said that I was his scion at Plutus. He was probably going to take this whole thing in a personal way.

I started by describing the face-off in the office and what George Gabriel said about being an advocate. Then I provided the backstory, which, really, was just the party at my house, and the three days in the office before that.

"That's it?" Richard tapped the table. "This guy doesn't talk to you for a week. Comes to your party. Then, the next workday, he's all, *Go home, see you, don't let the door hit you?*"

"That sums it up."

Richard grew quiet. Underneath the uncouth vulgarity, Richard's mind was a beehive of syllogism. I could see the processes shooting off in his eyes. He muttered like he was counting the Omer. I was always soothed when he did that, especially when he did it in front of me. It made me feel that I was protected by some ancient brotherhood going back to that firebrand who had risen against the pharaoh. It was the pluck and passion accumulated and strengthened over thousands of years of persecution. It was a cache that I didn't have access to, because I came from a people who had been defeated and never recovered and had nothing to give to those of us who had started a new life in the West. I folded my arms and waited.

"What's the guy's name? The one they brought in."

"George Gabriel."

Richard lost his grip on his cup. One of the children sitting near us let out a yelp and laughed. The spilled latte slid toward the edge of the table. I made a dam with a napkin. The children liked what I had done and clapped. A smile appeared on my face. Neither child looked anything like me. That made the smile turn hollow.

"George Gabriel?"

"Yeah," I said. "You know him?"

"I do. German guy. Married to a journalist at *Der Spiegel*. She lives and travels through all those -stan countries, exposing corruption, agitating for more openness. I know his wife a little better, but they are really very similar."

"In what way?"

"That whole generation of Germans," he said. "They feel like since they confronted the question of Hitler and accepted responsibility for it, they can now judge the rest of the world. They see fascism everywhere, though never in themselves."

"What was all that *dormant, latent, mysterious* stuff? If anything I was doormat, not dormant."

Richard added a second napkin to the dam. "Hard to say." He paused as the waitress came over to give us extra napkins. She was a young brown-skinned girl with pink Mohawk hair. Behind her apron she had on tattered fishnet stockings and short shorts. "I need to hear more."

"There's nothing more. I have been in the guy's company only twice and the second time was to let me go."

"At your house. Was Marie-Anne there? Did she, you know, rub him the wrong way?"

"She doesn't rub, you know that."

"Maybe he expected a little rubbing?"

I knew Marie-Anne well enough to know that she never gave off invitational signals. Even when I wanted her to be flirtatious she limited herself to friendliness. Ever since the illness there had been a drop-off there as well. "I don't think so."

We were interrupted by the Rach 3 ringtone of my phone. It was a number I didn't recognize. Thinking that perhaps it was someone administrative from Plutus, I excused myself and ducked into an alcove containing a yet-to-be-announced exhibition. The paintings seemed to be of no painter I had ever seen before. The cityscapes looked European, but I couldn't place which city it was. Even my knowledge of art history was disappointing today.

It was Candace. There was North Indian classical music in her background.

"Are you home?" she asked. "I'm coming to your house."

"No, I'm not," I said. "But why? I mean, why are you coming?"

"I remembered something else he said," she told me breathlessly. "When will you be home? I'm in a cab. I'm almost there."

"George Gabriel? I'm at the art museum. Across from my house. Come to the back of it. I'm there with a friend. Come over, come right now."

Richard and I stepped outside to wait for Candace and bummed cigarettes off a couple of college kids cowering behind a pillar. Upon seeing Richard's watch they demanded that we pay them for the cigarettes. Richard negotiated a two-for-one deal and congratulated them for being attentive to the ways of the world. "Fuck capitalism," one of the kids replied.

Candace emerged from the cab in the same peacoat from earlier and a red Siberian bucket hat with two small fur pompoms. Her delicate face was framed nicely by the hat and made her appear like a revolutionary intellectual. She tugged at her red gloves and waved as she paid.

"I hired Candace a couple years ago," I told Richard by way of explanation. "She says she has something to share."

"Cute girl," Richard said in a whisper before she got close to us. "But no rack."

"She isn't an offering."

I brought Candace over by the elbow and the three of us headed back to the café. We occupied the same table as before. The only difference was that Richard switched seats with me so he could stare at the waitress.

"So what do you bring?" Richard turned to Candace before she even placed an order for coffee.

Candace looked at me for confirmation.

"You can talk to him," I said. "He's like my lawyer."

"And former head of Plutus," he added.

She seemed relieved to hear that. "Well, like I said, Friday night at the party I was really drunk, and so was he, so take all of this with a grain of salt. But George was obsessed with the bookshelf. There was this one term he kept using. I had forgotten all about it till after I left you at the elevator earlier today. I sat down in my cube and opened my phone and saw this word I had saved in my notes. It's where I write down all the words whose meanings I have to look up."

She presented the phone and laid it on the table. There were a number of words there. *Arrogate. Quixotic. Ataraxia.* But the phrase she pointed to was at the very end of the list. *Residual Supremacism.*

My personhood drained out of some hole at the bottom of my feet. I remembered George using that term with me.

"I know what the words mean," she said. "But I wasn't sure if it was some psychological condition or technical term. He kept pointing to the bookshelf and repeating it. I haven't put together what it has to do with him firing you, but deep down I know there's a connection. That's why I rushed out."

"*Residual supremacism,*" Richard said. "It's causing me lingual perplexism."

"I know what he's talking about." I tapped my chin. "Do you remember, Richard, when my mom visited after my dad passed away? Well, one of her last acts in life was to stick this miniature copy of the Koran on top of my bookshelf inside a hand-stitched pouch. It's the kind of Koran you might get at an airport gift shop. I swear, I never once saw it there, not until George noticed it the other night. We were all drinking, so I didn't think anything about it. I just put it back where I found it."

"A Koran? What's the connection with residual supremacism? Did you read it to him? Did you try to convert him?"

"No, I didn't try to convert him. But I do remember George asking me why I was putting the Koran above the Nietzsche." My breath caught in my throat. My eyes closed in regret. "I'm right, aren't I? I fucked up when I put the Koran above Nietzsche. He even asked me why I did that. But I thought he was only joking. Maybe he thought mine was some kind of symbolic gesture. You know, like when people make a minaret higher than a steeple."

Richard twisted Candace's hat which she had set down on the table. "I don't know," he said. "I mean, the Koran thing is weird, but come on. That a Muslim has a Koran in his house is not entirely—"

I slapped the hat in his hand. It landed upside down as if jesters were about to erupt. "Muslim? I'm not a fucking Muslim." The children near me clapped. The waitress made a face.

Richard put his hands up. "We can go after Plutus."

Upon hearing about Richard going after her paycheck, Candace spoke up: "Do what when?"

Richard slammed a palm. "We allege discrimination. We link the things George said to you in the office with this residual supremacist crap. I think a court, especially an urban Philadelphia court, may be interested in hearing about a blond-haired German firing a dark-haired, dark-skinned subordinate based on religious discrimination—"

"No," I snapped. "I'm not about to go around claiming anti-Muslim discrimination when I'm not a Muslim."

Richard sighed and launched into a lecture on American history, invoking everything from the Declaration of Independence to Frederick Douglass and W.E.B. DuBois and JFK and Justice Brandeis and the X-Men and Ellen DeGeneres. He even tried singing the acronym "EEOC" like do-re-mi.

But I didn't hear him out. I vacated my seat and leapt from the art museum, taking the back exit overlooking the river. Richard was old and patient and didn't chase after me, and although Candace tried to, I left her behind very quickly.

I stepped out into the cold, my eyes fixed on the river. The ice was a dirty gray blanket with an occasional piece of knotted wood sticking out above the surface, like fingers pointed at me, accusing me of being a Muslim, the Fascist of today. And the disembodied nature of the incrimination meant that I could lodge no protest.

* * *

From the back of the art museum it wasn't a long walk down the hill to our building; but in my loafers, with the iciness caused by the perpetual northside shadow of the museum, it was treacherous going. I slipped and slid and stumbled through the stamped snow, using mental transference to take me to a giant green meadow somewhere, where I didn't feel any of the vertiginous vibrations of confusion, where the clouds made collages in the shapes of rabbits peeking and dragonflies bursting and the sky sang a libretto of soporific blue silliness. Not this gray. Not this cold. Not this weight.

Crossing Kelly Drive, passing the Joan of Arc statue, weaving through the scaffolding erected around one of the museum's annexes under refurbishment, I clawed and unclawed my hands. I imagined Marie-Anne examining my hands with pity, like she did that one sleet-splattered winter in Atlanta a decade ago. On one of our dates she had asked me why my fingers had a hookish bend to them and I had said it was because I had started writing love notes to her. That was the first time she had told me she loved me. And for a brief time I had been called Captain Hook. The world had been good then. The worst thing it turned me into was a fictional character.

It started snowing again. A flake landed on my eyelash. The smash of the eyelid made it melt. I became weary. The cold day seemed to flicker. I peered up at the lampposts. They looked like they wore helmets of smoke. I was reminded of nights in Bethesda, where Marie-Anne and I had moved after college, back when I was trying to fake it as a film director and she had been working on her first—and eventually only—attempted novel. We had loved smoking opiates. The world had been freer then. It hadn't cared to snare me.

I reached the apartment building. It was under construction as well, getting turned into a condominium. The new ownership had offered a 10 percent discount to all the current renters if they went ahead and purchased the apartment they were in. Marie-Anne and I had talked about it, because the mortgage would be less than the $2,250 in rent that we paid at the moment. I passed the number through my head a few times. It was going to be hard to make rent without my income. Student loans, car insurance, parking spots, credit card debts, Acela tickets, and a meager savings ate up all of our income. We hadn't exactly been paycheck-to-paycheck, but it had been pretty close, because that was what happened to those who lived above their means. I should have paid more attention when the brunette had talked about unemployment benefits.

I gave a light wave to Marlon. He was my favorite security guard. We had a bit of a conspiracy going: I procured varsity jackets for him from the Philadelphia chapter of the Emory Alumni Association and he distributed them to the homeless guys on Fairmount Avenue. Over the past two years a large group of men with an *E* on their chests wandered around the city.

Marlon wanted to jump up and talk about our thing, but I shook my head and plodded along.

The elevator was hot. The box strained and whined for a few floors and let me out. The hallway before me expanded and contracted like a scene viewed through a glass bottle. The smell of winter, that wet dog and burned bacon smell, permeated the air. They hadn't yet finished fixing up the hallway, and the peeling paints of the ceiling fell like the dead skin cells of a sardonic higher being.

When I entered the apartment the first thing I saw was Marie-Anne bent over to pick up a spoon. She straightened when she heard me. She was in a pink terry-cloth robe with bunnies on the lapel. The house smelled like she had been cooking. I moved past her without smiling and went to the kitchen, inspecting the source of the smell. The stove had four different blackened frying pans on it. Hot oil had splashed on the side of the fridge.

"I see you didn't go to DC yet," I said.

"It got pushed to tonight," she replied, and poked me with the spoon. "So I thought I'd try to make dinner. Total failure, as you can see."

"But you never cook," I said.

"I know, but I got some great news, so I thought I'd surprise you."

"What is this news?"

She giggled from a joy unexpressed all day. "So. MimirCo called. They said they want to shift me to sales. Not full-time or anything. But just go out and make presentations from time to time. Do you remember how Karsten King sent me out to Nigeria with Wu, Sharma, and Jones? That was to show me the ropes. Now they want to involve me."

"That sounds like a big deal," I said, and gave her a hug.

"Maybe. There will be more human interaction than when I'm writing those descriptions. If I help with a sale maybe I can get some commissions. All day I was writing the talking points down. It's how I burned the food. Twice." She rattled the pans in frustration.

"You will do great," I said. "This is what we've been working for all these years."

"It is, isn't it? I couldn't have done it without you. The best part is that we make another ten thousand a year. That's not including the bonus. That could be another ten."

"That's not paltry money," I said. "Especially now."

"Well, there will also be more work. I have to go to Virginia all the time. Maybe even abroad."

I gave her another awkward hug and then trudged around the house, taking off my clothes, unplugging the gadgets, lowering the blinds. I came back to the kitchen, found a pack of Bacardi Breezers in the fridge, and opened two at once, drinking from one, then the other. I was happy for her. The years spent commuting to Virginia, all those parties that we hosted for Karsten, all those trips we took to attend barbecues and birthdays—they had all paid off. They were willing to look at her as one of them, not just some creative writer, but as someone who could help them launch machines, someone they trusted.

As I stood in place I noticed a fly buzzing around. I followed its aerial arc with my weary eyes. It sat down at the edge of a bowl of milk-soaked cornflakes that Marie-Anne had failed to finish. I carefully took both bottles into one hand, picked up a frying pan, and smashed the fly into the bowl, ceramic shards flying in every direction.

"What. The. Fuck." Marie-Anne came into the kitchen in a total panic.

"I got fired from Plutus," I said in a deadpan, "so I am training to become a racquetball champion. I'm sorry for ruining your perfect day."

Two more bowls were shattered before what I had said registered with Marie-Anne. She extended her neck, tried to say something, and then pursed her mouth. Her forehead creased and smoothed and her eyebrows made a wedge. Eventually she grasped my arm and pulled me to her by the elbow; she could be forceful when required. Letting myself get swept, I put my head on her shoulder and brought the bottles to my mouth both at once, getting the fluid in me as fast as possible, spilling some on Marie-Anne's shoulder.

We stayed there, in the stinking kitchen, pressed together in silence like pages in a book, stained by alcohol.

After the initial confession in the kitchen, the evening was all empathy. Marie-Anne touched me, nudged me, said she loved me, and just hung around near me until we were sitting on the sofa drinking again. She said she didn't want details unless I wanted to share.

"I can share," I said.

"Okay." She sidled off the couch and moved to a chair that she flipped around and straddled. It was her favorite conversational position. "Tell me. I'm ready."

I told her everything, right from the start, in order. From the encounter with Candace in my office after lunch, to the specifics of the conversation with George, and then the subsequent meeting with Richard Konigsberg and Candace at the museum where she had told me about that awful phrase. Then I talked about the party and what had happened there.

"What did he have to say to all this?"

"Who? Richard?"

"Yeah. He's a lawyer, right?"

"He is thinking it's discrimination."

"He said that? But why?"

"Because apparently I'm a Muslim."

She made a face. "But you aren't a Muslim. Just like I'm not a Christian. We have no religion. We are about as religious as, I don't know, whoever is the least religious person in the world. We are spiritual only."

"That's what I told Richard."

"But," Marie-Anne said, almost continuing her thought, "maybe that's a narrow definition of Muslim? I mean, we do have a Koran sitting there on our bookshelf. And your name . . ."

"Yeah," I sighed. "Right at the top of the books. Above the Nietzsche even."

Marie-Anne's expression remained one of exasperation. "Aren't we getting ahead of ourselves? How can we be sure this whole thing is motivated by religion? Because Richard said so?"

"That's a big part of it," I said. "He knows about these kinds of things. And then what about those words that George Gabriel used that I told you about? Don't make me repeat them. But do you really think anyone would use those words on me unless they had been coming in with a certain prejudice?"

"What prejudice is that?"

"The one you hear on the news. The prejudice that Muslims can't be trusted. That a Muslim is sheisty, shifty, shady; undemocratic; hard to fit into the culture; a pariah."

"Again," Marie-Anne said with a great deal of calm, "you aren't a Muslim. No one who knows you could actually think that. Plus, you don't have a supremacist bone in your body. You are obliging even when you have a boner."

"Maybe," I said. "But that's the thing: George Gabriel doesn't know me. He doesn't know how I wield my bone."

We rolled into a deep and perplexed silence. A great burst of wind blew outside and a sheet of ice separated itself from some rafter and fell a long way down onto the dumpsters. In the echo I wondered if I had presented the wrong version of the story. Should I have been talking about how I didn't fit into the company? How my management style was found lacking? The character flaws that had supposedly prompted the release?

Marie-Anne picked up the remote and flipped to a cartoons channel. Yosemite Sam was chasing a feathered and war-painted animal and shooting wildly, without aim or direction. As the wind howled harder, more icicles bombed the dumpster.

"Wait a second," Marie-Anne said, and held up a finger like she had an idea. She turned toward the bookshelf and, after a couple of big leaps, brought the Koran and wooden holder down and put them on the coffee table. "If we are sure all this is about religion, what if you just gave George a call and explained yourself? Tell him that the Koran was a gift from your mother. And, really, that the gift was the pouch. The rest is just some religious stuff you don't care for. I mean, why don't we separate the pouch from the Koran? Tell him you lit it up, threw it in the river, something like that."

I pulled my head back and did a double take. This was hardly the position I had expected her to settle upon. "Why should I do that?" I sat up. "How would you respond if you had to tell your boss that you threw the Bible in the trash?"

She laughed. "Why would you ever have to do that? No one associates the Bible with the sort of things the Koran is associated with. The

Old Testament, maybe, once upon a time, was bad. But the New Testament, it's just some trippy-hippie stuff. I mean, beasts and horsemen? As harmless as these cartoons."

It was my turn to make a face. "So now you're saying that Christianity is better than Judaism and Islam? Are we really having this discussion?"

She shook her head. "I'm just saying that some books, like some movies, evoke certain reactions, while other books, like other movies, evoke another set of reactions."

"So the Koran is a horror film that makes men into lying villains, and the Bible is what? A romantic comedy? Disney? It makes princes out of men?"

Marie-Anne turned both hands at the wrists. "We are not talking about what these things are objectively. What we are talking about is what a book represents to George Gabriel. Not anyone else."

"So, ultimately, you agree with him."

She circled around the room and started loosening her robe. "Forget it. Think what you want. Don't take my approach. I have a train to catch so I am going to go get ready. Can you call me a cab in the meantime?"

"Yeah. Fine."

"And I hate to ask this, but I'm going to be in Virginia all week. I'm going to work out there. Do you have any poems for me?"

"No poems," I said. "I was going to write one over lunch . . ."

"All right," she said in a resigned voice. "I'll find some of the old ones."

I sat quietly, alone and increasingly drunk, until my eyelids and then my face fell to the side. I passed out and curled up on the sofa. Marie-Anne came by about an hour later. She smelled of black musk and her face had an aubergine darkness to it. She pulled my head back and looked me in the eye. "Did you get me the cab?"

"No."

"Fuck it. I'll just go out into the tundra with my bags and chase one myself." She slammed the door on her way out.

In a couple of hours I got up. Drool streaked on the side of my face. I wiped it away with the inside of my wrist, and headed toward the kitchen. Ignoring the mess already present, I opened the fridge and prepared a Parmesan, ham, and mushroom frittata, along with some salted beef boudin.

With each bite that went down to my belly, more of the argument with Marie-Anne came back. Her idea was the apogee of stupidity. I couldn't dis what I didn't even avow. Besides, a miniature Koran inside a cover, sitting on a stand unread, in proximity of clearly irreligious things like Nietzsche and Goethe, was just what I had said it was: a decoration. Nothing could be read into a decoration. It was just one of those things people had, like a mezuzah outside a door, or a cross between Lady Gaga's breasts, or a Balinese mask representing some ancient deity no one cared about. If Richard was right and George really was motivated by religious prejudice, if all he was doing was drawing me into the old wars of dogma and bigotry, I was simply going to refuse that game.

I picked up the remote to find some updated cartoons. SpongeBob and Patrick were on another channel. They had donned a pair of nun habits and ran after a curved-nosed villain with thin limbs and a potbelly.

I slept the night on the sofa. I woke up at the moment of quantum silence in the middle of the night when even the air in the house became devoid of movement. I was the only particle that attained motion. I went to the study and trailed my hand over the small desk from Antique Row. I toed the carved cabriole legs. I tugged at its handles. I inhaled it so hard it levitated. I had filled its drawers for Marie-Anne to browse through, with little mementos and keepsakes for her to discover. But she had run her hand over the desk and not delved into it. She hadn't wondered what she might find inside.

I sat on the chair, opened a drawer, and drew out the family albums. There was my family. The three of us seemed so negligible compared to Marie-Anne's mammoth clan. My family's pictures were almost all indoors, because for the bulk of their lives my parents were people who paid rent. Marie-Anne's family's pictures are almost all outdoors. They were people of land, people of substance, owners of legacy.

My parents made me smile. My small bespectacled father—meager lab technician—and my short-haired mother who stayed at home and raised me. They had come to America through luck, by having their name called in the immigration lottery. Because it was chance that brought them here, they always lived in fear of chance turning against them. The first job my father got, he held it, and the first role my mother had, that of raising me, she held that. Every now and then they would talk, in quiet tones, about launching a business, or aiming for another job, or getting financing for a house, but would veto themselves. "That's risky," my mother would say. "It's chancy," my father would add. That would be that.

The one thing they believed in was the myth of American meritocracy. That seemed to them to be utterly devoid of risk. "America is the only place in the world where performance trumps blood," my father said to me often, even if the stories we heard every day contradicted his belief. My parents were convinced that if I performed well in all the tests that America gives its children, then I would be able to reach the highest echelon of society. I was their one risk-free investment. And I was happy to say that as long as they were alive I more or less vindicated them. I did well in school, got a scholarship to college, and, after only a short period of aimlessness, found a stable job where I received a stable paycheck. I had done everything they had ever dreamed for me.

My decision to marry Marie-Anne was the only thing my parents ever questioned—because they thought it was a risky thing for a non-white to marry a white—but once I explained to them that she and I related to one another through our shared interests, values, and status as Southerners, they let go of it as well. If they'd had a problem with Marie-

Anne, if they thought they had lost me, they would've picked some end-of-life fight with me. Perhaps accused me of throwing away the past. But they didn't do anything like that. They came and tucked the past in a corner where no one would find it. And they left.

I was glad they were gone. If they were still alive they wouldn't have been able to handle seeing my American life decapitated by their inadvertent hand. It would've killed them.

Then again, if they were still alive I might have been able to borrow some money for the bills I was still responsible for.

The Koran had been sitting on the coffee table since Marie-Anne left. After breakfast the next morning, I sat down before it and made an inspection.

I started with the wooden holder. It was in the shape of a butterfly with rounded edges, made of mango wood, with intricately carved eight-pointed lattices in the wings. The color was a brushed plum brown, and there were hinges in the center that cradled the spine of a book, allowing it to sit open between the wings. I had once seen a black-and-white picture of my mother as a young girl, head covered, eyes lowered, sitting before such a holder. I put the holder aside.

Next I worked the cloth pouch. My fingers trailed over my name. The thread that my mother had used to do the embroidery was some kind of high-quality velvet. She must have remembered my fondness for velvet. The glittery cloth was also quite weighty, having a texture similar to an antique brocade sofa.

The Koran itself was the least impressive thing in the set. The zipper cover was made of cheap plastic and the zip got stuck at various pins. The calligraphic writing on the side and the dados on the cover were impossible to discern because dark green ink had been used on a black background. With my index finger I found the cloth bookmark and flipped back to the Chapter of the Hidden Secret. I skimmed over it for a moment. Purity and torment and guardians of the hellfire and blackened faces and donkeys alarmed by lions. It made no sense to me. I wrapped the Koran back up and returned it to the holder and resumed staring.

As a child I had never consciously rejected Islam. I simply hadn't cared for it, nor had it struck me that that there was any benefit in belief. The old religions were the politics of the past, lingering on due to the irascibility of ritual, the nostalgia of the adherents, and because appealing to certain dead men still led to good fundraising hauls. Since my interest was in the politics of the present, it had made no sense to bother getting involved with what was so evidently anachronistic. It had also helped that my parents, aside from preaching abstention from pork, and abstention from sex till marriage, hadn't bothered to impart Islam to me as a doctrine. This allowed me to see it as one of those things that foreigners did, like Soccer, or Kung Fu, or Bollywood. As a teenager, then, my focus had been on more secular things. How to hide my parents' accent (keep far away from them). How to make people blind to the color of my skin (stand close to Marie-Anne). How to best Anglicize my name (rearrange the syllabic emphasis). Once in college there had been Muslim students who had tried to reach out to me, but they hadn't been very persistent. They saw that I liked to drink and they backed away. Perhaps in other universities there were Muslims with greater evangelical zealotry, but not at Emory. The lack of a community meant that I met no Muslim girls who might have tempted me to learn something of Islam, perhaps as a courtship device.

For a brief instant, earlier in the decade, there had been a moment when I had been forced to confront the question of Islam. But not for very long. When the towers fell I simply attested to myself that I wasn't a Muslim—*There's no known god, nor is there an unknown god, and if there must be a god, then all are god*—and moved on from any feeling of complicity or guilt or involvement. I decided that I was nothing but a millennial, identified by my income, my profession, my consumption habits, living in this postracial America which through the burning of a Bush had become enlightened enough to follow a man from the Nile despite the fact that his name evoked not one but two of America's enemies. Then Marie-Anne had gone on to get a job working at a firm whose stated goal it was to keep America safe, and there came to be an additional buffer between me and Islam. As long as I didn't do anything to willfully attach myself to Muslims, I had figured I would be secure.

Except the security had been illusory. All along there had been a ticking time bomb on my shelf and now it had blown, collapsing the towers of my dreams, leaving me in the soot and ash. Maybe Marie-Anne was right. The best thing to do with a bomb was to pluck out the shrapnel and cry. Maybe explanation and apology was the way to go. Yet, even though I had always listened to her before, and our success was evidence that I should continue to, I couldn't bring myself to follow this particular command. It seemed like a slap in my dead mother's face. Given how hard Marie-Anne had taken her own mother's disowning, it had been shocking that she should ask the same from me. If anything, Marie-Anne should have had more respect for what my mother left behind, because my mother had at least accepted her into the family.

I picked up the Koran and the wooden holder and took it to the antique desk in the bedroom. I opened a drawer and thrust the whole set in there. Then I slammed it closed. Let the tan walnut consume the book into itself, the way ivy enshrouds a house. Let the memories of my mother be swallowed up and digested. Let the stories of the prophets and the Pegasi with human faces and the wars against the polytheists all be hidden. This was the best way of dealing with my troubles.

After all, was I not, as George Gabriel had said, a man inclined toward concealment?

Philadelphia got coated by a blizzard. The city emerged from the pristine blanket with all the grace of the Minotaur rising from his labyrinth. The scraped snow stank of road salt and of the sewage pipes that had burst in the morning freeze. The plows came in time to get everyone to work, but had knocked over the mailboxes on countless homes, and left snow piled, in some places, thirty feet high. By noon the senior citizens living along Pennsylvania Avenue brought out their Yorkies and terriers and poodles, and the cooped-up dogs defecated everywhere. On the ice rink that had formed, the poop was not easy to pick up. Many of the owners just kicked snow over the shit, leaving a nice surprise for the unaware pedestrians who came later.

The seniors reminded me of Richard, and because I knew that insinuations of aging upset him, I pushed away the blasphemous comparison. I hadn't seen him since the art museum. One time he had texted just to report that he had spotted the waitress from the museum walking near city hall. I had texted him back saying that he ought to pursue her. He wrote back saying that he had no intention of *hounding the sluts* anymore because *they always seem to outfucks me.* He didn't say it outright, but I knew him well enough to know that his joking, particularly about sex, was a way of opening me up and eventually picking up the conversation about filing a complaint against Plutus.

I didn't know how to respond. The short of it was that I was incapable of fighting. My coming of age in the eighties and nineties had been a protected one. I had witnessed no great civil rights struggle. The eloquent rabble-rouser of color who I had encountered wasn't the Pastor from Selma but the Fresh Prince of Bel-Air. The bespectacled gadfly from Chicago I had grown up with wasn't Malik El-Shabazz but Steven Q. Urkel. They weren't the sort of icons that made a man of color become inclined to rise up and resist. Their only concerns were to put on a good show and to be liked, the same qualities that I had cultivated in myself, the same qualities I would have been flouting by turning toward litigation.

But it wasn't just that. Deep down I also thought that I deserved what had happened. It wasn't as if the discrimination against me had occurred in a vacuum. Ours was an era that had to grapple with the dream of the nineties coming to a sudden and premature close. The nineties, when the great prejudices of mankind were said to have been overcome; the nineties, when the unfamiliarity between the rest of the world and ourselves was presumably erased through admiration of the things we created; the nineties, when the utopian magnitude of America had been at its apex. It had all gotten lost when New York got neutered. That September destroyed every American in a different way. And that included me. My destruction lay in the fact that when other Americans washed the ash out of their eyes and took a look around, they saw in my swarthy face a reminder of all those golden years eclipsed, the thief who had stolen the key to El Dorado, the brother of the devil whose whispers brought Paradise to an end. It was a testament to my fellow Americans, actually, that calling me a residual supremacist was the worst they had done to me. They could have tarred and feathered me. They could have hung me upside down like a bat in Guantanamo. They could have stripped me of citizenship. It was out of deference to their unexpressed wrath that I didn't want to be deemed some kind of ingrate. They could have done so much worse.

I didn't know how to convey all this to Richard Konigsberg, so I simply stopped responding to him. It was not that I didn't think he would understand. It was that I feared he would tell me to show some courage, to demonstrate some entitlement, to make boisterous demands rooted in moral outrage. I didn't have the heart to tell him that I was incapable of these things, that the reason I had made him my mentor hadn't been so I could learn how to be a force in my own right, but just so that from time to time I could hide behind the shield his ancestors had forged and bequeathed to him.

He was, in essence, not much different than Marie-Anne. A protector. But unlike Marie-Anne, who liked to know that I used her as a sanctuary and quite delighted in the role, Richard would have been greatly displeased by my eagerness to turtle up. He expected more from people. Not only because his ancestors had managed to rise up even against a pharaoh, but because he knew that struggle was how one got ahead. I often told him he would have made a good father. He always said he wouldn't have. "I'm too 'My way is the Yahweh' to be a decent parent."

Marie-Anne came back from Virginia, but she and I didn't talk about the firing. I wasn't about to make any overtures to George Gabriel and she didn't confront me about it. Our silence wasn't so much respect as anxiety. The first fight, the night she had left for MimirCo, had triggered hidden electrons of suspicion, and now they bounced around in oblong orbits within us both, as complex and twisted as the pipelines depicted in Marie-Anne's giant map in the bedroom entitled, "Cartographic Depiction of Major Pipelines of the World."

An unemployment check came for a month and stopped. The cutoff was preceded by the arrival of a renewal form. It required documenting the efforts I'd been making to secure a new job. I would then have to take the form to some bureau and stand in line and get approved for the next three months of payment. I decided the whole thing was too tedious, especially since anything I wrote about making an effort would be a lie. I let the form sit on the coffee table. Things spilled on it and made it brown and curl.

Marie-Anne seethed at my dereliction of the chore. She took the form and put it on the fridge. Then it moved to the mirror in the bathroom. Then it got to the TV. When even that failed to inspire me, it ended up on the toilet, hanging in the hole, arms and feet outstretched, taped to the seat. A pen on a string hung off the flush.

"Hostage audience!" I cracked open the door and yelled, and set about filling out the form. Once it was finished, however, there was still the matter of getting out of the house and going downtown. It took a few more weeks for that to occur. Once Marie-Anne was assured that the money was coming in, she stopped chasing me around.

In this period the image that best defined our intimacy was a scrunched-up face. Ours was becoming a domesticity of the darkest doldrums. Marie-Anne was unwilling to give me the satisfaction of her surrender, while I, not the janissary type, was incapable of infiltrating her defenses. When she came home it was as if she was hanging herself by the collar in the back of a closet while I sat on the sofa like a column of iodine or some other inert gas. She slept there; I slept here. The change occurred without discussion, without remonstration by either party.

Since Marie-Anne kept the door to the bedroom closed, I wasn't aware of what she did with her libido. Was it finger? Was it machine? Was it nothing? I couldn't tell. There were times that I wanted to rush into the bedroom, find her sopping wet, and enter her. But this was only a far-fetched fantasy. Not only because I wasn't capable of such aggression; but because Marie-Anne feared getting pregnant more than death and didn't want to take any risks associated with intercourse. The last couple of pregnancy scares, her cortisol levels had shot through the roof.

Marie-Anne had not always been afraid of getting pregnant. Babies were how we had bonded. While we had been dating in Atlanta, until we graduated and met her parents, we always played games coming up with the names we would give our children, what they might look like, what their characteristics would be. We would have three. Two boys and a girl. The boys would be musicians. They would form a boy band out of Florida. One of them would then turn out to be gay and go off to Europe. The other, after a bout with alcoholism, would revive his career on Broadway. The girl would be an astrophysicist and marry a Latino musician who reminded her of her brothers. But eventually we had to stop playing these games. The turning point had been the dinner at the steakhouse in Buckhead when I met Dr. Quinn and Mrs. Quinn for the first time. After the initial pleasantries had been offered and the steaks had been consumed and the wineglasses were on their third refill, Marie-Anne had announced that she'd brought us all together to get blessings for our engagement. It hadn't gone well. While her parents had done their best to feign politeness, the next few months revealed that they didn't think Marie-Anne and I would make a good pairing. The stated reason hadn't been, as we'd feared, anything related to race or nationality. Dr. and Mrs. Quinn were elites in the New South. They didn't subscribe to the old prejudices regarding coloration and ancestry. They had signed numerous petitions trying to take down the Confederate flag at the state capital. They even had a dog named Malcolm. Their objections to me had been far more ephemeral and, in a way, far more personal.

We thought our only daughter would marry a quarterback from Clemson, Mrs. Quinn had put it in an e-mail I wasn't supposed to read. *Even a black construction worker that could handle you like a husband is supposed to. What is this pretty little boy going to do if you fall down the stairs? He'd probably start crying.*

Marie-Anne had tried to reason with them, telling them that we didn't live in the ancient societies where women were shrinking violets and men were their strong-armed defenders. *The world belongs equally to women,* she had assured. *And I know how to make my way in it. The purpose of marriage today is companionship, emotional connection. He understands me in a way no quarterback or construction worker could. We connect in the mind.*

Dr. Quinn, who had a political bent and enjoyed talking foreign policy with me, accepted his daughter's choice. It became a regular thing between us to forward interesting political commentary to each other's inbox. He had forsaken his ancestral Catholicism and gotten involved with a Unitarian Universalist congregation and was eager to find places in the world where the message of his church might best resonate. He didn't really ask me for my input so much as he told me what his pastor had decided to do. I always suspected—and he made no effort to conceal—that he was far more dovish around me than he was otherwise. In this mutually indulged deception we formed an odd but comfortable connection.

Marie-Anne's mother, however, aside from the perfunctory appearance at the wedding, hadn't changed her mind toward me. Perhaps it was her own scientific background as a geneticist. Perhaps it was a traditionalist aesthetic dissonance about how men and women were supposed to look together. She had become more distant, more intractable. If Marie-Anne ever called her, rather than asking how I was doing, Mrs. Quinn instead tried to talk up some of Marie-Anne's old boyfriends. She went so far as to make a social media page inviting Marie-Anne to a get-together at their Charleston home where all the other attendees were big and tall twenty-something men from South Carolina and Georgia. For four years Marie-Anne dealt with her mother with patient perseverance. She took me down to Charleston three times a year—Independence Day, Thanksgiving, Easter—hoping that her mother would be won over. Nothing changed.

At last Marie-Anne gave up. She allowed herself to be excommunicated from the religion of family. She told her father that she wouldn't ever come back to Charleston. And she refused to break when her mother, in the guise of informing her about some tragedy in the extended family, wrote her long self-flagellating missives. It was an act of tremendous strength on Marie-Anne's part to resist her family for my sake. No one else in this life had ever felt inclined to stand up for me like this.

That was why I couldn't hate her for bringing pestilence upon us. The pull that our predecessors exerted upon us was a powerful thing. It was a force so strong that the only adequate release we had devised in response was to produce successors. But because of me, Marie-Anne had pincered the relationship with her predecessors into nothingness. Perhaps that was why she no longer wanted to look forward in time.

If things had stayed the way they were, we probably would've come around to getting a handle on the mess our family life had become. Maybe I would have been able to convince her that the solution to an imperfect family was not to kill the idea of family but to make another try, to keep pushing the aspiration of a perfect family life into the next generation. Something like that might have gotten us back to the baby talk. But instead the weight gain had struck. Marie-Anne's body image took a nosedive, and sexing up her mind was the only kind of intimacy she would accept. Bottom line: there was no room for making children when the only communion was verbal and manual.

Mind sex, as we called it, wasn't all that bad. What we lacked in physical performance we made up in narrative depth. We explored more of our subterranean interests. We were willing to say more deviant things in each other's ears. There was something of science fiction in our intimacy. Didn't all the scientists predict that in the future we would cease to have physical sex and be satisfied purely by the direct stimulation of our erogenous neurons using electronic stimulation? Marie-Anne and I decided that, as Sartre and Simone had been pioneers of the contemporary swinging culture, she and I were at the forefront of the kind of sex people would be having thirty years from now. At some point, she said, she would write a book about our experiences. It would be entitled *Mindtimacy*. Perfect for the virtual age.

Still, there were issues. Chief among the challenges of mind sex was that it was entirely reliant on conversation. When something created a mental barrier between two people it was impossible to appeal to physical connection to overcome that distance. Silence forced us to float away from one another. Each of us in separate quarters. Alone. Dissatisfied. Resentful of the other for withholding orgasms.

That was where we found ourselves now.

Being banished to the living room meant that I had plenty of time to become familiar with my surroundings. The first thing I did was reorganize the kitchen, reshelving everything from pots to wineglasses. Then I went through the bookshelf and familiarized myself with every book upon it. No more surprises. Next I set my sights on the two drawers underneath the television, which were filled with all sorts of film and music that we hadn't gotten around to. I took all the music, burned it onto our hard drives, and discarded the vast quantities of CDs. At last I moved to our film library, most of which was composed of DVDs that Marie-Anne had brought over from her Charleston home, simply sweeping them into a suitcase and dragging it over when her mother told her to clear everything out.

I had never gone through the collection before. I was surprised by it. It contained almost nothing from Hollywood. Many of the films had come down to Marie-Anne from her father. There was a lot of Italian neorealism. There was some early Polanski, including his first work, the taut and tense exploration of infidelity, *Knife in the Water*. Then I got to the bulk of the films. Almost all of them were French art-house flicks from the fifties to the eighties. With plenty of time to burn, I blew through them. It was an aspect of Western cultural history I hadn't consumed before. My favorite among these, from a cinematic standpoint, was *The Battle of Algiers*, about the French occupation of Algeria. Raw and violent. I liked it despite its overtly political flavor.

But it wasn't the most intriguing film in the collection. That mantle belonged to a mid-seventies film starring Isabelle Adjani. It was called *L'Histoire de Adèle H.* The container it came in contained a note from Marie-Anne's father addressed to her mother: *This is the actress that Martin Ryerson said you looked like. Take a look. I think the resemblance is uncanny.* The note had been written with a ballpoint pen, one that was short on ink so that some of the letters were without color. Marie-Anne had never mentioned her mother resembling any actress, so I figured she was either unaware of the film's existence or would never bring it up with me. I decided to go ahead and watch it.

In the film Adjani plays the second daughter of the novelist Victor Hugo. She spends her life chasing an indifferent British man around the world, subsumed in her love for him, destroyed in the end by the inability to attain him. The story wasn't what was compelling. Most of the magic of the film lay in Adjani. She really did look like Rasha Florence Quinn. Not identical twins by any means, but similar enough to be long-lost sisters.

My initial impulse was to hide the film, because if Marie-Anne were to see it she would probably suffer another bout of sadness.

The trouble was that I had underestimated my own reaction to Adjani. She struck me as immaculate. I found myself obsessed with Adjani's mouth. The way it curved downward at the edges, with that perfect lower lip like the hull of a prophetic ark or the arc of a perfect plot. Her eyes were compulsive. Peals of pain running across her pupils. A thorn jammed inside an iris. A knot in the cornea that couldn't be cut. Her body was like a tree, progressively twisted and gnarled by the gravity of her love. Adjani started stalking me, stealing upon me when I was sleeping, an uncontrollable apparition. Beauty. Every time she prodded my conscience I wanted to draw out the film and watch it again. That's precisely what I ended up doing. I tucked the film underneath the cushions of the sofa and proceeded to watch it whenever I was eating. The only time I withheld watching was if Marie-Anne was at home. There was no need to subject her to her mother's doppelgänger.

Seeing Adjani on repeat aroused in me all the dormant thoughts of Mrs. Quinn. I thought about the first time I had seen her. It hadn't been at the steakhouse in Buckhead, but a few months earlier, at our graduation at Emory. Marie-Anne and I had agreed that graduation wasn't the right time to tell our parents about each other. I had been with my parents and Marie-Anne had been with hers, just a few yards away, sharing a close embrace with her mother, who was wearing a printed sundress with a parasol hat in purple and had a champagne flute in her left hand.

While Marie-Anne had been holding her mother close she had peered over a shoulder, given me a wink, and pointed to her mother's back and mouthed the words *My mom!* in my direction. Then she had planted a big soft kiss on her mother's shoulder and given me a thumbs-up. There had been something vulnerable in Marie-Anne's need to make sure that she was linked to her mother at a moment like that. I had gone away from graduation equating Mrs. Quinn with the ability to unlock the deeper levels of my then-girlfriend's vulnerability, and with a separate wish; namely, to one day be close enough to Marie-Anne that she would want her mother to experience affection from me as well. Obviously that moment had never materialized. The next time I saw Mrs. Quinn had been at the announcement of our engagement. From then on she'd been nothing but a conniver and enemy against me. Against us.

The revival of the memory was upsetting. What kind of woman was Rasha Florence Quinn that she couldn't see how much Marie-Anne felt for her? How could she undermine her daughter's matrimonial decision? The only rational explanation was that Mrs. Quinn knew exactly how much clout she had with her daughter, that she was fully aware how weak Marie-Anne was in front of her, and she simply felt no remorse in taking advantage of it. Until now I had never let myself dislike Mrs. Quinn, believing that if I let rancor toward her settle into my spirit, then Marie-Anne would somehow manage to see it and be hurt by my judgment. But something about conceiving of Mrs. Quinn as Adjani, observing her from a third-person perspective, made it easier to let my resentment turn belligerent. I could conceive of her in all sorts of un-flattering ways and not feel like I was insulting Marie-Anne. I could let myself imagine violating her, slapping her, for the punishment she had inflicted on my wife. *You are a petty, petty woman,* I wanted to get on top of her and scream. *You have no idea how much suffering you've inflicted.*

The next time I watched *L'Histoire d' Adèle H.,* I paused it during an inappropriate scene. Then, aghast by what I had done, I hid the film underneath the sofa cushion.

One morning Richard Konigsberg surprised me at the apartment. He arrived at the building and buzzed on the aged speakerphone. It squawked like a duck with rusted vocal cords. Richard pressed the button over and over again. I knew what he was doing. He was making sure I was irritated. He said he enjoyed making people turn acid like vinegar, because vinegar was how you cleaned the urine and fecal matter of the world.

I met him in the lobby. He was not his usual self, looking listless and distant. His face was there but the eyes seemed reeled back into the head. His physique had lost much of its authority. The lines of his body and the void that surrounded him now all ran into one another, as if he had been left unfinished by some attention-deficient painter.

"Did a gold digger clean you out?"

"No, the Big Nonexistent did." He jerked his thumb upward.

His declaration came at around the same time a pair of toddlers across the lobby ran to the grand piano. They bashed their heads upon the lower octave.

I took Richard by the elbow and led him to the café attached to the building. I sat on the inside so he was facing the window. He made me switch seats.

"Twenty years old," he sighed into his latte. "In the military. Got blown up in Afghanistan."

"Who?"

"My son," he croaked.

"Your son? I didn't know you had a son."

I stared at him with a lump in my throat, the force of his announcement pounding through my body. We had never been men who dealt with the unexpected. Everything we did in life was the consequence of careful planning. Yet here we were, over the period of a few months, coming to each other slammed by the unpredictable.

Richard tried to keep his lips together, but they insisted on ripping their sutures. He choked a little. "I didn't either. I slept with this stripper in Chicago. She knew the whole time I was the father. But she didn't want to be connected to a Jew. Can you believe that? The kid was broke, so instead of college he became the few, the proud, the dead. Here I was. With all this money. He could have had it all."

Richard's face collapsed upon the bones. He was a bighearted man, gregarious and caring, who had been destined to go out as a shooting star, or in some orgiastic storm. But that was not what would happen now. He would shrivel up and become silent and find that when he tried to flick his eyes toward a fine female, his eyelids and his pupils simply wouldn't react. Here and there around Philly there were losers from Atlantic City who went and drowned everything in one fell weekend, and came back and sat in Love Park, or on the stone benches at Eakins Oval, and just rocked back and forth, without an identity, without money, the only papyrus in their possession the four-chambered one in their chest. That was what would happen to my friend.

"I'm speechless," I said. "What now?"

Richard's weakness spread like spiders on the web of his wrinkles. "I'm leaving for Israel," he said at last. It was the only firm thing he had spoken.

"What's in Israel?"

"What's in America?"

I felt insignificant; not only because I couldn't be of any use to him, but because my years of doting on him hadn't led him to think of me as a son. He was leaving everything behind without considering the possibility that I could fill the void.

I sat silent, desperate to find a way to rip off the wet sponge affixed to my skull. The jolt that Plutus had given me was a gentle stab compared to the waterboarding Richard received. I saw him seated before me, hemmed in by the limitations imposed by family and community. He seemed unsuited to the moment, like he was an aristocrat in a prison. The reason he had avoided a wife and family his entire life was precisely because he knew that they would cause him to give up his universality, his social breadth, and become a narrow man. That was why he had never considered moving to Israel, despite many of his acquaintances having left for Tel Aviv. "Israel is a narrow little place," he used to say, referring not to the geography, but to the feeling of being hemmed in by his people. He had always been scared of being crushed by the weight of a "We." All his life he had struggled to be the autonomous "I," and that was why he had thrived in America, which was an ideal place for those who could subsist alone. But now, upon finding that all this time America had been playing him, that he had been the victim of a twenty-year-long hate crime, one that concluded with the death of a son he never knew in a war that he had never paid attention to, it wasn't a surprise that Richard was going to the place where he could lose himself in homogeneity, in the inexorability of an eternal race, under the asphalt blanket that others in his tribe had hung for them to take shelter under. Was this why Zionism had been created? To give an aggrieved Jew like Richard a place to go and wail?

"You need to sue Plutus for discrimination," he said suddenly, as if remembering that our relationship was built around him imparting wisdom to me. Any other arrangement was not consistent with who we were. "You aren't the only American Muslim confronting nonsense like this."

I didn't have the energy to fight him. How was I to explain that I was an apatheist, indifferentist, materialist. The closest I had ever come to letting someone define me by an origin other than America was when I told some people I was West Asian, which covered anything from the Red Sea to the Himalayas, everything from Israeli to Iranian to Indian.

"I don't like your terminology," I replied.

"Sometimes you just have to become what people want you to be and then become a better version of that to get your revenge," he said.

"How did that work out for you? Could you erase the hatred they have poured into 'Jew'? Wouldn't it have been better if you had hidden your origin in something, like I am trying?" I thought about Chagall. When things were safe it was no big deal to believe that you ought to express your heritage. It was only when you got accused that you regretted giving up your hidey-hole.

We sat and murmured at each other. I expressed more condolence about his son; he told me not to overthink it. To change topics up a little, he told me about his exit plan. He had liquidated his shares, turned over management of a firm to a partner, and moved out of his apartment. He was on his way to hand his car over to the new owner and had stopped to give me a backup key to a storage room he'd rented over in Cherry Hill. I was struck neither by the finality nor the alacrity of it all. Richard was different from me. When he had a grievance he found a solution to it, rather than the gray abeyance that I languished in.

I tucked Richard's key into my pocket and walked him to his car. He had gotten a ticket for running over the meter by five minutes. The blue and white citation was tucked under the windshield wiper, slapped by the breeze. "Let me cover that," I reached forward.

He hit my hand and pulled me into a hug. "Don't save me," he said, "if you won't save yourself."

I was comatose in his arms. How similar Richard and I were. Both of us without children. We would have made terrible pioneers, terrible settlers. In the self-replicating mechanism of America we were aberrations and anomalies. Eunuchs unable to bring princes forward. Condemned to prop up people who did not owe us and we didn't own.

A couple of uncles who couldn't spawn.

* * *

That night Marie-Anne and I went to Rembrandt's for dinner, where we shared a shank of lamb and played a game of trivia. Afterward we walked along 22nd Street, along the massive walls of the Eastern State Penitentiary. The snow was piled in giant oily black mounds along the curbs. Marie-Anne had her hair up and wore a cardigan with a long skirt. I was in a tan corduroy jacket with elbow pads.

She had been a little reluctant when out of nowhere I proposed going out on a date. But I hadn't been willing to let her wiggle out. With Richard's departure Marie-Anne had acquired even greater import in my life, and I wanted to make sure things were shored up between us.

"I talked to Richard today."

"How is he? Dirty old man . . ."

"Was he ever dirty toward you?"

"Why are you talking in the past tense?"

"He left. For Israel."

"For. Ever?"

"Yeah. What do you think about that?"

"I'm not surprised," she said. "He wasn't happy here."

"Why do you say that?"

"Just, you know." She cleared her throat, sliding her ballet flat over a spot of ice. "He was always so active. So unsettled."

"Something wrong with that?"

"Nothing wrong with it," she said. "Just shows a kind of unhappiness."

"Maybe he was unhappy."

"He had everything. Yet even then he was always taking up some cause. Maybe if he wasn't suing everyone all the time he would be more settled. Act his age."

I was antagonized on his behalf. In Richard's willingness to eschew a settled life for one where he pursued giant class-actions against companies that defrauded their investors, I had always seen a sort of grizzled

Robin Hood. Instead of arrows he launched complaints. Instead of sher- iffs he annoyed CEOs. Maybe all of it had been a fruitless endeavor on his part; but it showed a willingness to align himself with those who lacked something.

One by one the houses around us turned down the lights. I decided not to tell Marie-Anne any more about Richard. I had thought that by telling her I would be able to cry out a little sorrow. But she didn't under- stand why Richard mattered. Men like him were rare. Today's man ei- ther pursued outright domination or opted for complete submission. Few offered their own slaughter in the game of bluff that produced justice. Marie-Anne had little sympathy for anyone who took risks on behalf of strangers and unknowns.

After dinner we went to Bishop's Collar. The bar was empty and quiet. We ordered a pint. Marie-Anne said she remembered something for work and needed to write down a note. She picked up a napkin and sent me off to find a pen. I made my way over to a new bartender, a bald, bearded fellow with tattoos of dragons and griffins. There was a pen in his front pocket, one of those where you could click five different colors. "Can we borrow that for a second?" I gestured in Marie-Anne's direction with my head.

"Yeah, sure, buddy," he said and handed it over. Then he grasped my wrist rather firmly and looked into my eyes. "Just make sure your mom returns it before leaving. First day at my job and I already lost my other pen."

"My mom?" I glanced back at Marie-Anne. "You think that woman is my mother? How could someone who looks like me come from someone who looks like her?"

"I don't know," he said. "Your daddy was black?"

"You nailed it," I said and returned to Marie-Anne.

She smiled. "What did that guy say?"

"Nothing. Just that we should feel comfortable keeping the pen."

"How nice of him." She raised a thumbs-up in the direction of the bar and proceeded writing.

Her note had something to do with the wording for a pitch she had been playing around with. "All these technical words like *unmanned aerial vehicles* sound so terrible during a presentation," she said. "I want to come up with something better to use when I'm just sitting with someone. Any ideas?"

"How about birds?"

"Birds?"

"Yeah. Just birds. That's all flying things are, right?"

"That's good," she said absentmindedly, as if she'd forgotten she'd asked for my input. "But I need something a little more descriptive."

We drank another round and headed home. The bartender tried to glare at me on the way out, but Marie-Anne positioned herself in between me and him. At our apartment building I noticed a new security guard stepping behind the front desk. She wore the uniform of the new owners of the building. Her arrival reminded me of Marlon's absence. But what would I have gained with his presence?

Once upstairs, I went to the kitchen. Marie-Anne was still thinking about work and went to the living room and put on the news. She was following the conversation about protests in a far-off West Asian country. Through the kitchen doorway I stared at her, absorbed.

I stood on one foot, the other raised and scraping the rough surface of the fridge. "I want children," I declared.

Marie-Anne turned to me, pulling her red hair back in a ponytail. "You know I can't, baby," she said. "It's too risky."

"We can manage the risks. Medicine today . . ."

"I am rotten," she said. "I don't want to pass this rot to our kids."

"What you have isn't genetic. It won't be passed on."

"I don't want to make them."

A flame passed over my body. It wasn't some misogynist insurrection caused by the way Marie-Anne made herself master over my virility. I, along with an entire generation of men, had ceded that sort of authority a long time ago. My rage had another locus, namely myself. Marie-Anne had become spooked about children only after her own relationship with her mother broke down, and the reason for the breakdown was me. Had I been less effete, less frail, more tangible, more of a presence, Marie-Anne would've never had to suffer her familial gulf, and without that trauma she would be busy reproducing, tightening her relationship with her tribe by expanding it, weaving herself into it in the manner matriarchs did. In that wave I would've been swept along as well. From her matriarchy my patriarchy would have arisen.

"But I really want to . . ."

"Why?"

"Because I need to feel like a part of the land. This land. For. Ever."

She looked at me like I'd thrown pie at her or smeared her face with cake. "You don't need children for that. I can get you a flag pin."

"You don't understand . . ." I synthesized a syllogism about roots, and putting them down, and children, and a clan, and creating a colony, and being an American patriarch from whom many generations emerged; not an average man, but a stud, like the sort Secretariat was, or his father, Bold Ruler, who was sired by a champion called Nasrullah. Something about bloodlines. But nothing like that came out. Nothing came out at all.

"I understand just fine," she said. "You've been stuck at home for months and it's making you disconnected from all the working citizens. But don't worry about that." She came and threw her arm around me. "No one can ever question your connection to this country. Because your wife is one of the people keeping the country free and safe and strong."

Despite my anger with her, despite her deft redirect of my feelings, I softened. I remembered the Fourth of July barbecues in Charleston.

The smell of charcoal and ribs and people sitting around discussing their favorite president, as if each one was an avatar of the same eternal god, one sent to us every four years to allow us to access infinity in a more intimate manner. Someone who might serve as an intercessor between the vagaries of human life and the transcendent ideals that stretched themselves over the Republic. Some of the political stories people told at the barbecues had an anti-Northern tilt. Some of them even came off pro-slavery ("It would have faded away on its own like in Latin America"). But the Quinn family's conception of the Civil War, which they referred to as the War of Northern Aggression, was something that came straight out of American history, and so it had always been palatable, even nice. In a way, that I was connected to the losing side of the Civil War was better than being on the side of the victors, because the losers were forgotten, and the ones who were forgotten were, in a way, more authentic, colored as they were by defeat. They had more in common with me, I who was descended of races that had been defeated as well.

"I like it when you talk like that," I said.

"Come." She pulled me to the sofa. "Lie down and watch this show and I'll tell you all the new technology we're developing."

She pulled off her skirt so she was only in panties and camouflage socks. Her thighs were like loaves of breads that giants ate. She talked quietly about how some of the new surveillance drones her company was developing were barely as big as a hummingbird. *"Drones,"* she said in an epiphany, "that's what we should call them." I rested my head on her un-dulating thighs and watched the old men from Harvard and Georgetown talking in front of the American flag. The screen changed and depicted protestors burning that flag. The newscaster played the image in a six-second loop. The repetitiveness of the image caused my eyes to blur. I didn't want to let myself go to sleep. I wanted to stay up and argue. But I couldn't bring myself to do it because I didn't believe in imposition. I didn't engage in coercion. I couldn't bring myself to make a demand. I wanted things, but I was too reticent to fight for them. I gestured toward them from a distance and hoped to get them, and if it all didn't come to pass, I wouldn't blame those who denied me. I would blame myself for not having hoped deeply enough. I was a new kind of man. I believed in surrender. I hadn't come to this conclusion as a result of a personal epiphany. I had come to it because I was cursed with having a Muslim name in America at a time when others with names like mine crashed shadows into America. As a result, I knew I had to do whatever it took to not allow myself to be likened to them, to never appear confrontational. The transformation had been an easy one for me because I had always been a bit of a coward. This was also why I remained so drawn to Marie-Anne. She had intact in her the aggressor, the assertor, the attacker who I sometimes wished I could be, who sometimes I needed to be. It was why I had always kept a flame alight under her power, propped it up, given it oxygen to thrive. I stood to benefit from it. I stood to be protected by it. She was my sword and shield. Behind her I could be naked. Under her I could be safe.

CHAPTER THREE

Spring sprang from snow. The days lengthened. The sky brightened. The trident maples and chokecherries began to display some color and the yellow forsythia, which flowered before showing leaves, started to bloom. The purple beech hedges were somewhere between winter copper and the purple bruise-like color of spring. It wasn't warm enough to go and sit out in the glades and gazebos along the water, but the rowers were out at Boathouse Row and the rollerbladers and cyclists were doing the six-miler around Fairmount in ever-increasing hordes. And at certain points in the day the art museum looked like it was erupting with golden spears.

Marie-Anne was busy during the spring. She got flown out to Doha—"the forward base of American foreign policy," as she called it—to make a couple of speeches about unmanned aerial vehicles, to analysts from Brookings Institute and *Foreign Policy* magazine. Later she visited Abu Dhabi for a defense technology convention. She also helped make a pitch for some drones to buyers from the Wazirate, a small oil-rich kingdom in the Persian Gulf. The trip was a big deal because previously it had been MimirCo's CEO, Karsten King, who would have gone to make the pitch to the Waziratis.

"Do you want to come along?" Marie-Anne asked before going. "Maybe look for a job in a warmer place?"

"I think I'll pass," I said, a little annoyed by her persistence in trying to get me back to work. I also had no intention of becoming an expat.

I was content at home. Marie-Anne's father called a couple of times, but I didn't bother answering. It would be impossible to explain the circumstances that had led to my firing. I spent my days playing video games; went down to the Bishop's Collar to drink and watch basketball; or hung out at the art museum. The brown-skinned punk girl still worked there and she gave me a curious look each time I came.

Marie-Anne texted numerous updates during the trip. Most involved mentions of some guy named Mahmoud. The frequency with which she mentioned him made me curious. Was she attempting to make him seem familiar? What was the reason behind such a move? Was it so that I would not ask any questions about him? Assume him to be a casual part of her professional existence? Despite the anxiety that came with the possibility of marital bonds getting tested, I experienced a brief tremor of excitement. It had been a long time since I'd been aware of any man gazing upon Marie-Anne as a sexual being. The possibility that somewhere out there, in a traditionally masculine industry, in a part of the world still owned solely by men, she might be objectified, pursued, seduced, triggered a possessory desire toward her. It was a validation I had not experienced since the start of her illness. It made me remember how much more I'd valued her when she had been healthy. Not only because of what she meant to me, but what the fear of losing her elicited.

Mahmoud became the first thing I talked about after Marie-Anne landed. We were on the sofa. She spooned me, curling a bit of her hair and dipping it into my ear.

"This Mahmoud seems to have replaced Wu, Sharma, and Jones as the leading singer in the we-love-Marie-Anne chorus. Is there attraction there?"

"Mahmoud knows how to make himself appear attractive."

"So you like him then," I said with a twinge of arousal in my foot and heart.

She almost never told me, despite my insistence, the names of her admirers because she believed she ought to determine when and how to spurn them. She certainly never went so far as to use the word *attractive* in relation to them.

"He is just resourceful. He introduced me to people at think tanks. To experts in surveillance. To journalists who all have great contacts with the military. I even ended up talking to him about your—our—situation. He told me I was wrong to ask you to ditch the Koran."

"Wait," I said, the tendril of sexual tension lost. "Let me be clear: I wasn't upset because you said I should ditch the Koran. I was upset that you wanted me to apologize when I wasn't the one who did something wrong."

"Baby," she said, twisting my wrist, "you don't have to let me get away on the issue of the Koran. I understand now how insensitive I was. Mahmoud made me see."

It offended me that my disbelief could be shrugged off because of the simple fact that my name sounded similar to his. It seemed that as long as you had a Muslim name you were presumed to be a believer. Your name was your blood and your blood was your faith.

"Let's look forward," I said out of exhaustion.

She clapped my thigh and kissed my cheek. "Yes, let's discuss how you should become a freelance promoter."

She made me reach for her purse and then she drew out a box of business cards. During her travels she had given my work a great deal of thought and decided that I didn't need to join an existing company. I could procure my own clients through initiative and references.

The cards were off-white with pale red trim and a kind of rubbery feel to them. The front had my name and contact information, along with the words: *Marketing Consultant. Social-Media Maven. Bon Vivant.* She also had the brilliant idea of miniaturizing my college diploma and printing it on the back of the card. "You went to the Harvard of the South," she explained. "Let's take advantage of that."

The cards made me appear like a kind of all-purpose hustler. Such people were pariahs. Low-end peddlers, pushers, pimps. Granted, in a capitalist world everyone was a salesman, but in my heart there was a great difference between being a solitary salesman working out of his house and a specialist with institutional support, someone with hefty patronage behind him. What was next? Was I supposed to put away my dress shoes in favor of sneakers?

I winced. Less at the deterioration of my status and more at Marie-Anne's desperation to get me back into the workforce, so that I'd once again be productive, an earner. It was an interesting reversal for us. Until a few years ago, before the break with her parents, when she still took stipends and allowances from them, I used to say that she was too casual with what it meant to be a breadwinner. Now she pursued the paycheck like she was its shadow. Her true turning point had been taking the job at MimirCo. Back when she had been a writer she fancied herself a kind of mystic in the world who, much like Rumi or Meister Eckhart, was compelled to be withdrawn from the exigencies of life, someone whose purpose was to root herself to one spiritual place, one's personal Yoknapatawpha County, and from there reach into her being and fling into the world, like rice at a wedding, invisible satellites made of empathy, tasked with sending back information to be processed at her heart. She had taken this idea of fiction as mysticism quite seriously. She even wrote an essay about it for some far-flung publication. The piece had evaluated ancient Islamic mystical orders, called the *tariqas*, and likened them to creative writing departments at our universities. She had found a great deal of similarity between the two institutions, both in terms of their guild-like structures, and in their emphasis on serving as a kind of spiritual pole to the world. But Marie-Anne wasn't that mystic anymore. With MimirCo she had chosen another guild. Its axis was money, not infinity, not empathy.

"To top it off," she said, "I think I even got you a gig."

I looked at her with rage. I deserved blame for turning her this way, for having seeped into her with my lust for acquisition and rotted the mystic in her.

There had to be a word out there for someone who slaughtered a saint.

My potential project involved a cohort of Mahmoud's named Qasim, a playboy princeling who was based in the Wazirate. He was hoping to launch a DVD in America. As a favor to Marie-Anne, Mahmoud had hyped me as someone Qasim might hire to promote his venture.

"Do you think you can do this?" Marie-Anne inquired.

I grasped her thigh and gave her a squeeze. If Marie-Anne had made the effort to juggle some balls for me, I didn't see why I couldn't take over for a little bit. She had many other acts in play as it was. For the first time I saw lines around her eyes. They were even beginning to creep to the edges of her lips. She had always warned me that she would age badly, her paleness chapping and cracking like the salt plains, while I would age better, becoming more polished, smoother, a well-trod wooden handrail. It was a little startling to be presented with the specter of her decline this early. "I don't see why I can't give it a go." She brightened at my acceptance.

I started that day. Qasim and I corresponded via e-mail and had webchats. He was a young man, in his midtwenties, dressed in a white *kandura* and a red Ferrari hat. His goatee was exquisite, almost painted on, styled more meticulously than the eyebrows of any housewife stalking Rittenhouse.

I worked from home. Qasim worked on the fly. I noticed that he streamed to me from his cell phone while driving around Wazir City, the reflection from the skyscrapers tessellating upon his face. One time he picked up a pair of women while we chatted, Russian by the look of them, and had them in the car with him while he raced some teenagers along streets with domes and minarets in the background. He told me that the Waziri Highway, which linked the only two major cities in the city-state, was the new Autobahn. It had a bridge that was the new Golden Gate. It had an airport that was the new Heathrow. Everything about his world seemed to possess novelty. It was as if their wealth had allowed them to elude the passage of history.

Eventually we got to his business idea. It was a health-and-fitness DVD that he'd recorded, with the Russian girls as background models. The name of his system was Salato. The name was derived from *salat*, the Arabic word for prayer. The *o* at the end had been added because yoga ended in a vowel and so did other exercises Americans enjoyed, such as Zumba and Tai Chi. He already had thirty thousand copies of the DVD ready to order. Now he needed press, exposure, word of mouth. He believed that gullible Americans were the best market for a new exercise craze, provided that there was enough noise to accompany the product.

"Creating noise is what I do. Why don't you overnight the DVD?"

Qasim pulled away from the phone for a few seconds, turned it around, and returned to the camera. "I just uploaded it to your e-mail. Follow the link to download."

"Your Internet is that fast?"

"Where do you think I am? In bin Laden's cave? Hell, even his cave turned out to be a bungalow. You guys need to update your stereotypes about us."

I heated up some nachos and cheesy salsa, poured myself a soda, and headed into the living room to watch the exercise routine.

The video began with a panoramic shot of a beachside resort, glittering teal swimming pools, a placid artificial lagoon. The thrum of Arabian guitar permeated the air. The camera came to a stop at an elevated space between two large golden fountains. Qasim stood in front, dressed in a shirt and loose trousers, and the Russian models were behind him in traditional black robes with sequins down the front. From the fall of the light it was evident they only wore underwear beneath. The production quality was high. The sound was excellent. It was evident Qasim worked with a script.

He started the viewer off on a small stretching routine and gave a short history lesson about the emergence of the Islamic prayer. "Official sources claim that the Prophet Muhammad took the full-body method of prayer that was already known to seventh-century Arabs, modified it, and from there over the centuries it spread to a billion people. So already we're part of a long history, a long legacy. Think of all your historical brothers and sisters. We are all going to join together as a community of exercise."

After stretching, he explained the various positions. Salato began in the standing position, hands folded. Then you bent forward with both hands on your knees. "Already you're cracking the kinks out of your cartilage," Qasim exhaled. Next, one stood back up, and in the same motion knelt down to the ground, folding both legs underneath the torso. "It'll be uncomfortable at first," he said. "But that is just your decadence complaining." Seated like this, one made two prostrations, head to ground, before standing back up. "You should already feel the spine aligning." Once you were back on your feet you repeated the aforementioned process again, up to four times, depending on what time of the day you were exercising. Qasim pointed out that there was a small chart available, at an extra cost, which revealed how many repetitions to make at what time in the day. Or you could pay out a little more and receive a small wristband that emitted a wail and reminded you it was "time to Salato." Due to the history of Salato, where all the leading practitioners had been men, Qasim advised that the routine leader should always be male. For the sake of tradition.

Now that the explanations were over, Qasim began in earnest. The camera zoomed in on his crisp goatee. His head filled the screen. "Normally one would be reading portions of the Koran during each movement," he said. "But we're simply going to focus on clearing our minds, focusing on the breathing, and exhaling the power word, *Hu.*" He demonstrated this for a moment. Then his voice took on an exhortative tone. "This is Salato! I am your Exercise Imam! Now say it with me! Hu! Hu! Hu!"

The Russian models nodded, smiled, and knelt.

It took me two days to come back to the DVD. It felt disconcerting to have fallen from watching films of Isabelle Adjani to this. But maybe the cosmos was speaking to me. Had I not always retained an interest in the film industry? A dream that I'd tucked away after Marie-Anne's attempted novel failed to materialize and took with it my own creative zeal? Well, marketing a kitsch infomercial-cum-documentary-cum-fitness-DVD might not lead me to the Oscars, but one could classify it as film work, broadly defined. It might serve as a gateway into other kinds of film promotion.

I decided to put together a PowerPoint presentation. This particular software program told us everything there was to know about how to persuade. With its bullets, tracks, columns, grids, it was chock-full of martial vocabulary. Even the name seemed to suggest that persuasion was an act of enforcement.

Once I told Qasim that I had a presentation ready for him, he became so excited that he said he'd be on the next flight to Philadelphia. *Such things should happen face-to-face,* he explained in his e-mail.

In the postscript he asked that I get in touch with Mahmoud so he could be present at the meeting as well. I asked Marie-Anne why it was necessary to bring Mahmoud in. She simply said that Mahmoud tended to get offended if his influence over a deal was not explicitly acknowledged. No one who ran a venture through him ran the risk of challenging his wrath.

Getting ahold of Mahmoud wasn't easy. He was a very busy man, though it was unclear why or how, especially as I hadn't found anything he had written, or even anything in terms of television or radio appearances. He seemed to be known without any effort. The best I could infer was that he was a sort of fixer or liaison who connected people in government and media and other important public institutions. A socialite and a promoter in his own way. But I failed to understand what he got out of it all or how he had attained his station.

I wrote to tell him that I was Marie-Anne's husband and that Qasim wanted him present for our initial meeting. He replied a week later and said he could stop by on his way to New York from DC. I suggested a couple of hotel conference rooms. But Mahmoud vetoed that option; he said Qasim wouldn't be comfortable with the possibility of someone hearing about Salato and stealing the idea. He recommended our place as the more suitable venue. I cleared the meeting with Marie-Anne, who was so happy to see me in the flow of work that she said she would come back from Virginia early and be present at the meeting as support.

On the appointed day I finished tinkering with the presentation and cleaned up the apartment. Outside an airy sleet settled over Philadelphia. The drops lacked volume. The ice was imperceptible, only visible against the reddest of brick, and even then seeing the drops required the assistance of the meek bulbs glowing in the alcoves.

The idea of having a get-together at home filled me with a peculiar anxiety. We hadn't invited anyone over since that fateful party. All day my eyes went to the bookshelf. This time it wasn't because of the since-removed Koran, but due to the Nietzsche collection and the works of Rushdie. It was unlikely that a pair of believers would like to see such work in the possession of a man they were doing business with. I swept my hand and moved the seven or eight volumes into the wine closet. I moved the Jewish writers too, just to be safe.

Mahmoud, Qasim, and Marie-Anne ran into one another down in the lobby and came up together.

Qasim was just as tall and fit in person as in the video. He wore a black suit and a gold tie. His watch was Swiss, loafers Italian, embossed handkerchief English. He kissed each cheek of mine with warmth. I pictured him having done the same to Marie-Anne, so when I greeted her I kissed her on the lips instead of the usual peck on the jaw. I regretted it as soon as I did it. I had forgotten that this was one of her pet peeves. When a guy kissed a girl in public it suggested ownership, and Marie-Anne was loathe to give anyone the impression that she was owned.

Mahmoud was much shorter than Qasim. He was also more muscular, with a craggy and severe face that suggested having spent a considerable amount of time outdoors. His eyes seemed fixed to the distance. He wore a traditional fitted black skullcap and his long curly black hair curved out from underneath. He shook my hand. He kept a scarf swirled around his neck. Dangling off his left wrist was a neon turquoise rosary that kept slipping out from underneath the sleeve. His smile was of a man who often found others giving themselves away to him.

During introductions I paid close attention to Mahmoud's interaction with Marie-Anne. He seemed not to notice her. There was no alchemy there. He only related to her as a contact. All the visions I had of him as an admirer of my wife tumbled away and broke. I was alone again. The only man in the world who persisted in finding Marie-Anne beautiful.

Initially it didn't seem like Marie-Anne was inclined to let me get to the presentation. She wanted to talk about the meetings in the Persian Gulf. Apparently, both Mahmoud and Qasim had been instrumental in getting MimirCo the private audience with a buyer in the Wazirate and Marie-Anne wanted to emphasize to both men how grateful her CEO was. It occurred to me that my work on Salato was, at best, some sort of quid pro quo, and quite likely a cover for future conversations on behalf of MimirCo. I wasn't against being Marie-Anne's tool in the advancement of her career; but I would have liked to have been apprised of my role.

It was Mahmoud who brought the conversation back my way. "Should we find out what sort of plan for Salato we have on the table?" he said, throwing open his old blazer and checking a watch on a platinum chain.

I gave his outfit a second look. Dressed in a V-neck sweater and tight denim jeans, I felt like a child ordered to perform before his father. I had not felt this eye—of evaluation, of criticism—in quite some time. People who used to come to Plutus had been so desperate for us to take them as clients that they used to fall at our feet. And they paid in advance. That assurance was missing now. I had to impress these men or fail to get paid. I became even more nervous when Marie-Anne dimmed the lights and sat down next to Mahmoud, throwing one leg over the other so her foot pointed at him. I stared at her foot so intently that water came to my eyes and in the blurry gaze her foot and his leg seemed to touch. But of course no man would be interested in touching Marie-Anne. I was the only man who could bring himself to do that.

I projected the images onto the wall above the TV and started talking. The first couple of slides detailed the kind of expertise I had. My contacts. My experience. Mahmoud and Qasim sat unmoving through this part, lightly scratching their faces. Qasim was intense. Mahmoud was casual; he evaluated *me* more than the presentation.

Marie-Anne, meanwhile, smiled in the way she did when she was trying to be supportive, like when I tried to enter her with a condom on and just couldn't muster the hardness.

The next few slides specified which particular outlets and personalities I'd like to pitch Salato to. These were followed up by specific examples of what previous campaigns I'd done.

Qasim raised his hand. "But what are you going to say to them when they ask what it is? I mean, is it Middle Eastern fitness? Arab yoga? Is it Muslim jujitsu? What's the hook? The catch?"

This was the inquiry I had set the presentation up for. Richard Konigsberg had taught me to build anticipation. It showed you weren't afraid to make the client wait, which the client understood as confidence. "It's kind of like what priests and rabbis do to sell God to us," Richard had explained. "They talk about everything but God, and we assume it's because they know God already."

I gave Qasim a confident look. "Well, I felt that given today's political situation, with mosques that aren't allowed to be built, with mentions of terrorism and suicide everywhere, with Americans caught up in numerous wars with militants, it would be best to avoid any mention of words like *Arab, Muslim,* or *Middle East.* The hook, then, is a little more ambiguous, meant to evoke mystery, to capitalize on intrigue."

I clicked the space bar and a slide popped forward. *WORSHIP, YOURSELF* the words said in calligraphic lettering. On three sides were images of Qasim and the Russian girls grabbed from the DVD, bowing, kneeling, and prostrating before the words.

I could tell something had gone wrong. Qasim curled his lip and paced the room, shaking his head. He sucked up the light in the room and turned it murky. He walked to the kitchen sink, ran the water, and dabbed his eyes.

Mahmoud, catching Qasim's drift, made a wincing expression and then moved toward the wall. "The execution is good," he said, "but the substance is not right."

"I'm sorry, but what's the problem? Is it the logo?"

Qasim tossed away a napkin, rushed to the projection, and rapped the wall with the back of his hand. It sounded like he might hurt his knuckles. "That slogan. I cannot believe. It is a fail. Muslims don't worship themselves. Worship of the self is the biggest crime in Islam. It is leaving the faith. I don't want to put a product out there that isn't Islamic."

"But look, there's a comma. That stops it from being a theological assertion. It's meant to suggest that Salato is something you can do alone, as opposed to other forms of group exercise."

Qasim shook his head and buttoned his jacket. "I think we are very far. I was told I should hire you because you were Muslim and would know exactly what we wanted. Instead, you gave me this thing, this idea of worshipping something other than God. There is a word for this. Maybe your parents never taught. It is called *shirk*. There isn't a Muslim out there who would find *shirk* okay. I am sorry, Marie-Anne, but we are very far."

It took Qasim a second between his final declaration and his ultimate decision to leave the apartment. In that brief moment the rest of us looked around as if seeing each other for the first time.

Mahmoud remained behind. "I am sorry," he said. It wasn't an apology as much as a phrase that was necessary to occupy that moment. "I will talk to him."

"What just happened?" Marie-Anne asked.

"Let's just call it a cultural gap," Mahmoud replied. "Qasim is smart enough to know that the only way to get Islam into America is to sell it. Like pizza. Like cars. But because it is Islam he cannot get past how dirty a business sales is."

"Selling is what he wanted me to do. It's a product."

"I know," Mahmoud said. "Like I said, I will try to talk to him. Maybe he will come back around."

Then, with desultory handshakes, he was gone as well. The pins of the door clicked back into place. The dishes in the kitchen stopped rattling. I turned to find Marie-Anne standing, ripping off the scarf from around her neck, tossing it down like it was a serpent from another world. She showed none of the anthropological reasonability that Mahmoud had exuded.

"That's almost six months of rent you just lost!" It was a scream, not a statement. It slashed into me like white noise in a broken transmission.

I wasn't prepared to accept blame. "You told them I was Muslim? Why would you do such a thing?"

"I did it to get you some business."

"You didn't do it for me," I replied. "You whored me out as a favor for hooking up MimirCo. You just wanted to impress your beloved Mahmoud."

"Yes, yes," she said. "So sue me for thinking that you having a Muslim name might be a fucking asset to me. Might be of some use. But obviously that was a mistake. You suck at being an asset. You can't even be yourself."

I was left alone in the living room, staring out the window into the sleet. The passage of time wasn't reliant on the consent of the living, but we could, often with our emotion, impress certain regulations on the experience of it, either speeding it up or slowing it down, or even stopping it if our will was of sufficient intensity. I slowed everything. Like streaming a video that buffered every second. I could see each tiny drop. Each one resembled the scarf Marie-Anne had hurled, or a lightning bolt, or a missile. Each one was aimed at some part of me, leaving a drop-sized hole.

I became a mesh. There, but everything passing right through me.

You can't even be yourself.

That sentence stayed with me. There were times it left me fetal. I lay on the sofa with my knees up, feet in the air, holding a big toe in each hand. Other times I went natal, my head sliding off the edge of the sofa, body straightening to a snakelike length, until I found myself crawling around the apartment on unpadded elbows. Sometimes splinters entered and didn't come out. I was absorbing back some of my spilled dignity.

Before long it was necessary to leave the apartment. To escape the visions of the second assault in my living room. To escape the reminder that my home was where I was most often and most severely ambushed. It created the paranoia that in some fundamental way I was unknown to myself, or worse, that after having known myself once, I was now lacking in that knowledge. In the arc of human awareness, which bended toward mastery, was I some sort of dead end?

There were very few places to go to. Out of town wasn't an option because that either required money or connections, neither of which I had. I wasn't an outdoorsman, therefore camping and hiking were out. I was afraid of going into Center City, lest I might run into someone from Plutus, or some other past I was trying to leave behind. The small size of Philadelphia's downtown, once an asset and a joy, now made it feel like a prison.

One day I walked out into the neighborhood behind the apartment building, toward Poplar Street. Just a couple of blocks south of Girard Avenue, that unofficial but well-understood demarcation between the Philadelphia of the professionals and the other Philadelphia, the one that didn't exist, that faded into darkness when the Comcast Tower and Liberty Place lit up orange to support the Flyers. The long rows of town houses, with blistered paint and white windows protruding like the bicuspids of witches, screamed at me, telling me to turn around, to go back. This was the Philadelphia associated with the forty thousand vacant properties. That itself was a legacy from a plan to try to house everyone in the city. But the city hadn't managed to fill the houses. It was as if the people of Philadelphia didn't want the city to be their home.

Eastbound on Girard, I followed the rails of the abandoned tram and reached Broad Street, where two Norwegian rats that had come into the port in Camden, literally larger than cats, poked their heads out of a hole in the wall of the Moorish Science Temple. Two men in long, beaded beards stood outside and called at me, telling me that the Freemasons downtown were not the real Masons, how America was still a territory of Morocco, how I needed to forget the history the white man had taught me. Passersby gathered around their cracked crate pulpit and listened, moved on.

I had always chosen to ignore this Philadelphia. This place where the cemeteries were in the sky—old sneakers tied to power lines—and where town houses slashed by time bled bricks onto the pavement. An old man dragged his chair while smoking a cigar as the chipped cement of the porch continued to crumble. The pigeons turned black to merge with the smog from the bus. Tattered plastic bags tumbled along the street and got stuck in the tram tracks. Shirtless boys played football in empty lots and celebrated touchdowns by clapping their knees together and kicking broken bottles of liquor. A police cruiser came out of nowhere, too massive for the street, too powerful, like the *Titanic* in a river. It waited at a red light and then ran it. The boys trailed it with insults and laughter.

I passed by a public school adorned with murals the students had made. The blue-hued art shone dull but proud. These were images of old men and young children who had grown up in these neighborhoods. The murals bore a glaze, if not of immortality, at least of substance, of meaningfulness. They were not marketing ploys devised by a bunch of bored and underemployed people for money and recognition and attention. They were just attempts at representation made on the sides of easily forgotten buildings. They seemed to say that the canvas was not important, and neither was the paint, and neither was the amount of response one might evoke. The only thing that mattered was to take all of what was inside and turn it into something that had a chance of glowing.

It became hard to remember how many successive days I floated around these parts of North Philly. The abandoned homes of Strawberry Mansion. The steaming sewers of Susquehanna. The knocked-over newspaper kiosks of Cecil B. Moore. I was there during the day; late in the afternoon; even sometimes in the evenings when Marie-Anne was at home making arrabbiata, or on the phone talking about taffetas and organzas with her Dixie friends. I didn't stop and speak to anyone. I didn't stop anywhere. I put my business cards—my sole form of identification—in my pocket and lost myself.

Yet I experienced a reticence in allowing myself this immersion. I couldn't help but think that without my own misfortune I would have never noticed this Philadelphia. Wasn't I only here to liken its emptiness and desolation to the failure that was my life? Didn't we seek hell only because it resembled the hole inside of us? My hunger for the hood felt fake, fatuous. If I were to continue coming here, I would have to face the fact that my sponging was parasitic and utilitarian.

In the streets I tussled with the Salato fiasco. Looking back at it now, I could hardly believe I had found myself in such a position. It was the first time in my career that a prospective client had refused my work outright. Aside from coming up with something new and different, there was no way to salvage the client. But I was afraid of even making that effort. I had been exposed and flayed for dissimulating, for pretending to be something I wasn't. It would be too difficult to go back. There was also the matter of first having to explain myself to Marie-Anne. It was a task I was unwilling to engage in. I resented her for throwing me among the sharks. She should have known better than to force me into something I didn't want to be.

One day, one of the Moorish men, in a floor-length robe with poof pants underneath, a red fez on his head, and beads around his neck, started following me around. He hadn't quite yet become a shadow— remaining respectfully distant—but it was impossible to shake him. I made getting rid of him into a personal challenge. With my newfound familiarity with the alleys, as well as the cover provided by an occasional passing truck, I tried to double back so I could follow him. But he was an elusive foe, and just when I thought I'd pulled off my trick, the two of us came face-to-face in front of New Freedom Theatre on Broad Street. There was a production of a play by Langston Hughes set to take place. Young thespians sat on the porch and recited lines.

The Moor and I were about ten feet apart. He was not as young as I previously thought. There was gray in his hair and beard. His eyes were a milky brown and his teeth were yellow. Nearby, a stubborn bag got caught upon a rusted metal railing, the iron spear lodged in its mouth. A puddle of water lapped at the Moor's feet like an obedient acolyte. There was a puddle near me as well, with motor oil passing over it, making it shimmer.

"You want your true passport?" he said.

"What?"

"It's free, ancient, and accepted," he sang. "Come on. You want your true passport?"

"No thanks."

"Every African should have it."

"I'm not African."

"Yeah you are. Light-skinned African."

"No. I am West Asian."

"So you're one of the Mooslims?"

"That's what my wife says."

"And what do you say?"

"I don't know."

He laughed. "Don't matter where a man is from. He always got to listen to his woman. You sure you don't want your true passport? Join the righteous nation?"

I told him I would have to pass on joining a new nation; I was having a hard enough time with the one I had.

The Moor clapped his hands and showed me his bare palms as if he had made something disappear. We walked down Broad Street together, all the way to Girard Avenue. The subway rumbled underground. This was where we parted. The Moor turned back to North Philadelphia, seeking someone else to invite to Moorish Science. I kept going, all the way to the art museum, to my wife, who had decided what I was.

I left the Moor behind, but my envy did not. He was from a people who, for all they didn't have, had in their blood hundreds of years of overcoming; they had established ways of dealing with the exclusion that the people in the skyscrapers imposed. What was Moorish Science but the erection of an alternative sovereignty? *Pretend that we don't exist in this America? Then we will pretend that your America doesn't exist either! Hell, America belongs to Morocco. Do you want your true passport or not?* The Moor and Richard Konigsberg had much in common. They both had a second passport to fall back on. A communal identity that existed underneath their status as Americans. One that they could appeal to if being American wasn't going well. I didn't have any such backup.

I just had Marie-Anne.

There was a word out there for when you belonged to a single person.

The Moor's pursuit put a stop to my aimless wandering. The next evening, when I went out for my walk, I headed straight toward Temple University, that oasis of familiarity in North Philly where the science took its mooring from Europe, from Benjamin Franklin, and from other men who didn't grow beards or put beads in them. The universities had always been a kind of sanctuary and harbor for me. The universities had this way of claiming ownership of everyone inside of them such that the classifications outside their doors no longer applied. They weren't bastions of democracy so much as sovereign protectorates where they could apply their own local despotism. In their case, the tyranny was aimed at keeping safe all those who could afford to be inside their walls. I wasn't a student at Temple, but by my appearance I felt like I could fit in.

I found a bulletin board in the film studies department. I might have gone wrong with Salato, but the idea of promoting new film projects still made economic sense. I was also taking a great deal of money from Marie-Anne's account, and every time we had a fight this left me humiliated. I might have become reliant upon her for housing and food, but my extra expenses I needed to cover on my own.

I walked to the kiosks and bulletin boards around the university and pinned my business cards all over. I forcibly channeled a sense of optimism during the task. Once I got paid for these projects I would be able to help cover some of our monthly bills. I might also gain a measure of revenge against Plutus. Any one of my clients, in five years' time, could become someone of importance and pick me to do their promotional work. I pictured myself running into George Gabriel somewhere—maybe he would be in the audience of a panel discussion I was leading. I would flag him down and carry out a mundane conversation about business without making the slightest mention of the original episode. I would pretend that the reason he had let me go hadn't so much as registered in my mind, which would be the best way to irk him. It would frustrate him to learn that he hadn't been able to derail my life.

But such fantasies were premature. No one solicited me for a project. The phone didn't chirp. E-mail remained dry. After a week of waiting I went back to the university and checked if perhaps the outdoor cards had been removed or misplaced. Not so. They were still there, stuck where I mounted them. The only difference was that they had dampened and become bloated in the rain. I set about replacing them with a new batch. After that I went to the film studies building and checked on the ones I had hung inside. All the cards were still there, in pristine condition, save two.

"It's pretty lame to put a diploma on the back of a business card," a male voice said from behind me. It was followed by the whir of a card flying past my head.

"I'm sorry?"

"Emory. Second tier. You can't show off with it, man."

I turned around to face the speaker. He was in a black trench coat cinched at the waist and a white turtleneck, paired with tan wool slacks falling lightly onto silver-buckled loafers. He wore his hair in a bun and his fingers were covered in a multitude of rings.

I smiled. University rankings were a coded way for Americans of a certain class to rib each other. It had been awhile since I had played that game. "It's not second tier. It's top twenty. One year it was top ten."

"But it isn't even Ivy."

"Then why do they call it the Harvard of the South?"

"Because Southerners are dumb and think that Cambridge is in Atlanta."

A class let out as we chatted. My eyes passed over a tall brunette. She was in hastily applied eyeliner and her ponytail was still wet from the morning shower; she wore flip-flops on undecorated feet. She reminded me of a young Marie-Anne. But there was one glaring difference: she seemed clueless to anything but her own presence. Marie-Anne, even at that young age, through just the exchange of a glance, had the ability to sniff out a person's dungeons, to suspect that a stranger had cata-combs. For a brief moment I missed her madly. It was a rare thing to find people in the world who could locate, much less suspect, your unspoken shame.

I saw another one of my cards in the man's hand. "So are you interviewing me for a job or are you just bored between classes?"

"I picked it up a few days ago for my friends. We were going to get together in a little bit to decide if we wanted to call you up. Then I saw you adjusting the card and figured you were the guy." He read out my name and came forward to shake hands. His arms were long and his eyes were suffused with a natural kindness. "My name is Ali. Ali Ansari. Like the Helpers."

"Helpers of . . . ?"

"You know . . ."

"Hamburger?"

He grew perplexed. "The Helpers, you know, of the Prophet? The *Ansar*?" He glanced down at the card and read out my name again, making sure it belonged to me. "I'm sorry," he said, "I thought you were someone else."

108 * Native Believer

The class cleared out. Left alone in the amber hallway, Ali Ansari and I stared at one another. He took a step back and folded his hands at navel level and passed my card through his fingers.

"I got into Emory," he said. "But I didn't go."

"Why not?"

"Because someone who goes to Emory is called an Emroid. I couldn't carry that crucifix."

"But Emory is among the top five most beautiful campuses, according to another ranking."

"Is that a reference to the architecture or the girls?"

"Well, the former," I said. "But I met my—"

Ali Ansari suddenly put his finger to his mouth. With his pinky he pointed to two people who had appeared from a side entrance. One was a bearded fellow, in jeans folded high above his ankles, wearing thong sandals. The other was a short, doe-eyed girl in a white hijab and cargo skirt with military boots. They headed to a plastic table at the entrance of the hallway and spread a tablecloth with a giant green crescent over it. They placed mugs on one corner that read, *Terrorism Has No Religion*, and, *Forgive Those Who Insult Islam*. The girl placed a giant pig teddy in front of the table. It wore a shirt that said, *Pig Protection Program*.

"I don't get the pig thing." I turned back to Ali.

"You got to go all the way back to the Roman Empire and the Jews for that. Pig was the favorite meat of the Romans. They sacrificed it as an offering to the god of war. It was also the symbol of Roman domination. When the Romans killed the Jews in Alexandria, the surviving women were forced to eat pig's flesh. And when a Roman emperor captured Jerusalem, the head of a pig was catapulted onto the temple to signal final victory. Muslims abstain from pig to follow the footsteps of the Jews. Hating pig is how the first Muslims showed they hated the Romans."

"I didn't mean the history," I said. "I don't understand what the shirt says."

"It just means that Muslims don't kill pigs . . . You really don't get it? Our propaganda needs work."

The pair spotted Ali Ansari and came over with a sign that went around his neck. It read, *Hug a Muslim*.

Ali made introductions. Hatim was the president of the Muslim Students Association, and Saba the secretary. Ali was an advisor to the organization and had encouraged them to reach out to marketing professionals for some work they needed.

"What kind of work?"

Sister Saba cleared her throat. "A campaign to put slogans on city buses. I'm sure you've seen how the neocons and the right-wing noise machine are coming after us. Passing these anti-sharia bills as if it's wrong for us to have religious weddings and funerals; asking our politicians to make loyalty oaths before they can get a job; holding congressional meetings to decide who is moderate and who is extreme; and preventing Muslims around the country from building mosques wherever we like. We want to do something about it. To make people aware that Islam is about piety and safety and caution and patience and peace."

"And modesty," Hatim chimed. "Most of Islam is actually about modesty. And marriage too. In fact, the Prophet Muhammad, may peace and blessings be upon him, said that marriage is half of the faith. So, if 50 percent is about modesty and the other 50 percent is about marriage, then the whole thing is actually about modesty."

Ali played with his bun and joined the pitch. "Twenty years ago, if you said you were a Muslim, people thought that was some kind of Latino. They used to see us as lovable street urchins hanging with fat blue genies. But now they see us as sons of a serpentine vizier attempting to poison the jasmines. Trying to hide who we are doesn't work, because nowadays everything is about identity, and we have been identified. The only thing we can do today is to clarify misconceptions. What better than way than advertising?"

I had little interest in subjecting myself to more believers. "The last time I ended up with this kind of work I was chewed out and not even given dick to suck."

"So you've done work with Muslims before?" Saba clapped. "That's great. We haven't found anyone with that kind of experience. No one wants to help us. Now Allah *azzawajal* has put you in our path. I only see a slight problem."

"What's that?"

"Well, you just said a bad word, and that's going to make you impure, so I think you should please go do the ablution before we continue. The bathrooms are that way. But be warned, they don't have a footbath. The university doesn't think it makes sense to install footbaths to accommodate us. Do you see the kind of oppression we're facing?"

The two students couldn't read my panic, but Ali Ansari picked up on it. Without breaking a wing, he took off his sign and pulled me up and away. "That's right. I will take him to do the ablution. But I just remembered, we have a lecture about Plotinus to attend. I totally forgot about that."

Hatim tried to join us. He was a philosophy major and his thesis sought to reconcile Western reason with Islamic revelation. "Did you know Plato was one of the prophets of Islam?"

"Plotnius, not Plato," Ali clarified. "This one the Christians already got."

Leaving Hatim behind, Ali and I rushed out and walked along Broad Street, past the frat houses, toward the movie theater on Cecil B. Moore. There was a pair of skateboarders avoiding the police cruisers whose job it was to keep them off the rails and the steps. A small group of black guys dressed in the finest new athletic gear came our way and headed into the movie theater.

Ali Ansari, it turned out, wasn't a Temple student. He was actually close to thirty and had graduated a few years earlier. Unable, or perhaps unwilling, to find any serious sort of employment, he also never got around to graduate school. Now he worked in the stacks at the libraries and as a security guard at one of the boutique museums on campus, while making films on the side. He lived in a small place on Diamond Street.

"A delinquent putting his salvation in film," I said. "But at least you chose a cheaper part of town to live in."

"It's not as cheap as it used to be." He waved his hand toward the intersection.

We purchased rotisserie chickens at the market and sat on a bench across from Assalamalaikum Barbershop, next to the abandoned Kabobeesh. Ali Ansari went up to one of the barbers standing outside and exchanged pleasantries, before coming back to report that Talib was off probation. A pair of black guys came out of a nearby house, in skullcaps, with checkered scarves around their necks, knee-length white shirts over khakis, both with chinstrap Sunni beards. "Cops stopped me the other night," one of them said. "No probable cause. Punched me in the face."

I turned my eyes toward the Hillel House. It emanated a soft blue light that seeped into the grass around it. I saw the Star of David and thought of Richard Konigsberg. He and I used to share moments like this.

"Sorry about before," Ali said after finishing up with his acquaintances. "I should have figured you out earlier."

I considered this man who hung out at a university; was familiar with the distinction between Plotinus and Plato; and could make jokes about gentrification. He had a name that was similar to mine, and he looked similar to me. This created kinship between us. I got the sense that if I were to tell him about being declared a residual supremacist he would understand me in a way that Marie-Anne and Richard weren't able to. To them, my being understood as a Muslim was a problem that could be made to go away, either by adapting to it through business, or by going to the courts. But to someone like Ali Ansari, being a Muslim in America was a persistent pain in the heart. The pain of being too visible. The pain of being perceived contrary to how you conceived of yourself in your thoughts.

Ali Ansari saw me staring and narrowed his eyes between bites. "Is this a date?"

"I don't know what it is yet."

We starting walking down Cecil B. Moore, past the point where the transgendered prostitutes congregated on 16th Street. I asked Ali if he knew a painting called *The Poet*. After he was done greeting the prostitutes he told me he did; he had seen it at the art museum a number of times.

We turned down Broad Street toward city hall, which glowed like a revelation in a cave. In hurried and desperate sentences I told Ali a story set in the shade of a Chagall.

Ali's swearing was a symphony that accompanied my shame.

Chapter Four

Marie-Anne was the "man" in the relationship and I was the presumptive "woman." We were aware that this was an atavistic characterization of our dynamic—why should anyone be the "man" or the "woman"?—but understanding ourselves like this made things easier to sort out when big decisions had to be made, or big fights occurred. Both of us were comfortable with our roles.

Troubles arose, however, when we were engaged in a cold war. In these periods, when resentment and moral outrage came easy, our usual clarity collapsed. Marie-Anne turned me back into the stereotypical man and expected me to behave in the chivalric manner of a herald or a knight, appeasing her out of some assured sense of honor, a stoic before her cantankerous digs. I, meanwhile, turned Marie-Anne back into the eternal feminine and expected her to fall at my feet like a geisha, to cease her petulance and be my concubine, telling me that I had been right all along. But since neither of us were trained in holding these perspectives—because she was the one who waltzed through the world with a broadsword and I was the one who navigated society using a perfumed handkerchief—what really ended up happening was more confusion, more disorder, more distance.

This sequestered apartheid was always difficult to negotiate out of, and it was precisely the place we found ourselves in after the Salato fiasco. My ambulatory escapes, along with Marie-Anne's increasing travel, wid-

ened our chasm even further. Perhaps our silence had had rational un-
derpinnings once. But like all rationality stubbornly adhered to, it had
turned into dogma, the syllogisms hardening into immutable edicts, our
psyches ruled not by term-limited presidents in dirty boots, but by dy-
nastic theocracies with executives in red leather loafers, as the caliphs
used to have.

All I could do was look upon Marie-Anne from a distance.

Each act of witness played out like an episode in front of me.

One night she came home crying, went to the bedroom, drew out a
copy of her unfinished novel, *Gaze of a Cyclops*, and with slumped shoulders pounded down a bottle of Two-Buck Chuck and eradicated a pack
of cigarettes. Never once did she actually write.

I wanted to reach out and straighten her shoulders and knead the
knots that roamed like subterranean monsters beneath her skin. But I
just couldn't do it.

A few nights later she had a verbal altercation with someone at
MimirCo. Instead of taking the call in the bedroom she went into the
hallway. She didn't realize I could still hear her. From what I gathered, it
seemed that the switch to sales was not going well. Her boss at MimirCo,
the former marine named Karsten King, had been upset with her for not
closing the deal with the Waziratis during her trip to the Persian Gulf.
Her failure with the client prompted them to put a lot of pressure on
her. It sounded like they were reconsidering whether she should've been
elevated from clerk to closer.

Under normal circumstances these sorts of difficulties would arouse
my sympathy. Ameliorative action. But not this time. I told myself that
Marie-Anne's crying and hallway conversations were theatrical fictions.
I wouldn't see into her psyche. I would limit her to being a lump of
performing flesh.

Marie-Anne wasn't as stentorian as me about observing silence. This
was because she needed me for something—namely, the poems that

would get her to the gym. Every few days she would come past me, idle, then linger until I became aware of her, making some comment about how she hadn't gone to the gym for a while, and if I had something to give her. There was no request in her tone, no supplication. It was all expectation. That made me dig in deeper. By now I had lost all notion of whether I was acting out of principle or stupidity. I only knew that I wouldn't put pen to paper. The closest I came to conceding was when I dropped an anthology of German romanticism at her feet.

My refusal to compose came to be considered the trumpet of war. There was immediate escalation. Marie-Anne harmed me the best way she knew how: she hurt herself. She refused to go to the gym, refused to do her breathing exercises, refused to write down the daily list of things she was grateful for, and ate foods high in carbohydrates and sugar. In the bathroom she didn't let herself break out into song. She never stomped her feet and moved her hips to music as the doctor had suggested. She didn't call her friends or even go out shopping. It was all aimed at heightening her cortisol.

She ballooned, again. The expansion started on the face, as it did always, and the cheekbones were submerged. Within a week her shoulders widened, her hips and thighs thickened, and there was a dour pudginess to her. In two weeks she went from brick to sponge. In the third week her hair started thinning, she developed acne on her face, a rash on her inner arm, and lesion-like bruises on her body. I glimpsed them in the bathroom mirror before she had a chance to close the door.

In the first few weeks of her vengeance she was reluctant to give up the years of progress, so she had, at least, eaten home-cooked meals. But by week four she ordered out every time. Greasy fries, greasier chicken fingers. All the salads and gluten-free things in the cupboards expired and grew stale and got thrown out. The only healthy thing she did was eat the vitamins from the unmarked bottle.

She had been good for so long. And now, while rendering me responsible, she had thrown it all away. She was taking us back to where we had been three years earlier. Except this time we didn't have any of the warmth, any of the trust, any of the fidelity that had allowed us to struggle together. This time she wanted my love turned into pity, and from pity an obedience to emanate. She wanted my obligation, not my ardor.

One evening during the fifth week she tore into her closet with scissors in hand, and disemboweled and exenterated all of her new clothes, the ones that didn't fit anymore because she had put on twenty pounds. She cried loud and wheezing, and sitting with my back against the wall in the hallway, hearing the slashing and the tearing, I cried too. Those weren't just clothes she was slaughtering. They were poems, they were the beauty of her recovering body, they were the memories of our united resistance against the insensitive and cruel imbalance inside her genes. Once, we had been good enough to bond and beat back millions of years of mitochondrial mutations. Now we weren't even good enough to talk.

One of these days she or I would pack our bags and go. It seemed as inevitable as the tyranny of cortisol.

My mother had been a subtle woman, indirect, of few words. Much of this had to do with her aborted career as a journalist in the Old World. Once idealistic and activist, she had been silenced by some landed interests—something involving a picture of a rape room—and from that day onward had taken to speaking in a roundabout way, fearful of persecution, cautious to a fault. Much like the Pilgrims of yester-centuries, she brought her circumspect inclination with her to America and carried it into the relationship with my father and then to communication with me. "Look, there is a grocery cart in the middle of the parking lot. I wonder if it'll hit a car." That was how Mother taught me morality. No pointing to codes or tablets or commandments. Just a roundabout way. I understood why she had tucked the Koran into a corner of the house.

Rather than having a conversation with me, it was better for her if I just had that conversation with myself.

The one time that Mother had dropped her preference for the oblique occurred the last time she visited. Marie-Anne had been unwell for some time. We weren't sure it was a cortisol spike then and had been giving her a diet that might resist hypothyroidism, the other possible diagnosis. Mother—as I called her—had gone with me to Reading Terminal to help buy some foods containing iodine, omega-3 fats, selenium, zinc, and vitamins A, B, and D. After she made a joke about how the letters a-b-d formed the root for a West Asian word for *slave*, she said that she needed to discuss Marie-Anne.

"I do not want you to be offend," she whispered.

"What is it?"

"She should not look like this," Mother said, puffing her cheeks and jutting out her elbows. "It is not good in marriage."

"What isn't good?"

"Bad appearance," Mother said. "It will kill feeling. It is known that men need attractive."

"She's beautiful. You remember her at the wedding."

"She was. But even then, very big and tall."

"She will be fine."

"What if it takes years? What will happen to you? A man cannot be with a woman who looks off."

"Nothing will happen to me. I love her. We will stay together."

"What if she never deflate?"

By this time I grew angry. I wanted to make assertive exclamations. To tell Mother how upsetting it was to have this sort of skepticism cast upon our love. It reminded me of what Mrs. Quinn had done. She had also doubted me on the basis of physicality. In her case it was something I lacked. In my mother's case it was something Marie-Anne lacked (or, rather, accumulated). I concluded that both mothers were the same.

They were not comfortable verbalizing the true bases of their prejudices so they highlighted alternative shortcomings in their children.

That conversation at Reading Terminal changed our relationship. I could see, driving home that day, as we wound through the falling cherry blossoms in Fairmount, that Mother realized she had rattled me. Remorse had been writ all over her, like fur on a wolf. But I didn't believe it was the right kind of remorse. She was aggrieved that I was upset. She was not upset with herself for her position. The recognition prompted me to adopt a posture of hermetic silence toward her, the same kind of taciturn stance that had marked her life. I maintained my silence throughout the duration of her trip.

Two weeks after she got back to Alabama, she passed away.

It was somewhere during that trip that Mother had booby-trapped my apartment.

CHAPTER FIVE

For the first time in our marriage, Marie-Anne and I ignored each other's birthdays. Marie-Anne gained reprieve from the apartment by going to the MimirCo offices as frequently as she could. It seemed like she was always in Virginia. Perhaps it was a prelude to her finding a place there.

Loneliness brought memories of Richard Konigsberg. He had been the one I used to get drunk with when things with Marie-Anne went sour. He had not been the biggest proponent of the institution of marriage; but when it came to Marie-Anne, he made arguments that impressed upon me the importance of stability and structure. He always said that making it in America was a multigenerational enterprise, and that it wasn't in the cards for me to achieve both social advancement and freedom at the same time. I had to choose the former. "It will be the next generation that will get to have the benefit of doing whatever they want," he'd said. "It's for them that your sacrifices must happen. It's for them that you must marry a good girl from a good, established family and stick it out." That sacrifice was the primary reason I wanted to have children. Their existence would legitimize the effort I had put into maintaining a loving relationship in the face of the longest odds. They needed to be born so that I could tell them all that I had done for them, much the same way my parents used to tell me all that they had done in order to leave their home country and make it in America. Progeny was how a debtor became a creditor.

Valentine's Day came and went without acknowledgment. Without Richard to mope with I reached out to Ali Ansari. When he learned that I didn't have plans with Marie-Anne he sent me a text with red hearts in it and announced that he was going to take me out. "Something to offset the internment!"

I met him on Ben Franklin Parkway, at the beginning of the alphabetized row of flags belonging to every country in the world. The only flag not alphabetically placed was Israel, which was on the pole closest to city hall, even before Afghanistan and Albania.

Ali and I started out at Reading Terminal and ate brisket at an Amish kiosk. With drinks in hand we sat on the steps of city hall and watched the workers on the scaffolding around the building as they wiped away hundreds of years of grime.

Philadelphia, Ali Ansari said, was America's pretty but rebellious daughter. She subjected herself to piercings and ugly makeup and tattered clothing and abstained from showering, as if there was authenticity to be found in shirking the established norms. Philly was shy inside, he said. She didn't want people looking at her; but the shyness came from wisdom. Philly understood that when you reveal yourself, the world starts expecting you to maintain yourself. Beauty is a slavery. But now Philly was washing up. Getting her hair done. Adding highlights. It was out of character. He said she would regret her decision.

"Maybe the city will attract more people. More diversity?"

"Multiculturalism? It's a recipe for estrangement. Everyone performing their pantomime. You just realize how different we are from one another."

The sun hit us on the face, energizing us to move. Ali suggested a trip to Northern Liberties. He wanted to show me something weird. We took the subway under the Galleria and the jewelry shops, under Independence Hall, all the way to the riverfront, until we emerged near the Ben Franklin Bridge. The river was pepper gray. It gave the sun no surfaces to twinkle in.

We stayed on this side of the river, looking out toward Camden. I had only been to Camden once, when Marie-Anne and I had gone to do a little circumambulation of Walt Whitman's grave. The lone man in history who had become one with America.

We soon arrived at a refurbished warehouse. I was expecting some kind of hipster convocation. What I saw instead was a roped wrestling ring surrounded by two levels of seating. There were a few stout men of Irish descent taking their seats, beers in hand, holding the fight card, placing wagers.

"The Extreme Wrestling Association of Philadelphia," Ali Ansari said, and nudged and pushed me toward the front row. The smell of turpentine mixed with sawdust and talcum; it had an intensity that brought the warehouse to life. The steel and stone and aching bone that had been used up in its past. The night shift, with minimal light, sedate faces hammering out metal parts and metal gizmos with which America armored itself and strode forth into the inhospitable world, manifesting a destiny outward after having mastered its interior.

We waited half an hour for the seats to fill up. Most of the audience members were factory stiffs and other longtime residents from Northeast Philadelphia. The show, meanwhile, had all the ingredients of the kind of wrestling popularized by the WWF, WWE, and Vince McMahon. But there was a twist—it was much more violent. The wrestlers bled more, threw themselves from higher ladders, and tossed each other into the bleachers in order to inflict pain that would be deemed more and more believable.

We had come to see the main event, which featured a massive, bearded wrestler named Marty Martel. He had a cross tattooed on his stomach. He entered the arena to Norwegian death metal music and carried a great broadsword in his hand that he handed off to his manager, a smaller guy wearing a crown and robes; his name was Charlie Main.

Marty Martel was a face. Once he was in the ring he gave a long speech about kicking out all the immigrants who were stealing good American jobs. This earned him a lot of laughter and support. In the middle of his speech he was interrupted by the heel, a masked Mexican wrestler named Gonzo, who lambasted Marty for denying his family an opportunity to pursue the American dream. The crowd booed Gonzo and cheered for Marty. They were egged on by Charlie Main, who walked around the arena swinging the broadsword and saying gibberish in mock Spanish. I found myself rooting for the heel, though in the face of Marty Martel's large following I didn't cheer out loud. Ali Ansari wasn't so shy. He stood and rooted for Gonzo, screaming at him to "choke the fucking cracker." It shocked me that no one else in the audience seemed to find Martel's commentary offensive.

After a number of super kicks and iron claws the fight turned in Gonzo's favor; he made Martel submit with a mean camel clutch. But the apparent victory was thwarted when Charlie Main jumped into the ring and distracted the referee by complaining that Gonzo was an illegal immigrant and didn't have the work authorization to be in the ring in the first place. The referee tried to tell Charlie Main that such bureaucratic things didn't matter in the ring, which was a place of honor, a place of equality. But as the two men had their dramatic discussion, thoroughly engrossed in each other, Martel was able to slither out of the camel clutch and pinned Gonzo with a suplex. As the reversal took place, Charlie Main excitedly directed the referee's attention back to the action and within seconds the referee was on the floor, counting Gonzo out. Not wanting to give the judges a chance to review the end of the fight, Marty Martel and Charlie Main ran out of the ring and toward the tunnel.

The masked Mexican wrestler, now all alone in the ring, with only Ali Ansari's support in the audience, was left stomping mad, clutching his hair, beating his chest. On his way out of the ring he took hold of the announcer's microphone and vowed that he would exact justice against the entire association, going so far as to challenge the referee to a match. That fight was scheduled for next Wednesday. The crowd roared their approval and booed Gonzo out of the arena.

There were more fights scheduled for the evening, but Ali Ansari said he had seen all he had come for and we headed back to Center City, for beer and mussels at Monk's.

"I had no idea these things were so political," I said.

"Wrestling represents the American narrative like nothing else. Any issue there is, it can address. Liberal versus conservative. Antiwar versus prowar. Man versus woman. Rich versus poor. Wrestling's got it all."

"All this time I thought it was just a bunch of fake pummeling."

"The fighting is fake," Ali Ansari said, "but that's not why people go there. People go for the story. It's social drama."

"I take it Gonzo is a friend of yours and we came to support him?"

"I don't know Gonzo. I came for Marty Martel. Whose real name is Martin Mirandella."

It turned out that Martin Mirandella had once been a wrestler in the WWE, where he'd played a heel called Hasan Hussain. He had been managed by the same guy who now played Charlie Main. Back then Charlie was called Rasheed Shaheed, though originally he was an Irish kid from Maryland. Their story in the WWE was that they were a pair of Arab cousins from Dearborn, Michigan, who were fed up with the way the United States treated its Muslim minorities, and wanted nothing more than to expose the manner in which they were denied their fair shot at the title.

"Basically it wouldn't matter who they beat," Ali Ansari explained. "The association would always find a way to deny them the title shot. This only caused Hasan to fight harder and beat more guys. After each fight he demanded a title shot and every time the association, playing the part of the racist, or the oppressive white man controlling the glass ceiling, turned him down. People loved it. Hasan became one of the best heels in years. But the more wrestlers he beat the more the other wrestlers turned against him. At one rumble that I remember, all nine of the other wrestlers stopped fighting each other when he entered the ring and ganged up to beat him up."

"Then what happened?"

"What happened next will break your heart," Ali Ansari said. "It's what prompted me to make a documentary on the guy."

It turned out that the WWE writers had gotten lazy with Hasan's act, and instead of keeping him going as a victim with some understandable anger issues, they started heaping terrorist imagery on him.

"It was as if they couldn't imagine a Muslim as honorable, as having a point, as being on the cusp of heroism. One Monday night, on Hasan's behalf, a gang of four men dressed in ski masks carried out a mock execution of one of the WWE referees who had cheated Hasan out of a sure win. The bit went too far. It evoked al-Qaeda and whatnot. Huge mistake. The network that aired the show flipped out and declared that Hasan Hussain and Rasheed Shaheed couldn't ever again show their faces on the network. Martin Mirandella lost his contract. His promising career was destroyed. All because he had the misfortune of playing the role of a Muslim in American wrestling. Now he's in this low-end independent association, playing the role of a European supremacist, the second coming of Charles Martel who fought Muslim invaders in the eighth century."

"And Rasheed Shaheed is Charlemagne, the king who backed Charles Martel . . ." I knew all the pivotal moments in the making of the West. "How ironic."

"It's not irony they are going for," Ali Ansari said. "They really hate Islam now. It's unjust what happened to these guys. I want to show that to the world."

"I had no idea."

"This whole thing played out in front of millions of viewers, yet people still don't know Martin Mirandella was born in Italy to Catholic parents or that Charlie Main's dad is Brian O'Brien from Annapolis, and runs a pub. Half of America watched these kids get screwed and forgot about it in the blink of an eye. I want to remind them."

"Are these guys even open to the documentary?" I asked. "I can't imagine he would want anything to do with Muslims anymore." I wasn't sure if I was speaking on Martin's behalf or mine. The scimitar that had swiped his head was the same one that had taken mine. I pictured the media executive who had cut Martin. He probably looked like George Gabriel. He probably considered himself on the frontline of protecting America, or the West, or "our way of life," somehow capable of identifying every sign of Islamic supremacism. If I hadn't been conditioned against it, I would have thought there was a central place where leading American men were trained to declare people infiltrators and traitors.

Ali Ansari sipped his beer. "Martin needs a little convincing. But Charlie Main is receptive. I went to high school with him. He's working on Martin. I think I can get him to talk about what happened. We probably can't get the character of Hasan Hussain back in the main events, but maybe Martin Mirandella can at least get another character. The guy is only twenty-four years old. He has his entire career in front of him. I like him. A soft-spoken giant. He works as a bank teller in Lancaster. His wife's name is Miranda; she's a janitor at Jefferson Hospital. Miranda Mirandella."

We drank and pulled up old videos on our phones of Hasan Hussain in the main events, entering to Algerian *rai* music or Pakistani *qawwalis*, draped in all sorts of West Asian headgear. Sometimes he yelled in Arabic, at other times in Persian or Pashto. I watched him beat contender after contender, only to be repeatedly denied the opportunity to take on the champ. The closest he ever came was when he interrupted one of the godfathers of wrestling, a grizzled veteran and former champ named Gold Bone who, after calling Hasan a whiny chump, did at least admit that Hassan's contentions were legitimate. Houston even gave Hasan a shot at a lesser title. To make sure the fight was fair, Gold Bone served as referee. Hasan ended up winning that fight. "That was the closest Hasan Hussain every got to the title," Ali Ansari said, and shut off his phone. "After that came the infamous ski mask incident and the rest is history."

"This is interesting stuff you're doing," I said.

"You think so? To most people this is nothing. Like my parents."

"They don't support you?"

"Why would they? They didn't come to America to see me become what I am—a nobody who has to fight for respect. They wanted to give me an opportunity to be important. Yet, I am the exact opposite. Last time we talked was when I turned down their offer to go to medical school in the Carribean."

"How are you paying for your life now?"

"I got some stuff on the side." He put a hundred-dollar bill on the table. The waitress came back with forty dollars in change. Ali Ansari left it all for her, along with a flyer featuring Marty Martel and Charlie Main.

I stumbled home drunk and disoriented, nearly getting run over in front of the Rocky Balboa statute. Marie-Anne wasn't around so I lumbered toward the bedroom. When I took a moment to stop by the desk and surf the web for more videos of Hasan Hussain, my knee hit against the drawer where I had hidden the Koran. For a moment, because of the conversation with Ali, I considered pulling it out. Then I passed over the thought. I poured myself a drink and fell asleep on the swiveling chair.

The next time Ali Ansari and I met, it was in front of a falafel deli on Fairmount, just off Broad Street. It was an easy spring day. The sky was between blue and gray.

Since the last time we had been together I had thought a lot about Ali's reference to an internment. To be a Muslim was not a physical confinement. It was an invisible concentration camp, where the bulk of our time was spent with each other, talking about ourselves, as if we were inherently problematic, in need of a solution. Maybe this was the nature of the twenty-first-century incarceration. It made you gaze at your own reflection, over and endlessly, until your existence became a torture, until you became unbearable even to yourself, until you loathed yourself and longed to be who you were not. All around us there was freedom. But it was not something accessible to us. The ones in the prison could only be one thing, which was themselves. When I was first introduced to the invisible concentration camp I did not want to believe that it existed. But more than that, I did not want to believe that I belonged to it. But I did. A will greater than my own had determined it. Maybe it would have been better if there were actually walls all around us. Clear demarcations between the ones free to be anything and the ones limited to being "Muslim." That way we would not have grown up thinking there were no walls. We never would have been mistaken, the way I was mistaken, and so the scar that came with getting herded wouldn't have been as bad, as ugly. Perhaps that was my role: to tell the next generation that there were walls, and for the most part they were impenetrable, and before insanity completely takes hold of you, you must find little pools of darkness around you, cavities that do not force you to look at yourself, and imagine them to be portals to a beautiful existence elsewhere, an entry point to a place of joy. Perhaps I was meant to be a messenger of this madness. Or, perhaps, it was nothing that special. Perhaps I was simply meant to stumble around until I found the mouth of a tunnel leading to oblivion.

The deli was close to the hulking Divine Lorraine Hotel, the ornately designed twin towers, more than a hundred years old, conceived by the renowned architect Willis Hale, who had gotten started in Wilkes-Barre but ended up designing a number of mansions and skyscrapers in Philadelphia. The Lorraine, as it was initially called, was his crowning achievement. Like the gaudy crown it was supposed to be, it resembled something that might fit well on the head of a giant sun king. Ali Ansari and I stared at the landmark from a window. Unlike the rest of North Philadelphia, where the old buildings were redbrick, this one was made of tan brick and limestone. It had two big towers joined together by a pair of round arches, one arch that went from the second to the fourth floor, and the other that went from the sixth to the eighth. Now the building was rough and raw and thick, like a medical surgeon returned from a civil war, the insides empty and shattered, a living thing utterly gutted and dilapidated by the ravages of the past. The alabaster railings clung to the building like breast-pockets coming off at the seams.

Ali Ansari had tried to meet Eric Bloom, the young developer who was trying to restore the building to its former glory. Once upon a time the building had been home to the richest Philadelphians. Then it got bought by Father Divine of the Universal Peace Mission Movement. Also known as Jealous Divine, he had been a black religious reformer who married a white woman at a time when such things were shunned. Even though he advocated extreme modesty between genders and celibacy within marriage, he made the move to desegregate the building and set up a public kitchen where people from the community—of all races, of all classes—could come and eat inexpensive meals. This was in the forties. At the time it was perhaps the only mixed-race high-end hotel in America. Though Father Divine died in 1965 his followers continued to live in the building until just a few years ago, when they were forced to sell and disappeared into North Philadelphia.

We stopped admiring the Divine Lorraine and went into the deli to eat. A sign on the door read, *Proudly Serving Halal Food Since 2000*. The zeroes were in the shape of crescents and carried stars in their arms. I leaned inside and the smell of shawarma and cheese fries bowled me back. There was a dark-skinned man standing in a stained yellow wife-beater with his hand on his hip and a remote control pointed at the high-definition TV hanging on the wall. There was a young white guy at reception with a hammer and screwdriver tattooed on his wrist. There were a number of young men sitting around, chatting with one another, betting on a soccer match. There was a smaller TV in the corner of the deli, dusty and unused.

Ali greeted the server: "Hey, Chris. You know I saw you with GCM in Northern Liberties the other day."

Chris gave a knowing smile. "I'm all about lust," he whispered and gave Ali a pat on the back.

When he went off to fill our order I asked Ali Ansari what GCM stood for. But he played it coy, saying I would find out when I was ready. This made me believe that perhaps it was some kind of code that queer guys used. GCM could stand for Gay Cute Male, perhaps. The possibility that the interest Ali Ansari and I had in each other might have to do with something other than our shared status as Muslims left me annoyed. I didn't want him to turn out to have been interested in me because of something physical. Not that it wasn't flattering; it just wasn't useful. America had no shortage of sex. What it lacked was communion.

We discussed some of the marketing campaigns that Brother Hatim and Sister Saba had tried to create. Ali flipped through the files on his phone. The first was an image of three Muslim children—one boy in a skullcup, one girl in a hijab, and one rather androgynous child, all of whom had eaten too much candy and appeared to be on the verge of throwing up. Above them it said, *Axis of Upheaval*, and below them was the information for the events being held during Islamic Awareness Week, which overlapped with Halloween week. The second ad featured a woman in a full black robe and face covering. Above her it said, *My Latest Design*. And below her it said, *Check out my website and find out what I'm wearing underneath*. The URL that was listed took people to Temple MSA's Islamic Awareness page. The third and final ad featured a criminal standing at a gun dealer's shop trying to buy a weapon, only to have his card declined, with the scary-looking store owner telling the thwarted man, *Payment declined. Your card is sharia-compliant.* It played on the idea that under Islamic law investing in firearms was illegal.

"You're right," I said. "Their propaganda needs work. The first one is too blatant. The second one is too slutty. The third one is too subtle. You should look at the adverts that the atheists are putting out."

"What a world we're in. In which even atheists proselytize."

"It's called commodification. Everyone has to do it."

"I only know how to commodify my penis."

"Well, start with your penis," I said. "How would you craft a marketing strategy for it? Then apply those principles to marketing Islam."

He laughed. A sincere and unabashed laugh. The laugh of a perverse man who considered laughing nothing more than the necessary consequence of feeling complete disregard for the opinions of the world. It was the same laugh that Richard Konigsberg had possessed. It became apparent to me that there was no sexual tension between us. If anything, we had a kind of complementary intimacy where our personalities, each missing something ineffable, indescribable, seemed to overlap in some middle space where we could both feel strong, masculine, more capable of throwing our fists against the skies that fell upon us. That might be what they called friendship. "That is hard to do," he said. "My penis is so much bigger than Islam."

We continued ribbing each other and finished our meal. We were just about to pay when the door opened and a customer made her way to the counter where Chris was working. I heard her ordering a shish taouk and did a double take because I recognized the voice.

I could hardly believe that the person before me was Candace. She looked radically different. She wore a gray headscarf tied stylishly around her face in layers, with its little sequined edge falling to the side. Her mascara was parrot green. It matched the nail polish on her hand. Her head was titled just a little to the left like there was someone there inquiring about her. She looked elegant, exotic, edgy. Like she was a model in an Islamic couture magazine. Perhaps it was the audacity of adopting a foreign fashion, but her face seemed to be filled with a greater, deeper vulnerability. I hadn't been this tugged by the magnetism of a face since I'd watched Isabelle Adjani in a film.

I told Ali Ansari to wait and got up to say hi to her.

"Is that really you?" I patted her on the shoulder.

She turned. Her face had a shocked expression. "I never thought I'd run into you at this place."

I spread my hands and gestured at Ali Ansari. "A friend brought me here."

She waved at Ali and paid for her order. "I'm really glad he did."

"I thought you lived in Center City. What are you doing up here?"

"Well, I only lived in Center City to be near Plutus and because I could afford it. But when I quit it wasn't important living there and I needed someplace cheap."

"You quit Plutus?"

"They were shuffling their staff in an unreasonable way. I just didn't agree with that."

"You should have reached out," I blurted.

She blushed a little. Her lips puckered and returned to flatness. "I figured you had your support system."

I bit down on my tongue. Was her remark an attempt to make me confess that I would have liked to have stayed in touch? I wasn't sure if I wanted to give her such a direct confirmation of my need. Even with things the way they were with Marie-Anne, I hadn't yet abandoned my caution around other women. Nor could I remove from my mind the night Marie-Anne and I had used Candace as part of our scenario. In a strange way it meant that Candace belonged to Marie-Anne.

"I guess I did."

"Good," she said. "I'm glad you did."

I glanced back at Ali, who was waiting expectantly. I didn't know whether to take Candace over to him or not.

Candace caught my uncertainty and decided she had made enough of an effort to connect. "So. I should go."

"Already?"

"Yeah," she said. "I got this new job I'm doing. Just popped in here for lunch."

"Well . . ." I lengthened the goodbye. "Your job sounds interesting."

"I'm with Al Jazeera. I'm a producer. For their video department. AJ+."

"Very exciting."

She smiled. "It was good seeing you."

I opened the door for her and walked her to the sidewalk. We paused, apparently hoping the other would say something, and then backed away from each other. I watched her leave and my eyes expanded to take in the world. The sun was clean and otherwise light, as if dangling on spiderwebs instead of engraved upon the mantle. Planes shot through the cirrus and the clouds curled up and made mustaches.

I came back to Ali Ansari. He gave me an inquisitive smile.

"Just an old friend," I explained. It was aimed more at myself than at him. "She wasn't like that," I waved my hand around my head, "back when I used to know her."

"I didn't even ask," he said. "Just be careful with the converts. They come into Islam and forget to bring their cynicism along. Pretty dangerous, being around adults experiencing innocence."

Ali paid, refusing to let me even look at the check, and we headed out for a walk. I spied a good number of hundreds in his wallet. Combined with the immaculate clothes he wore—almost all designer by the look of it—I had to wonder how he had so much money. Working in the stacks had never paid well, as far as I could remember.

* * *

We headed down Broad past the Masonic Temple and walked around city hall, cutting through the alleys between Chestnut and Walnut, toward Rittenhouse. A gleam off the skin of William Penn, standing regal atop city hall, blinded me for a moment and I had to take Ali Ansari's shoulder.

Farther on we passed a stretch of pavement made of diagonally lain brick. Many had been loosened by time and water and now sat on the moist earth with barely concealed enmity, waiting for just the right toe to stub and become an even more dangerous hurdle.

The length of the walk I thought about Candace. The way she had characterized her departure from Plutus made me believe that my firing had played a role in her decision to leave. I guess I wasn't the only one who had been affected by George Gabriel. I regretted having run out on Candace that day at the art museum. I regretted not using her phone number when things got bad for me. Perhaps we could've been there for each other. Instead she had been forced to channel her frustration in another direction, eventuating in her apparent conversion to Islam. Her conversion, if that's what it was, seemed to say that she had made up her mind in opposition to the Philadelphia of skyscrapers, which was full of people in peacoats and fur-lined hats and stylish gloves. There was in her clothes, as well as in her decision to move into North Philly, the sort of naïveté that the ironic and much younger hipsters in the Northern Liberties area would find kind of sad and desperate, and with a straight face they might even accuse her of being an agent of gentrification. But I was drawn to it. She showed a willingness to challenge convention, to rip out her own upholstery and try a different pattern, a characteristic that had been squeezed out of Marie-Anne and me. Our aim went in the other way. Toward stability. We couldn't change our designs.

About a block from Rittenhouse Park, near a condominium, a doorman came out from a canopied building with scissors in hand and set to work cutting out the shriveled brown branches from a row of pots containing bright purple flowers. As we stopped to watch we saw two girls come out from an ice-cream shop. Both had waffle cones and licked them simultaneously. One girl licked with the tip of her tongue while the other mashed the scoops against the flat of her tongue.

"Only white girls have the ability to tell you everything about themselves through single acts," Ali Ansari said. "It's as if they mastered sexual symbolism before being born. It's nice but it takes the mystery away."

"I don't know about that," I replied. "Maybe East Coast girls are different than Southern ones."

"What makes you an expert?"

"I live with one."

Ali Ansari grasped my shoulder and punched me hard to enough to sting. He took my phone and started interviewing me on video. "Sir, sir. Is it true that you're with a white girl?"

"Yes."

"Do you realize, sir," he said, continuing to film, "that makes you the modern-day Ahab, except you caught the whale?"

"I think Marie-Anne would object to that comparison."

He kept the camera on me. "How does it feel to be more of a man than us? You make our penises shrivel in homage. You are the godfather. I must pay you protection money."

"Marrying a white girl didn't protect me from George Gabriel."

"Fuck George Gabriel." I foresaw a rant coming and turned the camera at him. "Sometimes I wish I could kill every George Gabriel I come across," Ali said. It was too serious for me to laugh. "You know, selective extermination. That kind of thing." He went on about his preferred ways of killing. Most involved disposing the bodies in a river so they would wash up in some beachside town where other white people could look upon the corpses and experience a warning. Vengeance had to be systematic or else it was pointless.

"Got it out of your system?" I asked.

"Not all of it. The rest will only be washed away in the final bloodbath."

"Anyway, tell me," I said and shut off the camera, "is a white girl really such a big deal?"

"It makes you unique," he said. "The generation of Muslim immigrants that came before us—the first generation—they used to be able to get white girls, easy. Their accents did it, their funny mustaches did it, their patriarchy did it. But for us, the second generation, it doesn't work like that. We're associated with terrorism and the bad kind of patriarchy—you know, stoning and stuff—instead of hot patriarchy, like casual spanking. If we go abroad, yeah, maybe we can get a white girl. But here, in America, to get a white girl after this War on Terror is no longer possible. Every now and then, sure, you hear of a brother getting one. But she's usually one who got manipulated into converting to Islam first and now she's lonely and afraid because she didn't realize what a terrible thing it is to be a Muslim today. Those girls don't count. Sometimes I wonder what is this world in which my nerd father had an easier time nailing white girls than I ever will. The increasing absence of white girls dating and marrying Muslim guys is living evidence of an emerging American apartheid."

"How did I get one then?"

"She's probably a PBL."

"PBL?"

"Pre–bin Laden," he said. "It's how we refer to the Golden Age. Back when Americans didn't have prejudice toward us. A PBL white girl is one who isn't just white, but is also capable of seeing a Muslim man as an individual, as someone distinct from the collective. Granted, you have to be careful in protecting her from this society that will try to make her change her mind."

"I wasn't able to protect Marie-Anne from that society," I said.

But Ali Ansari wasn't interested in my lament. "I bet your PBL is real dirty in bed too. Muslim girls don't know how to be sexy. A girl needs to have some infidel in her to be sexy. Or have been sexually abused in such a way that she becomes a nympho. Of course I don't advocate abuse. But if an abused girl gets in my bed I am not going to throw her out."

I raised my eyebrows and said nothing about the hard freeze between Marie-Anne and me.

"So you told me about PBL," I said. "But are you going to tell me what GCM stands for? Or would you have to kill me?"

He hopped up. "I don't need to kill you. But I would have to take you to the Mainline."

"If you take me to the Mainline, wouldn't I just want to kill myself?"

He shushed me. "Careful talking about killing yourself in public. You are someone people would believe. And they will think you are going to take them along with you."

We walked toward 30th Street Station and passed over the Schuylkill. The pale purple sun set in the distance. Below us, in the grassy area along the river, joggers and walkers stopped to watch a film projected onto a big screen. Some men stood nearby with fishing poles in hand. At a distance, in a large brick building, one of the old converted warehouses, a doctor stood in the window putting on his blue scrubs, watching the scene play out below, seemingly about to leave for a night shift at the nearby hospital. I imagined him happy and comfortable in his life, with just that slight bit of envy the established feel toward the wanderers.

Ali Ansari purchased the train tickets. At the platform he took out a book from his bag and offered it to me as reading material. It was a volume of poetry called *Love and Strange Horses* by a Haitian-Palestinian writer named Nathalie Handal.

The train arrived on time. It was full. We took the last available bench seat. I sat by the window and put the book on my lap. The train chakachoochooed forward. On a trail along the river a team of riders in red uniforms headed toward Manayunk. Through the junipers lining the shore they resembled the streaks associated with Jupiter. That red was also the color of the three horses painted on the cover of the book. A description on its back said that the painting was based on Chapter 100 of the Koran, which was called "Running Horses." I could only chuckle at the way the Koran had made its way back into my hands. I turned to Ali Ansari to see if he had given me the book as a joke or a taunt. But he had put on his headphones and was blasting music.

I opened up the book and started reading. The poems were short and brisk, as light as croissants, and just as warm. They were the kind of poems Marie-Anne would have liked for me to be writing. The themes included unrequited and sexual love; languorous moments of passion and loneliness; the ache of being an exile and a wanderer.

But there was also something unique. The poet had a strange fixation with the number nineteen. One of the poems was called "Nineteen Harbors." Another was called "Nineteen Arabics." In another there was a line that read, "Nineteen is the infinite." In another she mentioned "the nineteen beats" inside a Bulgarian orchestra.

Of all the possible things that could've captivated me, I found this numerical repetition most fascinating. It gnawed at me. It was part riddle and part paranoia. I simultaneously wanted an answer and feared what I might discover. This was because the only significant instance of the number nineteen I could think of was that it was the number of men who had been involved in the attacks on New York. Was this book some kind of morbid propaganda? Was Ali Ansari perhaps part of some strange deathly Islamic mysticism that had created an entire theology around violence and the number nineteen? I suddenly wished I hadn't read the poems.

I turned to Ali Ansari and reexamined him. Was there something I had overlooked before? Perhaps his clothes and intellect were a put-on? Perhaps he was part of something if not outright dangerous, then at least unsavory. Perhaps he was being followed by someone from the Department of Homeland Security. Or worse, perhaps he was an informer for the FBI who had put the poetry book in front of me to see how I would react, to see if I would start a conversation about the number nineteen. The train compartment seemed to be collapsing around me like a crushed soda can. Never before in my life had I felt the kind of fear I felt in this moment. It was as if everywhere around me there were hidden sleeves inside the air, and within them sat official sort of people who were watching me, observing me, possibly even toying with me. I had never given in to the possibility that America was a police state, with agents and assets scattered around the train cars, the streets, the cafés, the universities, whose sole purpose it might be to watch me. But that had been before I was rendered a Muslim. Now even I myself thought I needed to be watched, because there was no telling what I was about.

I took the mysterious poetry book, inspired by a chapter from the Koran, a book possibly filled with references to terrorists, and put it in my jacket pocket. Publicly giving it back to Ali Ansari or throwing it in the trash would've only drawn more attention to it.

Perhaps it really was true what they said about Muslims.

We were shady.

At the small train station along the Mainline we were picked up by a young brown-skinned guy, extremely skinny and tall, with a bullring in his nose, and both ears fitted with discs. He wore a tight shirt that said, MANWHORE, with mirrorwork stitched into the lettering. He wore a turban: a white muslin cloth wrapped around a red borderless hat. There was a gem in the turban; it contained a Disney character.

Manwhore was with a girl in a cardigan and long white slacks. She wore French barrette hair clips with iridescent crystals, the type of accessory that an heiress might be handed down from a grandmother.

Ali Ansari introduced us. The guy was Tot. Girl, Farkhunda. She had a tattoo on her lower back. An Islamic inscription woven into the tramp-stamp. It was the *bismillah* verse that preceded most chapters of the Koran: *In the name of God, the Loving, the Merciful.*

We drove into a large subdivision with hilly roads; lawns with sprinklers that seemed to bloom from the earth; wrought-iron lampposts along the driveways; enormous multistory mansions with fountains, pagodas, and bulbous balconies.

Tot pulled up in front of the largest house and dropped off Farkhunda. She went to the door and met up with some sort of adult, waving back in our direction, gesturing that it was all right for us to leave.

We drove away—but only to circle back around the other side of the house, from where we could see a light come on at an upstairs bedroom.

"So I guess we're just waiting for your girlfriend to sneak back out?" I asked.

"She's not my girlfriend," Tot said. "She just sucks my cock after school."

Farkhunda's father was Mushtaq Hakim, a millionaire physician-turned-philanthropist who founded Crescent Compassion Charities after the genocide in Bosnia. Before long his international aid network spread to Chechnya, Kashmir, sanction-era Iraq, Palestine, and anywhere else Muslims were victimized. The nineties had made him rich and elevated. Jesuits even invited him to give talks at their universities in order to learn his global mobilization techniques. But a year after 9/11 he was indicted by the federal government for providing "material support" to terrorism because one of his charities had given money to a destitute family that had produced a suicide bomber. Mushtaq had argued that there was no way for his thousand charities to know which families in the world contained criminals. He even pulled in a major law firm from DC to make his case. The government told Mushtaq's lawyers that if they persisted in their defense they would also be indicted for "vicarious material support." Left without counsel, Mushtaq pled guilty to all forty-seven counts against him. Rather than sit in jail the rest of his life, he showed the authorities that he was still on his green card and hadn't yet become a naturalized citizen, which meant that they could deport him. He ended up in the only country that would take him—namely, Saudi Arabia. The mansion had survived because Mushtaq divorced his wife right after the indictment and signed it over to her name.

"Farkhunda has PTSD," Ali finished. "Post-Terrorism Sentencing Disorder."

Farkhunda came out of the house, this time dressed in a sleeveless red top and a small plaid skirt with stockings and black pumps.

"How old are these people?" I whispered to Ali.

"Tot's twenty-five. He looks young because he's so femme. The girl is like seventeen."

"Sixteen," she said, settling down in the front seat again, crossing her legs.

I examined her bare brown thighs. "Isn't that kind of illegal? You and Tot?"

"Everything's kind of illegal," she laughed. She saw me looking at her and angled her legs toward the gearbox in order to show them off. "How old are *you* anyway?"

"Way older than you."

She turned. "Older is hot."

It was undeniable that Farkhunda was beautiful. She had a kind of ambiguous expression on her face, someone seeking docility, as if in being subsumed by someone else's authority she came closer to discovering herself. But it wasn't a fatalist surrender on her part. She connived for it. I wanted to give her what she sought.

"Older is wiser too," I parried. "Get at me if you ever want to talk about your dad. I'm sure you miss him. My dad passed away not too long ago."

"That's not the same thing. Your dad was taken by Allah. My dad was taken by America. I can pretend Allah doesn't exist. But I can't pretend the same for America."

She leaned forward and raised the volume on the music. It was a local band called Gay Commie Muzzies. This was the GCM I had heard about earlier. They sang a dissonant mixture of punk rock and rap with reggae riffs. It made any follow-up conversation impossible. The song that was on was called "LUSTS." It was an anagram of the earthly form that Allah had taken; namely, sluts.

"God is all the girls in the world," Tot shared. "That's what God did, bro. He poured himself into women. It would have been too much beauty for the universe to handle otherwise. The attraction we feel toward women—lust—is the tug of the Divine on our heartstrings."

I listened to the rap. The lyrics involved ejaculating the smoke of the soul—"I cum / Dukhan / My gun / the Koran"—on the mirror that was the world and letting it turn into a powder to be snorted via the two-eyed phallus that was the nose. Tot was the lyricist, though he preferred the hybrid term lyrymystycyst. He hoped to be bestowed the mantle of the most prolific Sufi poet of America. But out in Houston there was a group called the Fatwawhores that kept friending and defriending him on social media and stealing from him the necessary emotional quietude to compose high-quality verses.

"Where did he study Sufism?" I asked.

"Never did," Ali said. "But if you want to connect something modern to Islam and don't know how, you call upon Sufism. Tot is better at that than anyone."

Tot, meanwhile, had pulled Farkhunda's head in between his legs and was muttering into his digital recorder the poetry that came to him. One time he slapped the back of her head because her slurping interfered with his recording. I had my eyes toward the window; but a few times I stopped to stare at her legs. It would be so easy to just reach over and touch her. Maybe Ali Ansari could join in as well.

After fifteen minutes through twisting residential streets lined with evergreens and finely trimmed hawthorn hedges, we reached a subdivision. We pulled up to a house much like Farkhunda's, but a little farther back into the woods. Instead of going to the front of the house, we drove along the side where a long row of cars were parked. At the end of the driveway a garage door was open and people dressed like Tot and Farkhunda were coming in and out to smoke cigarettes. The plumes from their mouths looped like punctuation marks and dialogue boxes.

Ali Ansari led me in. I was buffeted by the smell of weed. There was a ping-pong table where members of the Gay Commie Muzzies—who seemed to have as many members as an orchestra—were playing with two paddles in each hand. Tot and Farkhunda passed through a mesh spring door and Ali Ansari and I followed them farther into the basement of the house. GCM ranged from West Asians to North Africans to Southeast Asians dressed in vintage sixties and seventies clothing, with the occasional white convert in foreign clothing.

"Your basic suburbanite Muslim society," Ali smiled. "I call them Asymptotes. As close to white as possible, without touching the line."

The basement was immense, carpeted in thick wool. Hunting guns from VO Vapen sat on shelves, along with ornamental daggers and embossed serving trays. The pool table had platinum leaves on its legs and was made of tulipwood and brushed aluminum, designed by Vincent Facquet. The wealth came from the first-generation parents who sat upstairs somewhere, reading news about the old country, oblivious to what transpired in their basement. The partygoers sat on beanbags or on each other's laps, watching movies or strumming on guitars. Here and there were bongs and water pipes; groups of dolorous and nodding people kneeling near.

"I never thought that the guy who introduced me to Brother Hatim and Sister Saba would bring me to a place like this," I said.

"But why? These are Muslims too. Just of a different sort."

"So you have a foot in each world."

"I do," he said. "Because they both need each other. They just don't know it, preferring instead to hide."

"What are they hiding from?"

"Same thing that makes you and me hide," he said. "From being distrusted. From being thought of as the enemy. From having false motives heaped on them. So they try to prove their harmlessness. The fundamentalists think they just need to show how pious and peaceful they are. These guys think they just need to show how naked and cool they are. Sucking cock is the best way to prove to the government you aren't a radical."

Ali's voice increased in volume, became shapely, oratorical in inflection and emphasis. GCM ears perked up.

"It's sad how we ended up here. Sad. Those towers went down and suddenly everyone started pinning their gripes on a thing called a Muslim. The word became synonymous with *devil*. With every goddamn evil thing America has fought. I'm surprised they didn't compare Muslim to imaginary villains. Never mind, they did that too, like when they made the hordes of Mordor look like Muslims, or when that bastard Frank Miller made the pre-Islamic Persians look like Muslims. And the rest of the world fell in line with this new game. If you're Indian, pissed off about Pakistan complaining about your occupation of Kashmir? Hey, just call them Muslims and get them declared a terrorist state. If you're Israeli and you don't want to release an inch of the West Bank to the Palestinians? Hey, just call them Muslims and you don't have to move your tanks. If you're Russian, struggling with a bunch of Chechens telling you to stop raping their women? Hey, just call them Muslim and blow them to bits. If you're Chinese and struggling with a bunch of poor Uighur demanding some respect from the Han? Hey, just call them Muslim and jail all their leaders. If you're European and you've got millions of illiterate

Turks and Moroccans and Algerians and Libyans who you didn't allow to become citizens for decades? Hey, just call them Muslim and declare them Fascist or lazy or criminal or all of the above. And if you're American and you want to fly around the world and bomb the boogers out of countries that object to you taking their oil and resources? Hey, just call them Muslim and go to town."

Ali Ansari had a beer in one hand, a joint in the other, and a crowd around him. He put his foot up on a keg.

"But I guess compared to all of those Muslims, we Muslims in America are lucky. They don't bomb us. Yet. They don't put us in prisons. Yet. All they want from us is to keep our mouths shut and not object to their name-calling. It's only an internment of the soul. Our suffering is of a man who is drowning but cannot drown."

The Gay Commie Muzzies had heard the speech before and they knew exactly how to reply: "Long live the empire! Long may we suck her!" Their slogan became a chant and their chant, accompanied by someone playing a snare drum in a military march, became a song. The drum then went silent and another member took up the guitar, playing the *Marche Funèbre* by Chopin.

I looked at Ali Ansari. He had moved off to a corner of the basement, near the bathroom. He winked at me with a cloth in his hand and gestured for me to follow him inside. He said he wanted to play a game with me. I trembled and followed. After his speech, I wanted nothing more than to please him.

The bathroom was dark, lit only by a flashing strobe light. The mirror had been scratched up and had black paint thrown over it. The window was boarded shut, though I could hear the screechy scraping of a windblown branch. The toilet had been duct-taped shut and resembled an iron throne. The unused duct tape sat on top of the seat.

The most obvious modification was the bathtub. There was a long, inclined wooden board over it. Ali Ansari grabbed the duct tape and handed it to me. With his mouth near my ear, in a whisper, he instructed me to tie up his wrists. I obeyed him without thinking, making three turns around. Next he had me duct-tape around his chest, pinning his shoulders to his sides. The first time around I was too limp with the tape and he pecked me on the cheek and told me to do it harder, stronger. I accepted his challenge and, with one arm around his torso and arms, wrapped him so hard that he needed to take multiple long breaths to adjust his breathing.

Once he was tied up he walked over to the wooden board and laid upon it. He put his feet on the elevated side. Between deep and steadying breaths he told me what needed to be done and how to do it. I told him I wouldn't be able to do what he wanted. But he looked at me with pleading eyes. Said he needed it. It was his only drug. When I demurred further he told me that this was a prerequisite to joining the Gay Commie Muzzies. If I wanted to stay I had to perform. I had to serve.

I placed the cloth over his forehead and ears. I took a watering can sitting on the ground, filled it up, drenched the cloth, then lowered it until it covered his nose and mouth. Per his earlier instructions, I applied a little pressure to the cloth so it went into his mouth, and counted to fifteen. During those fifteen seconds I continued pouring water onto his head from the can. Around the tenth second Ansari's feet started twitching. Around the fifteenth second a grotesque gurgling sound came from his throat and he started maniacally shaking his head and twisting his body, trying to remove the cloth, trying to make the water stop. I was unprepared for the violence of his movement and dropped the can. The cessation of the water allowed Ali Ansari to get his bearings and he wriggled out from under me, sitting upright, gasping, laughing, crying, wheezing, mewling. He opened his eyes big and blinked as if in a daze, then coughed. He pointed to a pair of scissors sitting on the windowsill and had me cut him loose.

When he was free he took a deep and steadying breath and put his head on my stomach, kissing it feverishly, telling me I was welcome, telling me we had shared something special, telling me that I would never again be alone. I held his head against my body. I wanted to fit him inside me, so he could live within me, so he could teach me how to survive a drowning.

No one had noticed our absence and when we came into the basement, we were quickly swallowed by a group about to start a video game marathon. There was something wrong with the console, however, and Ali had to wade behind the trolley to untangle the cords.

Tot took our separation to sidle up close to me. "Hey, bro, you want to hear about the Divine Cunt?"

"The what?"

"The Divine Cunt," Ali called out. "Yes, Tot, tell him all about it."

Tot adjusted his turban. "I want to talk to you about the relationship of the phallus to the vagina. You see, the purpose of the penis is to penetrate and the purpose of the vagina is to receive. Right? This seems straightforward. But what happens when we take this question into the realm of rape, into the realm of consent? My view is that it means that rape isn't real, rape doesn't exist. You see, since it's the vagina's inherent characteristic to get wet in order to receive the penis, it doesn't matter whether consent has been established or not. The vagina will get wet even if it is entered in a state of aggression. In fact, it will get wetter the more insistently the cock enters it. Are you following?"

My face twisted. "That is a juvenile opinion and a medical falsehood. Sex is about love. Not aggression."

Tot tittered in Ali's direction. "What if I told you I can make a whole theory of love from this? It goes like this: Since a vagina gets wet even when the penis enters without consent, it means that women are the most merciful and forgiving creatures in the universe. It stands to follow that God, who is the height of mercy and forgiveness, must be a woman as well. In other words, God is the Divine Cunt, the place of absolute warmth and unquestioning moisture."

"Divine Cunt!" some members of GCM shouted from a distance.

Tot ignored them and continued, pulling Farkhunda by the hair toward his groin. "Now if God is the Divine Cunt, that makes God the woman. We humans in our wickedness and selfishness are the equivalent of the male. We are the penis. We penetrate. We do these nonconsensual things. But the Divine Cunt gets wet no matter what we do. Wetness is forgiveness. It is salvation. It is woman. It is love."

"That's self-serving, if you ask me," I said.

"You think I'm just talking shit?"

I turned to Ali, pleading with my eyes to start the game. But he wasn't finished subjecting me to Tot's treatment. Even Farkhunda took longer breaks to look up at him.

"Well, it's not shit, bro," Tot declared. "This thing I am telling you explains everything in the world. Down to September 11."

"This I would like to hear," I said.

"Well, it's pretty simple. I posted it on my blog if you want to read about it. But basically it goes like this: Most people that evaluate September 11 think of the two towers as America's phallus and the two planes that knocked them out as a kind of blade that emasculated America. Now all America can do is to arm up and go out into the world to try to recover its lost masculinity by engaging in all sorts of violence."

"That makes sense to me," I said.

"Total nonsense," Tot offered. "Those two airplanes in New York, they are the phallus. The two towers, standing right next to one another, a few yards apart, are like the vaginal lips of America. The penis forced itself in between the lips. It was not emasculation. It was sex. America has just been the recipient of thorough intercourse. One that it enjoyed!"

"If America liked it so much," I replied, "why did it make plans to go out and bomb everyone and their mother back to the Stone Age?"

"Because America wants more," Tot said. "After centuries of watching the Muslims of the world fornicating with Europeans, America was finally probed, and it liked how it felt to be the object of desire, the woman. It liked it. The only way to get more was to take off the chastity belt and go out among the rapists. That is why America will go into one Muslim country after another. Afghanistan. Pakistan. Iraq. Yemen. America is like that virginal girl who becomes a nymphomaniac after she's taken by force for the first time. Kind of like Farkhunda here. Everything America does from here on out will lead to exacerbating this conflict. If America was really serious about avoiding violence, it would shutter up and shut up. But what it wants is more of what transpired. More intercourse. Through the lack of consent, a consent has been established. Isn't that right, baby?"

Farkhunda nodded, gagged, and nodded some more.

Ali Ansari came over and started the video game.

Hunter Two-One ran through rubble and shrapnel and automatic gunfire toward a rooftop fortification overlooking a village tucked between stone and sky. He was limping from a gunshot wound and his voice relayed through the radio was heavy and raspy. He held before him a small green briefcase, handling it like a waiter holding a tray. He climbed the broken ladder at the back of the charred mud house. It connected to a ramp leading to a sanctuary. He dragged his dirty and muddy body to a small viewing hole in the northeastern corner and blinked hot and desperate a few times, gazing out at a caravan of trucks coming toward the village, the beds of the trucks filled with turbaned men. His health meter was running low and the screen was red to indicate his likely imminent death. Hunter Two-One opened up his briefcase. It revealed a small stick and a series of lit-up buttons. He put his hand on the controls and pressed a button.

The screen switched to black-and-white, a slightly digitized satellite view of the village and the surrounding environs. There was a metallic hum in the background. The little mud structures of the village were highlighted with complicated alphanumeric text. Little red squares started to ping over each one of the villagers riding in the trucks. And the squares became red halos as villagers stepped off the trucks and started milling about and talking in some foreign tongue that sounded like barking dogs and bleating goats.

"Neutralize all enemies," came the order over the radio. *"Hunter Two-One! Blow them to sticks! Keep them away from our boys!"*

Hunter Two-One pressed a button. The screen switched to the camera affixed to the incoming projectile. The ground came closer and closer. Hunter Two-One used his stick to deliver the payload in the tightest grouping of red halos. The camera shifted back to the earlier screen, the one with the metallic hum in the background.

"Direct hit," congratulated the voice. *"Ten-plus kills. Good job!"*

When all the turbaned men were dead, the screen snapped back to the earlier one. The health meter was at a comfortable green, getting fuller with each kill. Over the next five minutes Hunter Two-One proceeded to launch a series of five or six more missiles from the robot hovering overhead. The kills were confirmed by the disembodied voice of the captain. Five-plus kills, ten-plus kills, fifteen-plus kills. There was no certainty to the count. There was no certainty to the destruction. Trucks, camels, sheep, women, children, other such nonessentials. The goal was to have a higher kill percentage than Ali Ansari. In this I succeeded.

At the end of the mission the drone hovered into sight and the American flag fluttered above the shattered village. A cut scene showed Hunter Two-One going home. The skyline suggested he was from Philadelphia. But it could've been any other American city. Just as Hunter Two-One could've been any American.

Ali Ansari and I rained drones well into the morning.

Farkhunda fellated Tot nearly as long. Every now and then I was compelled to look over. His cock was the longest I had ever seen, a snake that Farkhunda nuzzled like a scarf around her neck. Once she caught me looking, put the long cock around her face, and asked if I liked her hijab.

I woke up in a heap of tawny bodies. It had to be a little before dawn. Groggily I searched for Ali Ansari. He was awake, standing in a corner of the room, bowing and prostrating, murmuring and whispering, lost in prayer. My only recent experience with Islamic prayer had been through Qasim, whose aim had been to sell it, who had made it appear like a performance. Ali Ansari's prayer wasn't like that. It was a purposeful abstention from everything, a temporary secession from the world of will and violence. I wondered if he experienced something mighty in there. Or perhaps it was simply the harmonious hum of nothingness. Even that wouldn't be so bad. Isn't that what we sought when we read Proust, for example? I looked away. People didn't like being stared at when they were reading.

There was stirring among the bodies. It was Farkhunda. She was in panties and a men's button-down shirt. Her neck and thighs had bite marks all over. She hopped onto the sofa and hurriedly put on her shoes, at the same time trying to shake Tot awake so he could drive her home. She had the car keys in hand.

"Just drive yourself."

"I can't. Don't have a license. Not even a permit."

"I thought these things were only *kind of* illegal."

"The cops out here sit at the intersections waiting to jump on us. It's discrimination."

Farkhunda went off to look for Ali Ansari. When she saw he was in the middle of prayer she let out a moan. She threw the keys to the ground and sat on the sofa, staring at her phone, waiting for the inevitable call from home.

"Get up." I swept up the keys and her wrist in the same move and dragged her to the car. "I'll take you. Just tell me the directions."

We flew through the winding streets. The atmosphere had a subdued morbidity to it, the trees looming, the streets disappearing into fog-filled turns, the stop signs having been decapitated by rapscallion children. The fear of Farkhunda's authority figures only added to the trepidation in the air.

"Your mom is kind of bossy then?"

"It's my sister. She's a bitch."

"She's protective?"

"She's religious. She used to be normal. But when my dad got taken, she changed. Now she thinks women represent honor and other shit like that. And we should be covered head to toe and we shouldn't date or talk to boys or eat anything but halal. It's all her Islam. It's too much."

"What do you think women represent?"

"Whatever the fuck we want. Just like men. We are equal."

"But Tot doesn't treat you like an equal."

She turned to me with a pitying expression, the kind of know-it-all smugness that teenagers tend to assume. "Do you think I don't cheat on Tot? At the end of the day, no one treats each other equal. What matters is whether you are getting shamed in the process or not. Islam shames its women. That's why I don't believe in it. It's built on the idea of sin. That your fuck-ups have a greater meaning. They can't just be fuck-ups. Sin doesn't let you forgive yourself until others forgive you."

I grew somber. "I hope that one day no one has to live in shame."

Her face was jaded. "Won't happen. The world is Shameistan. Anyway, there's my sister, my executioner."

I looked in the sister's direction. It took a moment to register that it was Sister Saba. I immediately lowered myself into the seat.

"What's the matter with you?" Farkhunda said.

"Your sister. I know her."

"You've met her before?" she nearly yelled, putting out a hand to help me steer. "I didn't know you were one of the fundamentalists. By your age the fundamentalism disappears. They call it Salafi Burnout."

"I'm not a Salafi," I said. "I'm not even sure if I'm Muslim."

"Of course you are. You have a Muslim name. That's all you need to be Muslim. Anyway, I don't know why, but you knowing my sister is kind of hot. Isn't it?"

"Is it?" I said, peeking over the wheel, slowing the car even further, rotating my eyes in her direction.

Farkhunda put her tongue in her cheek and nodded. "Remember earlier? When Tot dropped me and parked on the other side? You do the same. I'll just go inside and come back. Over there, around the corner. Got it?"

"But why?"

She popped her mouth with a finger and told me I wouldn't regret it.

I pulled over as much from shock as excitement. Farkhunda patted me on the thigh and ran out to mollify her sister. I drove around the house and parked under a couple of oaks. The branches moved a little in the breeze. Otherwise the morning was still. In the calm I fell into a nap.

She came into the car an hour later, dressed in flannel pajamas, an off-shoulder sweatshirt, and teddy bear slippers. I had regained enough composure to remember that she was just sixteen and that I wasn't up for that, no matter how tempting the vessel. Getting declared a sexual deviant and having my name published on a website was the last thing I needed. Perhaps the only thing being worse than a Muslim in America was to be a pedophile.

"You're sixteen."

"18 PA 6301, section D, subsection 2," she replied.

"What?"

"I know you're worried about my age. That's your loophole."

"I don't understand."

She rolled her eyes. "In Pennsylvania, if a minor is between sixteen and eighteen, then it's a defense for you to say that you thought she was over eighteen. A lawyer told me that."

"Did you suck him too?"

"Of course not," she spat. "He was non-Muslim."

I pressed my lips and accelerated out of the neighborhood. Farkhunda pulled out her phone and gave directions. It was a forty-five-minute drive to where she wanted to go. I didn't bother asking where we were headed. We were well outside the suburbs soon.

With the sun out, spackling light upon our windows, we came upon a wide grassy clearing. Farkhunda put a hand on my arm and had me slow. She pointed to the right and I gasped. A large white-domed structure in the center of the field, set off by hedges, surrounded by evergreens, shone like a star in an emerald universe. There was a garden near it with a freestanding wooden structure for vines. A crescent and star protruded from the top of the structure.

This was the mausoleum of a mystic named Bawa Muhaiyaddeen. He had come to the United States in 1971 and established a Sufi order that drew hundreds of followers. By the time he passed away, the group had enough resources to field a mosque in Overbrook and to build this mausoleum to perpetuate his legacy. Farkhunda said that some of the great American translators of Sufi poetry had been inspired by the saint. I said that I hadn't been aware that such a place existed. She told me a story about Bawa's spiritual predecessor, Abdul-Qadir Gilani. Some highway robbers had taken him hostage when he was a child in Iraq and searched his pockets for money, only to be thwarted because his mother had sewn his money on the inside of his clothes. The robbers were about to leave Gilani alone when they proceeded to ask him if he was hiding any money. Gilani was so truthful that he told them it was sewn to his clothes. The robbers were sufficiently impressed by his honesty that they immediately converted to Islam and renounced their crime. The moral of the story, Farkhunda said, was that when you are held up by criminals, you should volunteer to get naked.

We got out of the car and stepped onto a private road. Taking off her slippers, Farkhunda ran ahead, the dewy glinting grass crushed under her feet and springing back when she moved off. I ran after her. The building was farther than it appeared. I was winded from the chase.

By the time I came upon the door, Farkhunda was on her knees. She had a couple of keys in her hand and was picking out the one that might allow us to get inside. She said the keys were jealously guarded by Bawa's fellowship, but awhile back someone from the GCM had dated someone who knew the locksmith who serviced the mausoleum. As a result, the shrine had become a reliable place for GCM members to have early-morning or late-night hookups, provided that the caretaker didn't show up.

It took a couple of tries before the door opened. We were let into a large room with four Persian carpets. In the space where they met, there was a central grave covered in a black sheet. The sheet was stitched in gold and contained an inscription I didn't understand. The symbol of the Sufi order, a rose with a six-pointed star in the middle, was etched on each corner of the sheet. The ceiling above the grave opened into the octagonal underside of the dome. Its interior was painted a cool green color. Koranic inscriptions and Allah signs hung on the walls and gave the room an even more sacred atmosphere.

Farkhunda stood and offered a prayer before the grave. Both hands up; quiet invocations. I was puzzled by her behavior. She had held herself out as a sinner, yet here she was, engaged in supplication. I could only stand back and watch. Perhaps belief wasn't a declaration or a negation. Perhaps it was a disposition, an inclination, one that emerged in each person at their own accord, like an exhale.

She finished and brought a pair of cushions used for congregants and pilgrims and turned them into her kneepads. She pulled down my pants and took off her top. I could see her *bismillah* tattoo reflected in the window. She didn't like that my back was to the deceased and turned me around so we had the grave to our side. I was small at first and she held me with two fingers and a thumb. She stroked hard, with a pinky extended, and kissed and slurped the head. I became large enough for her to have to use her palm. My eyes were fixed upon her knuckles and the cuticles. They were dark brown, nothing like Marie-Anne's pale fingers. Not that my wife ever performed this act. The thought of doing something I never got to experience caused me to let out a groan of encouragement and I leaned forward over Farkhunda, holding her hair, her black hair, up with my left hand, taking my right hand down to her breasts, her bark-brown nipples. I made my brown belly press against her brown forehead. My thoughts turned to the night before. First in the car and then on the couch in Tot's house. I remembered how Farkhunda had knelt among us—ours to behold—and enjoyed being in that position. On exhibition. Displayed. My eyes flickered over her body. I imagined me, Ali, and Tot sitting around her, making her slurp in turn. Farkhunda could be our gathering place. Our bond. Our mosque. It was appropriate, for all of us who were in various states of disenfranchisement and isolation, to find congress in an underage girl whose life had been destroyed by a scared president's war upon a feeling.

It wasn't very long before I came. I held Farkhunda's head and clenched my toes and stared at the dead Sufi's grave and released in her mouth. I caught my breath while leaning on her head.

Before I had a chance to stop shivering, she jumped up, sat down on the grave, and asked me to lie her down on the sheet and finger her just a little. But after my orgasm I was in no mood to entertain her demands. I told her it would be better if she took care of herself back home. "Ali Ansari would've done it," she pouted.

"You should have brought him then."

We drove back in silence. She sat with her feet tucked up. I occasionally turned my head to look at her underthighs. With the mountain-walls whipping past us on the highway I gave some consideration to the violation of the vows I had made to Marie-Anne. But not a lot, because I didn't consider Farkhunda a competitor to Marie-Anne. She occupied a different place. Someone to be taken advantage of and used. Like I was used by my wife, Farkhunda was used by me, and that was just the way hierarchy worked for all of us who played the role of the slut in America.

I came home and went to sleep after texting Ali Ansari the details. He was happy I had liked his gift.

CHAPTER SIX

The next few weeks were hot. Light shone upon the skyscrapers and created a separate city made of shadows. Shirtless children wrapped each other head to foot in cellophane and hopped their way up the art museum's steps. There was news that a Sikh man had been killed for looking like a Muslim and the Sikh community organized a parade and festival, with turbans bobbing on the horizon, dancing drummers in pink and purple, and little boys with long hair. Later on there was a street fair for the Fairmount neighborhood. Older women came out into the streets, with coiffed hair and in ruffled shirts and pretty floral headbands, carrying the coxcomb ginger flowers that have long served as scepters to the empresses of Philadelphia.

I didn't do much those days. Mostly Ali Ansari and I played video games or watched old movies and drank. This led to more conversations about Marty Martel and other related topics. It recalled life in high school. Sometimes we even put on Boyz II Men, or Shai, or Wreckx-N-Effect, and belted out the best songs from the early nineties, which Ali called "a time of peace, a time of free-ish love, a time when America was perfect, a time when the names of guys like Hussein, Khomeini, Gaddafi were associated with a song written by Tupac Shakur instead of guys like you and me." Tupac's group was aptly called Outlawz.

We always met at my apartment. Ali wanted to go the Mainline often but I feared running into Farkhunda and vetoed the idea every time.

I wasn't certain if it was my guilt toward Marie-Anne and our vows that prevented me from going back, or because I felt a separate hatred toward myself for having taken advantage of a girl who had been victimized by an overeager prosecutor desperate to make his name in the golden age of the American dragnet. It was my weakness that had made me go off with Farkhunda. The weakness of the need to be superior. I used to get that fix at Plutus, and losing it had made me desperate. Was this need for superiority something that existed in me as a result of my connection to Islam? Or was it something that was part and parcel of my position in America?

I tucked the memory of that morning at the mausoleum into the cloudy folders where I kept inappropriate dreams. The dream where I had been the Minotaur and murdered the Theseus who looked like George Gabriel. The dream where Rasha Florence Quinn was an old witch and I was a young boy and she had promised to turn me into a superhero only to stab me with a sword. The dream where the Koran was my magic flying carpet and I trusted it to carry me over an ocean but it dropped me and let me plunge into the deep.

I also kept Ali Ansari away from Marie-Anne, sending him back to North Philly well before she'd be home for the weekends. For those couple of days I wouldn't communicate with him, I'd avoid references to him, try not to think about him. I became a man with two lives. One with my actual partner; one with my partner in procrastination.

Their meeting was a prospect I wouldn't allow. She would question everything from his affiliation with Gay Commie Muzzies, to his obsession with video-game drone warfare, to his simultaneous affection and flagellation of Muslims. But most of all she would question his clothes, his demeanor, his diction. I could envision her calling him a dandy. To flit around, purely as a servant to some aesthetic ideal, was difficult for her to accept, largely because her own creative career had stalled. Maybe because she wasn't able to be an artist, because she had to do labor like the rest of us, in order to make herself feel superior to artists, she told herself that she was the real humanist, the one truly moral person, whereas a dandy was just a decadent who didn't care about anything bigger, who had no access to certainty. I had warned Marie-Anne that holding this kind of certitude was dangerous for someone who worked in international surveillance, where declaring someone a suspect, someone worthy of reconnaissance, simply required assertion. Fruitlessly, I had tried to tell her that those who watched others from a distance became inclined to liken themselves to gods, and wrongly concluded that since their vision was limitless so was their judgment.

I didn't want Marie-Anne to subject my friend to that kind of determination.

As the summer deepened, Marie-Anne opened toward me. It wasn't the warmth in the air so much as the imminence of our tenth wedding anniversary.

Our wedding had taken place at Canon Chapel at Emory. The reason I had picked the chapel was because it served as a kind of interreligious and intercultural meeting point for the university, and we hoped that its universalist ambiance would seep into our congregation and keep things civil and polite. We shouldn't have feared. Our wedding was the model of decorum. Some of the peacefulness was due to the fact that from Marie-Anne's side only her best friends and her parents came out because her mother had refused to call any of the society from South Carolina. My party was a little larger. But none of the invited, except for my parents, were immigrants. Perhaps ashamed, or perhaps wary of what their immigrant friends might do or say in the presence of South Carolina elites, my father decided that he would only invite his highest business contacts. A few older white couples, a lot of paisley and seersucker. Our wedding, then, had all the tension of a weekend business convention. The congregation gazed upon us as if we were a PowerPoint, or a rather boring panel that had to be endured before we could get to the food. Marie-Anne and I hadn't cared. We had even liked the formality of the event. It had made our union seem more legitimate. As if by having fun we might have unwittingly said to her mother that this was just a youthful indiscretion. A little stiffness gave a more serious imprimatur to the whole thing.

For our honeymoon we were supposed to go to Hilton Head. I screwed up the reservations, so we rented a car and drove down to Key West instead. Marie-Anne got food poisoning somewhere near Ocala and we veered off toward Orlando and ended up at Disney World.

The first time we had sex was when we got a little too drunk from the minibar. I was wearing Mickey Mouse ears and Marie-Anne had on a tiara. In the middle of the sex I made the mistake of calling her "my princess," and she grew angry by that insult and put the tiara on top of my head and pushed me away a little. It wasn't much of a push, but because it was a gesture of disapproval during an act of intimacy, it made me lose my mind. I accused Marie-Anne of trying to emasculate me and stormed out of the hotel room, going down to the bar to have a drink named after a cartoon dog. A few hours later Marie-Anne came up behind me, hugged me hard, and told me that we needed to go back up and try again. "It's just nerves," she had said, and was right. During the act we talked lovingly about making babies in the future, growing old together, other things that virgins said.

The morning of the tenth anniversary, as I sat at the antique desk flipping through my phone, Marie-Anne came up to me dressed in a black shirt and boxers and flicked my ear.

"We forgot each other's birthdays."

"I know."

"But we are old. Birthdays aren't as important as the date we became responsible for each other."

"Right."

"We should go out somewhere."

"We should."

Fifteen minutes later we were headed out to Friday-night jazz at the art museum. We sat in the atrium, wineglasses in hand, pressed next to each other. I was dwarfed. It seemed inappropriate to be so close, as if she was forcing herself onto me without having addressed any of our underlying dissonance. The only upside was that the music was continuous and the breaks didn't give an opportunity to talk.

The artist was from Turkey and played soaring pieces celebrating Atatürk. They had a kind of postimperial grandeur to them. The songs of a state that remained prideful despite losing ownership of the world. It wasn't music appropriate for America today. We still maintained seven hundred military bases around the globe. We still knew how to take children from other nations and remake them in our image. Our music didn't need to fill us with pride. Just to have a beat. Pride was something emperors could take for granted.

I wanted to go home before there was more drinking, before inhibitions and resentment dissipated, before I ended up telling bedtime stories; but Marie-Anne was in her ballet flats and eager to stroll downtown. We walked toward the Franklin Institute and headed into Center City, past the Whole Foods, past the adult cinema still clinging to its little slit as skyscrapers and condominiums and culinary schools swallowed it up. It reminded me of the green-domed church on JFK Boulevard, with similar desperation holding on to its location across from the crystalline Comcast Monster.

I went along despite myself.

We continued toward Rittenhouse Square, taking 18th Street. The Friday-night crowd was out. The heat made the women minimalist with clothing. Men stood outside the various bars and restaurants, smoking and staring at the women. Different lines went into the various lounges, the bouncers dour, the doors barred. The longest line belonged to a small restaurant called Byblos. They had a couple of tables out on the pavement where people smoked flavored tobacco from a water pipe and poured mint tea for each other. When the coals on the aluminum foil covering the head died down, a man from inside the restaurant was summoned. With the authority of a Catholic altar-server swinging a thurible, he came brandishing a long-handled coal-scuttle. Using a pair of tongs, he replaced the expired coals with a new batch of ember eyes. The smoke from the nozzle became more bulbous, heavier. The smokers thanked him.

"A hookah," Marie-Anne cooed. "I had one at the W Hotel in Doha. You up for trying?"

"The coal seems carcinogenic."

"Seems like everything is."

Most of the patrons were children of immigrants. They spoke English, but threw in the occasional foreign word. But only nouns; their connection to languages other than English wasn't complete enough to allow for verbs. Eyes flickered over us. They went from Marie-Anne to me, from her ring finger to mine. The women were far more obvious than the men. I tried to look into Marie-Anne's eyes to see if she had a comment, if she'd even noticed any of it, but she showed no expression. She was more focused on drawing a waitress over and persuading her to let us go to the front.

My ears burned at her maneuvering. I got the sense that if Marie-Anne and I were successful in jumping ahead, then all the patrons would regard me and think it was only because I was with someone possessing pale skin, someone who they associated with privilege. I cursed Ali Ansari for putting such thoughts in my head, for introducing colors into my once-innocent myopia. I wished I hadn't met him. This limb—of being identified as a Muslim—that had grown from my back out of nowhere should've been amputated at the first sighting; instead I had let it grow muscular and now it had the ability to smack me upside the head.

Marie-Anne was successful and we got seated immediately. As I received the hookah I noticed all the eyes inside Byblos boring into me. Hoping to offset the disquiet, perhaps to extend a sort of middle finger to all the people who were staring, I cupped my face and turned to focus on Marie-Anne.

"Is it just the two of us?"

"It's our anniversary."

"Well," I said, "if it's just us, I might start thinking about things you don't like to hear. I might get drunk and bring up the B word."

"Not this again. Haven't you noticed that I've gotten worse?"

I had noticed. It was the most obvious thing about her. She was in no condition to get pregnant. And that shattered me, because we had almost gotten her to that point, of healthy weight-loss, where it would have been possible to talk conception.

"I blame you for letting yourself slide," I croaked. It wasn't something I thought too long about, otherwise it probably wouldn't have come out; when it came to Marie-Anne I wasn't capable of premeditated dissent, only periodic prods that were less assertion and more whine.

"You're blaming me for something I can't control?"

"You're lying. There are parts of this you can control. We did control them."

"But then it fell apart."

"You let it."

"I guess you checking out of life had nothing to do with that," she said. "Besides, even if I was all right, I'm not sure I would have been up for having children."

"Why not?"

"You won't get it."

"Make me understand."

She pulled on the nozzle of her hookah, exhaled a cloud, and set her eyes on me. The fog contained dissipating roses. "I'm just not sure we would be the best parents to them. Maybe you think you will be good.

But I know I won't. What happens when I fall out of love with them?"

"You can fall out of love?"

"Look at us."

The coals upon my hookah, once howling in heat, had put on a silver fur and no longer warmed the head. I prodded them with the tongs, trying to undress them, trying to revive them. The ember at the heart was tiny, embryonic, disappearing.

When I glanced back up, Marie-Anne was sliding from the booth, headed out of the bar.

I stayed put. Byblos on a Saturday night had a kind of intimacy that demanded that you be there with a date. I was not against sitting with Ali Ansari in such a place, but before I tried him I sent a message out to Candace Cooper instead, asking her if she wanted to join me for some genie smoke. She replied after a little while and said she was at a book reading near Rittenhouse and would come on over as soon as she was finished.

I busied myself with the music videos and talking to the waitress about the hookah. A song by Myriam Fares played on the screen. In the video the curly haired singer played a dancer, a ballerina. She was in Paris, chased by a taller version of me, even though I had never chased a girl like that.

"That's hard core," Candace said when she arrived. "Smoking by yourself."

She wore a volumized white scarf and a white dress shirt tucked into a polka-dot chiffon maxi skirt.

I pulled some smoke and blew it at her. It spread over her like a cream.

I helped her sit and ordered wine and hookah for her. She vetoed the wine saying she didn't drink alcohol any longer. I tried to downplay the faux pas by giving her a little lecture about the hookah based on what little I had learned from the waitress; but Candace put up her hand and said she knew all about it. She'd smoked it in Dubai and Turkey and even frequented a Palestinian hookah bar in her neighborhood in North Philly.

"I like your look," I blurted out. "I loved it at the deli too."

She smiled and lowered her eyes. "You always made fun of my clothes."

"I'm not doing it now."

We sat together and Candace blew O's which I both popped and wore on my fingers like rings. She gave me a rundown on Arabic pop music. How Lebanon produced the starlets, Egypt the musicians, and a recording company in Saudi Arabia launched the indecency upon the world. The videos that were released during Ramadan were particularly licentious. As evidence she showed me videos of Elissar and Nicole Saba. Squinting into her phone required sitting together, our legs touching lightly. Candace said she had started taking belly-dancing classes.

"I had always wanted to do it," she said. "But until I converted I felt it would be stealing someone else's culture."

Her comment gave me the opening I needed and I prodded her about how she had taken to Islam. She went on to detail her own coming of age in the suburbs of Atlanta and DC. Her parents, both half-black, were part of the new black elite who turned their backs on her when she decided that she didn't have a similar love for "black tribalism" that they did. It started when she refused to go to Spellman in Atlanta and opted for a public university. It worsened when she told her father that she imputed no inherent superiority to a black man. Race, she said, was an oppression created by those who profited from making divisions in the world. To agree to belong to a race meant affirming that basic oppression. She couldn't do it. She needed to belong to something built around inclusiveness, something that erased the differences between people. The natural thing to do would have been to turn to the Christian God, who welcomed all to His flock. But the problem was that she couldn't erase all of her blackness, and Christianity belonged to the white man. She turned, therefore, to the God of the nonwhites—Allah. Choosing a universalist deity based on somewhat racial reasons was not completely consistent with her initial rejection of the very idea of race, but it was better than living an entirely racial life of the sort her parents led.

We smoked two more rounds before she started wrapping up.

"Are you going home after this?" she asked.

"No. I have this crazy friend in North Philly I'm going to go see."

"Same guy as from the deli?"

"Yeah," I said, and in my excitement I pulled up the video of him threatening to kill George Gabriel. "Total original."

"He's very . . . loud," Candace said.

"He lives near you. We can go up together?"

Candace appeared interested. But decorum still made her cautious. "How is Marie-Anne?"

"Things between us are ending," I stated. "Are you down or what?"

"Sure, sure," she said. "I'm down, I'm down."

We paid the bill and headed out from Byblos toward Walnut Street, where we intended to catch an eastbound bus that would connect us to the northbound transportation. I staggered with an arm around Candace and tried to liken her to paganism, asking her if she had any connections with Rastafari or animism. She laughed and said not at all, she had grown up a good Baptist girl and then transitioned into Islam. God, she said, was a secret she couldn't ever forget.

I told her if that was the definition of God, then my God might be a girl I just smoked hookah with.

She laughed and told me I was intoxicated.

The commute took about two hours. There had been a shooting on the Broad Street line and the buses were running forty-five minutes behind.

Candace exchanged messages with the newsroom and mobilized a cameraman to go out and find footage. Places like North Philly were neglected in American media and it was her duty as a journalist to illuminate what was concealed. The world deserved to know how the heart of the empire was full of gunshots.

It was well past midnight when we made it to Ali Ansari's building on Diamond Street. Candace told me that the area used to be a hub for art deco and for jazz, until the race riots of 1964 which began when a pregnant black woman was killed by a pair of white police officers. Since then this part of North Philly had known nothing but murder and mourning.

The front door to Ali's building was wide open and we let ourselves in and headed up to his second-story apartment. Candace kept the back of her skirt cinched with two fingers like a wedding train. Outside Ali's apartment there were two women standing in the hallway. Both were topless, texting on their cell phones in heels and thongs.

Candace turned to me and asked what kind of illicit business my buddy was into.

"I thought it was Islam."

"He's not a pimp, is he?"

I was about to ask the women about the apartment owner when the door opened wide. There was Ali Ansari, wearing his usual slacks but only a sweat-soaked white undershirt with them. There was a small bowler hat on his head and he held a miniature digital camera. Behind him I could hear the sound of a couple men talking to one another. Ali Ansari hadn't looked at me or Candace just yet, and proceeded to give one of the girls instructions about her scene. The only words I made out were "Obama" and "hymen."

I cleared my throat. Ali Ansari's eyes bulged upon noticing me. He came over to give a hug.

"Ali Ansari, Candace Cooper."

"I thought the wife was a different complexion."

"Definitely not the wife," Candace laughed.

"You know," Ali put an elbow in my rib, "Muslims are allowed up to four—"

"If there's anyone who should be talking about polyamorous relationships, it's you," I interrupted, gesturing at the two women. "And what's this about Obama and hymen?"

"Osama and Ayman," Ali Ansari replied. "Not Obama and hymen. Come in, come in. Let me introduce you to Talibang Productions."

He panned his hand across the room and led us inside. Tripods, reflectors, flashtubes, and camera batteries were strewn around the bedroom studio. I saw two guys who looked vaguely like members of GCM get undressed and head into the bathroom. The room was covered with other paraphernalia as well. Ejaculating sheaths with hand pumps; bukkake lotion; brushes for concealer paint. Candace nearly stepped into a half-empty jug of piña colada mix and Ali rushed over to save the backup fake sperm. From the bathroom one of the performers complained loudly about discoloration. Ali yelled back and said some discoloration was normal after girth-enhancing fat transfers.

Candace and I leaned against a dresser. The only decorations in the room were a pair of picture frames with stock wedding photos. Ali explained that the scene he was filming involved a couple of Mainline widows of 9/11 who had an inexplicable desire to experience terrorist sex with Osama bin Laden and Ayman al-Zawahiri.

Candace and I wanted to watch the scene, but Ali said our giggling was going to be a major distraction and told us to sit in the hallway until he finished. We went outside and sent the housewives in.

"Aren't you glad you came?" I asked Candace.

"Literally the greatest night ever."

We sat down on the carpet and shared a cigarette. Candace rambled along about how little money she had. The Al Jazeera paycheck was not enough to cover her expenses, much less help make a dent in her student loans. When she was in journalism school, two of the biggest loan checks issued to her were actually private loans from a bank. The name had sounded very official, very governmental, and she had thought the loans were part of the federal cornucopia. Except they weren't. The private loans went into default less than a year after graduation. There she was, studying investigative journalism, all while getting hoodwinked. The default became a permanent blight on her credit. Buying a house was out of the question. So was renting at most corporate buildings.

"It doesn't matter," she said. "I get to be in North Philly. Feel like this is supposed to be my community."

"Maybe you should've stuck it out at Plutus. Money was good."

"What about principles?"

"What about student-loan default?"

"What about principles?" she persisted. "What George Gabriel did to you was wrong. If he could do that to you, then under different circumstances he could do it to someone else as well. To a mixed-race girl with a lot of debt. I wasn't about to live in fear for the rest of my life." She eyed me with sudden admiration. "I'm kind of surprised to see that you're doing so well. Surprised, but glad."

"You've no idea how bad up I've been." I gestured toward the door. "First off, I'm unemployed. After that, what can be said? I'm sitting in a slum in North Philly with a woman not my wife outside the door of my only friend who's inside having a couple of terrorists fuck a couple of whores pretending to be Mainline elite. I'm not even including the part that he's trying to convert me to some numerical ideology that might have to do with celebrating terrorism."

Candace perked up. "Numerology? I am the god of numerology. What are you dealing with here?"

I didn't have the poetry book on me, so I had Candace download it onto her phone. I showed her the repetition of the number nineteen. "I'm thinking there's something celebrating Islamic martyrdom."

Candace laughed. "Are you saying that the guy filming the terrorist porn inside is some kind of secret jihadist? He's got a sleeper cell?"

"I didn't know he made terrorist porn until tonight. Who knows, that could be his cover, a very good one."

She patted me on the back. "I don't think you really believe any of this. He just seems like a suburban kid gone lost to history. Just like the rest of us."

We came back to the question of the number nineteen. Candace said that when she had first converted, the Internet had been her major source for acquiring knowledge about Islam, and one of the websites she used to frequent had a theory about the number nineteen. She pulled up a website and put it in front of me. It referred to something called the Mathematical Miracle of the Koran. Apparently there's a mysterious verse in the Koran that reads in full, *Over it is nineteen!* For centuries no one understood what the verse meant, until an intrepid mathematician came along and postulated the theory that the "it" in the verse referred to the Koran. The number nineteen was supposed to be a sort of key, a hidden secret, that hung "over" the Koran, waiting to be inserted, unlocking countless secret treasures. The mathematician, by the name of Khalifa, had found numerous instances of the number nineteen and its multiples making a showing all over the Koran, from important verses to instructive tales about the prophets. And then one day Khalifa, who was living in Arizona, got killed in Tucson, which to many only went further in supporting the viability of the Mathematical Miracle.

"Wow."

That wasn't the only association with the number nineteen that Candace knew of. Nineteen was also the number of words for "love" in Arabic. She pulled up another web page and showed me the list. From *tarrafouq* to *hubb, gharam* to *ouns*.

"Wow. Numerology really is your thing."

"You were about to wrongly accuse someone of having terrorist sympathies. I would think you'd know better than that."

"Guilty," I said. "But in my defense, I wasn't entirely serious. Why else would I continue to be his friend?"

"You tell me: why are you friends?"

I hung my head. "I'm ashamed to say this, but maybe I was secretly hoping he really was some kind of terrorist sympathizer. Or, to be more accurate, that through him I might meet someone who was plotting against America. Then I could turn that person in and feel like I had done something to deserve being in this country."

"Like earning kudos?"

"Yeah."

"But why?"

"To belong."

"You don't feel American?"

"Only a part of me does."

"What percent?"

"I don't know."

"Well, guesstimate."

"More than 50. But less than 100."

"Three-quarters then?"

"Less."

"Three-fifths?"

I smiled at the reference. "More than that."

"How much more?"

"I would say I feel five-eighths American. 62.5 percent. That's exactly how American I feel. E-R-I-C-A."

"Erica? Who's that?"

"I just picked five letters out of the eight in *American*. ERICA."

She smiled. "You could have picked some other five letters. Like maybe A-M-I-A-N."

"That doesn't make a name."

"Not a name," she replied. "It makes a question."

Ali Ansari finished an hour later. To thank us for our patience he took us to an all-night Ethiopian restaurant. It was off Cecil B. Moore, near a broken-down food truck and next to a lot where men gathered and played chess. Before we went inside Ali pointed me to a well-kempt house next to the restaurant. Masjid ud-Dukhan. That was the mosque he sometimes attended. Candace said she liked going there as well. She was particularly fond of the preacher, Sheikh Shakil, a former felon and archburglar who had given up his nefarious ways in jail. Unlike some of the other religious leaders in North Philadelphia, Sheikh Shakil actively engaged in the political sphere, and had gotten a number of programs up during Mayor Street's time.

At the restaurant there was no bouncer or cover or even a line as had been the case in Central Philadelphia. All were welcome, at any time, without any orchestration or intercession by an attendant. As a Honduran jazz pianist performed upstairs we sat down on rickety high-legged chairs. Candace's legs angled between my open knees. There was a draft in the establishment and her skirt kept rustling against my ankle.

I directed my attention toward Ali. He wanted to tell us about Talibang Productions so that we wouldn't make fun of him.

Like every dandy before him, Ali Ansari became obsessed with aesthetics due to his own lack of attractiveness. In early puberty he was short, bespectacled, with a massive Adam's apple and black peach fuzz. When he grew tall, the unattractiveness only became more visible to the people around him, including his own mother, who chastised him for not being the sort of exuberant, assertively masculine man that her uncles and brothers back in the Old World had been. Once, for example, she noticed that when shaving he didn't pull his skin down with his off hand like her uncles used to, and she told him that his shaving style wasn't manly.

Compounding his insecurity was that he was the sole West Asian at his high school. There was a group of white kids and there was a group of black kids. Neither accepted him. And if they did allow him in, they never elevated him, which was what he really wanted. Being dark-skinned, he couldn't achieve the social popularity that leading white guys could claim. And being of small stature, he couldn't possess the physical authority exuded by the leading black guys. He therefore became interminably jealous of two things at once: white charisma and black strength. "That is the sexual yin and yang of America," he said, polishing off a Stella. "And I didn't fit into either."

The college years were a time of depression. He tried everything from joining a white fraternity to joining a black stepping group that toured historically black universities. But because he always felt that in these pursuits he was not locating something essential about himself—something he hadn't yet learned how to define—his efforts never brought him peace. In the end he stopped trying, became a hermit of sorts, and indulged his doldrums by watching interracial porn. Strong black men having intercourse with pretty pale-skinned white girls. In masturbating to the American yin and yang—the inaccessible—Ali Ansari finally found a bit of relief. He dropped out of his premed program and set about getting trained in film.

After college Ali Ansari told his parents he was going to Dominica to study at the medical school; instead he moved out to North Philly and sent his résumé to various pornographic websites specializing in interracial porn. One company, Aphrodiesel Spanktertainment, based out of Baltimore, recognized his name from the subscription he had bought and renewed at the gold level for four years. They decided to give him a job. Ali was assigned to travel with a Jamaican-American former wrestler named Blake Nails who, due to his fragile mental state and repressed homosexuality, needed a more encouraging cameraman than the one he had. Managing Blake really meant getting him cocaine, holding his hand when he got male-enhancement procedures done, and stroking him until he was hard. "I used a glove at first and then one day I didn't," Ali shrugged. On these trips Ali developed his directorial craft. Looping a scene to extend the pounding. Doing the money shot first. Learning to hide the ejaculating hand pump. The use of glory holes and prosthetics. Point-of-view tricks. Camera angles. He also learned about the most up-to-date male-enhancement medical techniques, everything from penile widening to suspensory ligament incisions to platelet-rich plasma injections and glandular grafting. Together Ali and Blake traveled across the country, from motels in Miami to hotels in Houston, from casinos in Las Vegas to private homes in Montana. Under Ali's management Blake also started freelancing, answering swingers ads from the web. Everywhere there were men eager to give their white wife to a black porn performer and pay good money for it. The freelancing became lucrative and allowed Blake to transition into physical therapy and let Ali buy his own film equipment.

During his travels, Ali also met others similar to him. People seeking inclusion in America through sexuality. One, like a Kashmiri-American girl named Shazia, believed that she was actually a white girl, and proved it by being contrasted against black skin. Blake Nails had her regularly. Another, like a Persian-Swedish-American named Mitra, demanded that she would only be with white guys, because she was pure Aryan. Both girls eventually devolved into a glassy-eyed sadism. Shazia ended up a sugar baby in Las Vegas, getting five thousand a month from a forty-seven-year-old lawyer and accountant who liked to be forced to eat his own semen. Mitra got pregnant by an Egyptian plastic surgeon who lied and said he was Caucasian. She killed herself and left the baby in Tijuana.

At some point in the middle of the decade Ali Ansari started to wonder why there were no Muslim men performing in porn. He figured the answer was that there was no demand. No one got off on the idea of seeing a Muslim boning a white girl. He wanted to know why not. The answer he settled on was that America simply didn't recognize Muslim masculinity. The only image of Muslim men America saw was of those at the receiving end of invasion, at the receiving end of the torture like at Abu Ghraib, or simply exploding themselves out of desperation. The Muslim was the butt of humiliation. Ali Ansari decided he wanted to change that.

And so Talibang Productions was launched. Ali envisioned a Muslim version of the interracial porn that he had made with Blake Nails. Husband humiliation. Cheating wife. Forced entry. Abduction. Inexplicable erotic romance in the men's section of the mosque, with the entire congregation. He imagined nothing less than a revolution in the way the Muslim man was viewed by America.

In order to find performers, however, he had to do the hard task of wading into Muslim communities. He started by getting a hold of some cab drivers and chefs, but all of them were new to the country and wanted visa sponsorships before committing to anything experimental. Ali then turned to the second-generation youth, finding them at Sufi orders, Salafi mosques, progressive circles. He hit the big conventions, the ethnic speed-dating services that parents set up to get their children married off, and the lecture circuit where the Islamic pundits peddled books that blamed American consumerism for all the world's ills. It turned out that finding Muslim guys eager to get into pornography was not very easy. Even more difficult was the persuasion that followed. He had to convince men who had attended mosques and listened to sermons about chastity their entire lives to unshackle themselves from their restrictions. It was next to impossible. Even the promise of touching naked white girls wouldn't convince them.

In the end, the only group of Muslims he found who didn't care what their community thought about them were those loosely affiliated with the Gay Commie Muzzies. They were open to performing for Talibang Productions. But as aspiring intellectuals they could only do porn ironically. It had to be meta. It had to be self-reflexive. It had to have something that undermined the very idea of "pornyness."

At first Ali was resistant to these requirements. But as a playwright without players he had no other choice than to consent to the limitations that his performers imposed. Within a few months of working together, Talibang Productions and Gay Commie Muzzies put out their first video, entitled *Gangs of Abu Ghraib*. In it, a fictional and much hotter Lynndie England was put on a leash and passed around from cell block to cell block at Abu Ghraib prison. That was when Ali met Tot, who ended up playing the Iraqi prison guard who groomed Lynndie to share her body with the prisoners. The entire thing was filmed at Eastern State Penitentiary.

The film ended up being a modest financial success. There were ten thousand downloads and nearly a thousand people paid to subscribe to Ali's video channel. He was pretty sure most of these subscribers were Muslim kids around the world. The bloggers hailed him for pushing back against the image of the Muslim male as abused, hungry, tortured, subservient. He had gotten the image of the naked victims of Abu Ghraib out of people's minds and replaced it with machismo. Galvanized by the reception, Ali quickly directed *The Terrorist*, which was about a skinny Muslim guy with a small penis who started sleeping with white women and found that, compared to the men they had been with before, his penis was massive. Partly because of the uniqueness of the venture and partly because of the international network that the Gay Commie Muzzies possessed, Ali started making a good deal of money. Subscriptions made it necessary to come up with new projects, of which *Osama and Ayman in the MILFline* was the newest.

But while everyone agreed that Ali Ansari had the exceptional ability to turn the War on Terror into a joke, he hadn't actually set out to be a jester. Deep down he still longed to make sizzling and serious works of interracial erotica, to introduce new shades into the American spectrum, to create a new sexual aura for the Muslim man. He firmly believed that until the Muslim man was also given the right to access the beauty of the white woman, all the platitudes of American equality would remain hollow.

During his narration, my thighs started touching against Candace's. Her legs were light and delicate, belonging to someone inclined to flight, someone used to running, someone adept at escaping, very unlike Marie-Anne's legs, which were powerful pillars, rooted, sedentary. I hadn't been with a woman this light, this tiny. I wanted to pick her up and lay her down.

"Would you be interested in being in a movie?" Ali asked Candace. "There is some demand out there for hijab-domme. Putting white guys in leashes while wearing a veil. That kind of thing."

"Leave her alone," I pushed. "She's not crass like you."

Candace laughed. "Actually, I'm pretty crass. Which is why I first need to ask whether you sleep with your performers."

"I keep it business . . . Now that we've taken care of that, what about gang bangs?"

"Sure. But only if it's with *nineteen* guys and I represent New York." She emphasized the number for my benefit. "But you know, even if Islam allowed it, I could never do porn. I can't take birth control, and your guys can't do condoms."

We all laughed and the moment passed. But I held onto it. I feared that some kind of connection had formed between Ali and Candace; as if they both realized they shared something—the ability to take everyday motifs and make some kind of a social joke about them. I was grateful when Ali saw a pretty East African girl with a shaved head and went toward her to do his strut and worship.

Left alone with Candace, I let myself imagine being married to her, because marriage was the only way I had ever known how to understand a sexual connection with a woman. If Candace took me home, her parents wouldn't make up excuses to try to keep us apart, because they would know that inclusion was better than exclusion. With Candace I could talk about how un-American I felt. We could even play word games about it. With Candace I wouldn't have to believe that acts of prejudice against me were my own fault. With Candace my friendship with Ali Ansari and his theory of the American yin and yang wouldn't be something I would have to hide. When Candace saw me wronged she would fear that the same thing might also happen to her. Marie-Anne didn't offer any of that. How in the world had we lasted ten years? We were so different, situated in distinct levels of the American caste system. She came from the priestly class, from those who were presumed to be born with access to divinity. I was from something far lower. Perhaps even an untouchable place. My one hope had been to merge my dirty blood with her pure blood and dilute myself in a new generation. Even that hadn't worked out.

I was just about to fashion all my thoughts into an indirect compliment when Candace looked at her phone and face-palmed.

"Shit."

"What?"

"I just remembered. I have to get some footage of this thing in Old City."

"You need to go?"

"I do. The story was my idea."

I took one more shot of whiskey and paid the tab. Ali Ansari was nowhere to be seen so we went outside without him, staring at one another. Far down the street I glimpsed an old church I hadn't noticed before, its walls caved, its glass shattered. In the faint glow of the restaurant's sign I turned to Candace and tried to kiss her cheek.

Before I could make my move, however, she grasped me by the collar and hopped a couple of times. "Why don't you come with me on this thing?"

"Me?"

"Yes."

"Are you sure?"

She put her right hand in the air and made a C. Then she lowered it to her chest and nodded.

She called it "stamping crescents on the heart." It was meant to replace "cross my heart and hope to die."

The time before dawn. We headed out. Our fingers laced together, a stitch to fix the wound of loneliness. We were a unity and before us the contradictions of North Philly spread out in every direction. Here there were lofty pillars and buildings that seemed like they were carved out of rocks. There the earth had been leveled, pounded, and crushed as if rank upon rank of icy angels had been tumbling to their demise in Philadelphia.

We caught a cab in front of the Divine Lorraine. The driver was an old man in a skullcap blasting Koranic recitation on his radio. He was happy to see Candace and said salaam to her. She replied effusively and touched her palm to her chest. When I failed to respond, she gave me a little rap on the knee, and had me offer the driver blessings of peace. The man's English was not very clear; but from the sound of it he wished us well for the sacrament of marriage and for avoiding the fate of the shameless people who only wanted to "fuckchu."

Without any traffic we flew across the city, the driver weaving through the numerous potholes, nearly running over a pair of homeless men stumbling onto Market Street. Candace took a mini–video camera from her purse and tried to pull a shot.

We disembarked at the Federal Courthouse on Market Street. The

Philadelphia History Museum was just about coming to life, a solitary worker in the cafeteria mopping the floor. Candace directed us toward Independence Hall, where the Declaration of Independence and the Constitution were hammered out and presented. The horse-drawn carriages that took tourists around Old City had started to arrive. The breeze that swept off the Delaware River wasn't as intense as usual. It was also humid. A slant of light from the cloudy sky cut at the buildings in Camden.

I asked Candace where we were going. She asked me if I remembered Ken Lulu, the guerrilla marketer. It turned out that after she converted, he revealed to her that he was also Muslim. Ken was short for Kenz, which meant Treasure, and Lulu meant Pearl. When she left Plutus she had delivered to him the names of a couple of her clients. In return she had requested his help for a vision she needed to execute. I asked her what it was, but she just pointed the camera in the direction of Constitution Hall and put a finger over her lips.

Suddenly, without warning, I heard the beginning of the Muslim call to prayer. Clear-throated, well-pronounced, loud, but with a slight musical accompaniment behind it. There were a total of seventeen lines recited. Then the call, rather than ending, transitioned into a rhythmic drumbeat, followed by a symphonic melody featuring a flute and piano. The composition sounded similar to some of Liszt's *Hungarian Rhapsody*, except there was a chorus of men chanting *"Hu! Ya Allah!"* at regular intervals. Much like *Boléro* by Ravel, which began pianissimo and rose to a crescendo to fortissimo possibile, the chant expanded over the ostinato rhythm of drums, which stayed constant through the piece. The end came in the form of an explosive *"Hu!"* that rang loud, true, and immense throughout Old City, a reverberation. My pulse raced from the rhythm, my blood felt as if it might explode out from my cuticles. My cheeks were hot enough to make the rest of my skin feel cold. A deep exhale escaped my lips.

The sound, however, was not the entirety of the piece, or even its primary vehicle. The action was in the visuals, a light show projected onto the walls of Constitution Hall. As the call to prayer and music played in the background, a giant *Allah* written in Arabic appeared on the wall, winking and blinking, ominously gaining in size, until it sat at the top of the building in big bold lettering. After that, one by one, ninety-nine pieces of Arabic calligraphy appeared on the wall, flickering and expanding in size like the initial *Allah*, but disappearing after a second or so. The music picked up and so did the pace of the projection. The names scrolled to various corners of the wall, like birds upon a tree, almost as if they had been etched into the redbrick monument, until they started to coalesce, the calligraphy interlocking to create an eight-pointed arabesque, then breaking up and reorganizing in the first *Allah* that had appeared on the wall, expanding and contracting like a beating heart. A beating. Heart.

A small crowd had formed during the light show. They snapped pictures and made videos. People as far away as the courthouse and the Liberty Bell Museum had stopped in their tracks to witness the projection. Even a pair of security guards posted in the area were riveted. Each time a word passed over the building I felt my insides collapsing and then exploding out into the city. By the end I felt like I had been splattered upon the streets.

Candace turned off the camera, gave a thumbs-up to Ken Lulu in the distance, and turned toward me. "You aren't saying anything," she pressed.

"I'm at a loss for words."

"Is that a good thing?"

I didn't know. This was the most intriguing thing I had seen in a long time. To place, in today's paranoid and prejudiced world, the name of the God in the tongue of the terrorists, onto the walls of America's most hallowed building, was nothing short of audacious. If this was Candace's personal attestation of faith, it was more powerful, more inventive, more astonishing than any other spiritual rebirth.

I pulled her against my dark body. She was light.

The apartment was still when we entered and stayed still as I pushed Candace against the wall and we threw tongues and sighs upon and into each other. A boiler gurgled in the walls and a high neighbor blasted James Blake's falsetto into the halls. Midkiss she pushed me away; as I told her I missed her lips, she retreated toward the bed and my arms elongated and tore her clothes. Underneath she was all rib and clavicle and sternum and bone. Her spine a series of edged diamonds going down her back. My fingers filleted through the rest of her. Her hands measured me like she was a seamstress. I dug into her gaps and spaces, prodding, testing, confirming her frailty. She was sparrow. I was snake. She was doll. I was child. I had never squeezed anyone so hard. I wanted to take her gasps from her. We got naked and I opened her up. There were no barriers between us, manmade or divine.

I woke up with my face toward a wall. Candace wasn't in the bed. The room was humid because there was no air conditioner. There was a poster of Kunta Kinte looking down at me. It was the scene from *Roots* where LeVar Burton is whipped by his master because he refuses to change his name to Toby. I met Burton's eyes and thought of Marie-Anne. This was the first time in our marriage that one of us had stayed out the entire night while the other was at home.

Candace came out of the bathroom. She wore a full-length purple dress with heels and had cinched a pale purple scarf around her head. There was a chunky bracelet on her right hand and a thin rosary around her left wrist. She brought a cup of coffee and a kiss and sat down on the edge of the bed.

"You didn't want to get up for the morning prayer? I tried waking you."

"I've never done it," I said, taking hold of the cup and her waist.

"It could be something we do together," she said.

I heard the sound of a bus sloshing in the distance. I pulled her in and leaned around to look at the rain. "There will be a lot of things we'll be doing together."

We headed out to Strawberry Mansion and ate halal food at Crown Fried Chicken. Candace was convinced that meat tasted better when the blood was drained from it. We walked up 33rd Street and she pointed out John Coltrane's row house. Under the influence of a Wahhabi magazine that started showing up magically after her conversion, Candace had become convinced that music was the tool of Satan and stopped listening to it. It was Coltrane who had brought her back. Prior to her return to jazz she had always feared that her love for it had been conditioned into her as a consequence of her parental nationalism; but to rediscover jazz because it was a source of transcendence, a method of attaining closeness to God, was quite another discovery. When she had come to Islam she thought it erased everything that came before it, like Muhammad erased the Ignorance. But then she realized that Muhammad kept wearing the same clothes, speaking the same language, using the same names as the Ignorance. If he could keep all those things, couldn't she at least keep jazz?

"When a Muslim child is born you are supposed to speak the call to prayer in their ear. I intend on playing Coltrane to mine."

I had never shared with anyone other than Marie-Anne how much I wanted children. Candace's comment made me grow despondent and my insides wilted into melancholy. Years ago in Love Park, Richard had introduced me to the concept of quantum entanglement. It occurred when two particles, despite being thousands or billions of miles from each other, looked and behaved in the exact same way. Einstein, a skeptic of entanglement, had called it "spooky action at a distance." Whereas Richard had meant to teach me the concept as a way of elucidating modern electronics, I had tried to read human intimacy into it. If only I had some way of finding the other simulacrum of myself, somewhere out there, maybe in a distant galaxy, maybe in some other time period that existed concurrently with ours. It would mean so much. Perhaps if I knew I had been replicated I wouldn't care so much about reproduction.

"Time for prayer," Candace whistled. "Shall we?"

"Shall we what?"

"Shall we pray?"

"Where?"

"Right there." She pointed to an abandoned lot, full of glass, mounds of dirt. The shingled roof from the shattered house next door had slid off and made a staircase into the lot.

"In front of the whole world?"

"All the world's a mosque and all the men and women are merely prayers."

"I think you might be plagiarizing."

"I don't think so. The Prophet Muhammad said, *The whole world is a mosque.* If anything, Shakespeare plagiarized *him.*"

"I'm neither player nor prayer. How about I just watch?"

"If praying here is bothering you, we can go to a mosque. Only the believers will be there. No one to watch us."

Candace reached for my hand and bit the tip of my finger. The pressure from the teeth cut through the gelatinous force field I was ensconced in. Despite myself, I assented to her proposition, and without a pause we were taking long strides up to Cecil B. Moore, toward Sheikh Shakil's mosque. Each step drained vitality from me and the usual reservoirs of replenishment receded in the face of the scorching fear that came with stepping into a mosque. It was one thing to have gone into the sanctuary of the Gay Commie Muzzies and seen Ali Ansari praying, by accident, in one corner of a house, while the rest of the group engaged in sexual fore-play. That seemed to me a safe way of experiencing Islam: one that didn't arouse suspicion; one that wasn't likely to be equated with something foreign, dangerous, different; one that didn't lead to your name being written in the ledgers held by informers. It was quite another to be taken to the mosque of a former felon escorted by a convert who had gone so far as to excise music from her life and who was comfortable performing prayer in front of the rest of the world.

We stepped into the mosque and passed through a group of young black boys wearing white robes and white skullcaps, coming out from the basement where a madrassa was located. Candace knew most of the boys and asked them how their Koranic memorization was going. The interior of the mosque had a kind of damp sandalwood smell to it, mixed with sawdust and the sweat of men coming in from some outdoor work. Candace pointed me in the direction of the men's entrance and then gestured with her head that she was going to the women's side. I asked her if there was a middle place where we could sit together. She shook her head and whispered: "There's only brothers and sisters, no middle place. Besides, only husband and wife can sit together; we are fornica-tors." Reluctantly, I took my shoes off with everyone else, tucked them in a cubby, and then went to the bathroom to perform the ritual ablu-tion. There was a row of dripping faucets against a wall and pair of older men with cracked feet were squatting on wooden boxes. I squatted down near them and from a corner of my eye watched them wash their hands, arms, heads, and feet. One of them caught me looking and smiled. "The grandson of the Prophet once repeated his *wudu* three times so a shy convert who was watching him could get it right." I nodded at him with a smile of my own. The old man touched me on the back with his wet hand and left a cold imprint.

The prayer hall was split in two halves with the men on the left, the women on the right, a few yards between them. A simple chandelier hung down from the rafter and there were Arabic inscriptions and pictures of global mosques all around the room. I looked at the sisters' side, hoping to spot Candace among them, but with big prayer shawls covering their bodies it was hard to tell the women apart. I scanned to the front and spotted Sheikh Shakil. He was an elegant and thin man, with a shapely mouth that was not overwhelmed by his fist-long beard. He wore a white robe and leather socks and carried a fat cane. He helped the men "align the ranks."

Prayer was an exercise in silent emulation. I lined up with all the other men, folded my arms as they folded, and bowed and prostrated as they did. Unlike them I didn't know what to recite or when to gesture with my fingers or when to turn my head. I had only seen my father pray once—at the funeral of a man we had known from a grocery store. I tried to pull that memory back to me, the body lying in front of the all-male congregation, the act of raising my hands to my ears and then down. Nothing more came to mind. I had been twelve then and found the entire pageant so farcical that I had never again let myself near a religious gathering.

Once prayer was finished, Sheikh Shakil stood up, tapped the microphone, and said that although it wasn't Friday he had a simple message that he wanted to convey to the congregation. It had come to him the night before, during a conversation with a brother who had gone astray. The milling and whispering quickly died out and the crowd anticipated his talk.

"Religion," he said, starting slowly, with a hoarse throat, "is a glue." He looked around, sighed, and was content with the attention he commanded. Then he started over.

"Religion is a glue that God gave mankind so we could stick to each other. Without it we would be broken. Spread apart. Isolated. The religion don't need us. We need it. We need it because we ain't meant to be alone. We need it because we *can't* be alone. Who alone got the power to withstand loneliness? Allah *azzawajal*. He took it upon Himself so that the rest of us wouldn't have to. That is Allah's sacrifice. The rest of us, man, all we can do is find ways to stick together. Now some of y'all might say, of all the religions out there, of all the glue y'all can sniff, why is it that this brother is trying to preach Islam? Why not Christianity? Rasta? The religions of our African ancestors? I tell you one simple reason why it is Islam: Not because it's the truth. I know y'all better than to tell you the difference between truth and falsehood. Y'all wouldn't be here if you didn't already know it. All I'm here to do is tell y'all that in this age. Age of nudity. Age of incarceration. Age of war. Age of drugs. Age of booze. Age of world domination. There's only one religion that is feared. One religion that all of the peddlers and all of the pornographers and all of the fat cats fear. They know, deep in their hearts, that if you gave us the opportunity we would bring justice and purity and cleanliness to this world. They see us, five times a day, washing our bodies, making ourselves pristine in order to stand before Allah, and they fear our prayer, and they fear our hygiene. They don't fear nothing else. They don't fear Osama. They don't fear the Taliban. Hezbollah. Qaeda. None of them. They got no reason to fear them. They fear belief in something higher than them. Something other than them. Something that ain't subject to their power. If y'all want to go join them. If y'all think you can rule the world through their devices, I ain't gonna stop you. You go and do that there. But if you wanna be one of the people who stand on the Last Day, the Day of Judgment, *Yawm al-Akhira*, and tell Allah *azzawajal* that you took measure of your age and you put up your hand and you said, *Stop in the name of the God!* then you got to stick with Islam. It will give you the only pathway to bring change to this world. All the other religions gave in to corruption and wealth. They give in to vanity and hedonism. Islam will give you the brotherhood you need to stand up when you weak. It will give you the discipline you need to survive the prison that is this world. Most of all, it will give you the rope of God. If you got that, then *alhamdulillah hi rabbil aalameen*." He snapped his fingers. "The prison walls disappear. Now y'all gotta remember that this system, this system of resistance, ain't gonna cost you no money. But it's gonna take all your labor. For it to become your biggest asset, you got to put all your self into it. You gotta sign all your belongings to it. Your spouse. Your children. Your soul. And the way you start that transfer is through the Witness of Faith. You say that statement, and right then—boom—the transfer starts. You start uploading yourself into Islam and it starts pumping its powers of resistance back into you. You stop wanting to get naked. You stop doing things that take you to jail. You stop going to war. You stop them drugs and booze and vice. Say that *shahada* then. Say it now, my brothers and sisters in Islam: *Ashadu Allah ilaha illallah Muhammad rasool Allah*."

The entire crowd murmured the testification of faith, first in a quiet manner and then louder, until it became a collective chant that climaxed with *Mu-ham-mad ra-sool Al-lah* being sung between the male and female parts of the congregation. Muhammad was not a living person, but in that song he had more life than a thousand presidents. I thought of my father again. He had never taught me about Muhammad. He had never made me chant the *shahada*. How had my father resisted the inexorable power of this Muhammad who could otherwise move to music a group of citizens of an empire whose predecessor empire didn't even exist during Muhammad's time? Was there something in my father that was immune to the charisma of great men? Or was it simply that he had erased the love of Muhammad from his heart in order to carry out the lifelong project of settling in this country? Perhaps it something darker—perhaps my father had sought control over me so completely that he considered even Muhammad a competitor. I wished he was around. I needed an answer as to why I was unmoved by Muhammad.

Sheikh Shakil got off the podium and walked around the mosque, nodding and smiling at his people, mouthing the *shahada* with them, shaking hands, asking little questions about family. In his other hand he carried a straw skullcap that served as the collection tray. He sent it into the river of rows and it got passed around the mosque. He trailed after it slowly, greeting, laughing, and sometimes embracing. When the cap passed before me I put all my cash into it. Sheikh Shakil watched me from a distance, with a smile on his face, and then suddenly pointed at me. "You got to recite the *shahada*, brother."

Air trapped in my chest and became a knot. My eyes hopped across the mosque. I experienced the gaze of the believers upon me. Could they tell I hadn't recited the testification? What did they think of Sheikh Shakil outing me in front of them? Was he about to make an example of me? Or was shaming me sufficient? My temples started streaming sweat and my armpits filled with moisture. My face contorted into a strange and terrible smile and I made my lips move in the same *bur-bur* sound others were making, trying to give Sheikh Shakil the appearance of my witness. Every movement of my lips stung me as wrong. Not because I was cheating, but because I was afraid of getting caught. Was I making my lips pout too much? Did I need to make my tongue roll more? Did I need to rock like the others were rocking? Did I need to elongate the round sounds? Flex my neck more for the guttural ones? The panic was intense and nauseating. As soon as Sheikh Shakil turned to the sisters' side of the mosque, I got up and went out into the street, forgetting even my shoes. In a dumpster across from the mosque I threw up the halal chicken from earlier.

It was a long and painful vomit. Sulfur cobras. Corpse fingers. Shit shavings. At any moment I expected Candace to show up and hold my hand; but she was either too occupied with the chant or had not seen me rush out. I was alone with my pain. In the middle of my heaving, when my eyes turned back, I saw Independence Hall pass before me. I saw Ken Lulu packing up his equipment, throwing a backpack over his shoulder, and exiting the scene. The light show that Candace had put on replayed like a strobe light. Accompanied by the tremendous symphony.

This time it wasn't exhilaration; it was a tremor of disgust that followed. Something recoiled and regurgitated along with me.

Could we just waltz over to the building where the Constitution had been written and spray it with words inspired by the Koran? The Constitution was supposed to be a blueprint for a new order that had sought to break away from the Old World, the one to which Islam and the Koran had belonged. How would the Muslims feel if one day we walked over to Mecca and took off its black shroud and replaced it with a cloth covering on which the Constitution was embossed? Wouldn't they rightly think of it as an act, if not of war, then at least of insult? Didn't we, not just as residents of America's foundational city, but as guardians of the Constitution, owe the symbol entrusted to us some modicum of exclusivity— dare I say, supremacy? Or was the Constitution not sacrosanct? Was it just a document that could be played with? If that was the case then why even hold onto it? Why enshrine it? Why treat it as central to our identity and sovereignty? Tomorrow perhaps the Chinese could come and project images of Confucian wisdom on Independence Hall. The day after we could invite the Hindus and let them throw the Vedic swastikas all over it. Like that, little by little, the gift handed down by Franklin and Jefferson and Madison and all the others who had gathered in the hot summers two hundred years earlier would be slowly whittled down, watered down, perhaps even completely altered. It might be personally appealing to me to regard Independence Hall and see upon it images that would bring a smile to my mother's lips, to my Candace's lips, to the lips of my new friends; but the Constitution and the principles that it represented were supposed to be bigger than my personal satisfaction. They were supposed to be holy. I wasn't certain I appreciated engaging in this blasphemy that Candace had wrought. She seemed less like the harbinger of newfangled freedoms and more a criminal dragging me into a secret lair. She wanted me to sever the rope that bound me to the dream in whose name my parents had sacrificed everything, even their past. Candace's promise was that I would be more at home in a space that affirmed Islam. I did not believe her.

My shirt was as soiled as my mouth. I needed a change.

I did not wait for Candace to emerge from the mosque.

Chapter Seven

I came to the apartment and rushed to the shower. Marie-Anne was in the bedroom, sleeping with her phone on her chest, a plate with scraps of chicken tenders next to her. The phone had slipped between her large breasts, the light from the screen making her veins glow blue. When she snored, the phone rose up and hit one of her chins. I picked it up and stared at the screen, wondering if there were unsent messages to me. I found instead a series of e-mails from her boss.

I slept in the living room late into the afternoon, moored to the sofa. Marie-Anne woke up and brought a little storm around, stomping through the living room, trying to create awareness about herself without having to explicitly demand my attention. It didn't work. I kept my face pressed in the cushions and waited for the waves to recede. They came in the form of the front door slamming.

As soon as Marie-Anne was gone I checked my phone. Candace had flooded me with messages, inquiring where I had gone, if I was all right, if I was mad at her.

It isn't you.

Then what?

It's the glue.

I don't follow.

You follow too much. That is the problem.

I shut her out after that. She deserved my anger. She had betrayed me before even allowing me the chance to give her my trust. Her cosmopolitanism, her vulgarity, her social expertise, her sexual liberation had fooled me. Misled me. She wasn't a libertine; she was only a sinner. I was not what she sought in the world; I was only the consequence of a temporary disorientation she suffered on a bizarre and surreal night. The moment that Candace authenticated herself she would look at me and see a mistake. Then she would either remove me from her presence, or worse, in an effort to make me conform to her chosen principles, force me to experience corrective judgment. She didn't just have Sheikh Shakil to enforce her writ. She had entire congregations.

I got up and waddled around. It was raining outside. That mysterious Philadelphia rain where the drops were all interconnected so it seemed like a slab of mist had propped itself between earth and sky. Like a presence had descended.

I ended up in the study. My eyes fell upon the desk. There was a gift-wrapped box sitting on it. I looked around, reached for it, and checked the card. It was addressed to me. I undid the ribbon and tore open the purplish-pink paper. A bound book was inside, with a hefty black cloth cover. The title said *Falsipedies* and underneath it was my name. I opened it up and browsed. The book was a collection of 114 of my gym-motivational poems for Marie-Anne. They were laid out in reverse-chronological order. The later ones, belligerent, related to persistence in the face of pestilence; the earlier period, when I encouraged Marie-Anne to fight for the sake of our love; the first ones, where I addressed her illness obliquely, as if it wasn't real. The inscription inside the front cover was written in Marie-Anne's messy hand.

I can't always tell you how I feel, but you have always been able to tell me how you feel, and that has made all the difference.
    With love, your wife?

M-A

I texted Marie-Anne and asked her to meet me at the gazebo at Schuylkill River, the one overlooking Boathouse Row. There were still a few hours left in our anniversary weekend. She texted back a single four-letter word to dismantle my heart: *Fine.*

My eyes turned back to the desk. I skittered toward it, running my hands over this little investment, this little emblem of my fidelity to America, pulled back the chair, and opened the drawer. Sitting underneath the pile of papers was the Koran inside the pouch my mother had sewn. It seemed so long ago when I had tucked it in here, out of sight. How circuitous the journey had been since then. How uncertain. I reached for the Koran and brought it close.

It was odd. Touching it now created no insurrectionary thrombosis in me, didn't fill me with rage. Just a distant shame one feels when having hobnobbed with friends no longer worth one's time. I picked up the Koran, with the pouch, and I tucked it into my pocket.

I also picked up the wooden book holder and opened it up into its X shape, running my fingers over the designs. I blew the residual dust off and brought it out into the living room and put it on top of the bookshelf. I had never noticed it before: the wood was the same color as the bookshelf. The book holder belonged here. It was what had sat on it that did not.

I texted Marie-Anne an update and ran out of the apartment, hustling through the dog park, past the flying-horse swings, down the slope that would bring me to Kelly Drive, where a man with a cauldron sat hidden behind some bushes, asking passersby for lighter fluid. I ran through the night traffic without so much as a glance for my safety. It was the abandon of childhood, when we used to play capture the flag in Mobile, sweating and out of control in the acrid air stunk up by the paper mills. Or later on, when we were older and raced our lowered pickup trucks on the flat highway outside of Citronelle, swerving into the shoulder, toward the oncoming trucks belonging to the rednecks who were looked down upon by rednecks. It was the confidence of youth, when you believed there was a sacred covenant with the earth that held you and the passion that compelled you—and neither would ever let you suffer harm. It was the trust one felt toward one's birthplace.

The gazebo constituted itself before me. I picked up my pace and reached my destination, parting the little curtain of water that nature had drawn around the structure. I went into the dry area and called out Marie-Anne's name. Once. Then twice. "Here I am," she replied from over by the railing. I put my arm around her and my face in her neck and we were together there, staring at the river, the line of trees, the entirety of the north. There was a strange brightness in the water underneath us and it flowed fast, like the blood of a living creature—not quite an abyss, but evocative of its mystery.

I turned back to Marie-Anne and put my nose deep into her neck again. She smelled of smoke. It belonged to Bishop's Collar; I could tell from the vague bit of teak that made up the smoke's heart notes. I held her even harder. While I had gone off to cheat on her, she had gone off to our neighborhood hangout to have a drink and a drag. She had always been the loyal one. The fixed one. The sun. And I was always acting the part of the envious asteroid, burning myself in fierce infernos that might, even just momentarily, rival her persistent splendor.

"How come we met here?"

I reached into my pocket and pulled out the pouch. With slow fingers, like a pickpocket trained to lift rose petals from bowls of water, I drew the Koran from the pouch, until it sat on my palm like a particle of dust, or a feather, or an eyelash found on a lover's cheek.

"I wanted you to see me do this."

"Are you serious? You don't have to."

"I want to." With a smile I tilted my hand. But the book didn't budge. It was fused to my palm with the weight of its history, with the immutability that it had acquired over fifteen hundred years of significance, through the adoration of millions of mothers. There was a ghost inside every book, and like a parasite it wished to latch on and feed upon the reader, driven by the imperative to achieve endless replication.

I tilted my hand again, further this time, but the collection of revelations didn't wish to be let go. It strained against my decision. It couldn't accept that it was no longer the blueprint for empire. It couldn't see that it wasn't ascension toward Allah that animated the people today but the pursuit of American happiness. Like some ancient mariner unwilling to hand off the helm of the battleship to a younger, more capable captain, the Koran screamed out in anguish at the prospect of being sent off to a final resting place.

Then, without waiting, I used my left hand to swipe my palm. The Koran went pirouetting through the air, spinning downward toward the river. It sat on the surface for a moment, like a memory in the mind unwilling to let itself be forgotten, and then was pulled along to a little depression where the water cascaded toward the reservoir. The current released its invisible electricity and threw its threads around the Koran, and before long it was taken down into the depths, drowned into the river on Philadelphia's left bank.

"Happy anniversary," I said. "I love you and I love us. I'm sorry I went crazy for a while."

"Don't be," she replied. "It's just the things our parents do to us."

We stayed at the gazebo for some time. The lights from Boathouse Row shattered and fused in the rain. Then, holding hands, we headed back, my head on Marie-Anne's shoulder. She tried to spread her hair over me. I told her I loved her. My beloved giant with her invasive disease.

We came home and Marie-Anne helped me put the poetry collection on top of the bookshelf. It fit in the book holder just fine.

We needed a beach vacation. Toes dug in the sand, the lilting of the oceanic breeze, a story of zombies in our hands, and beer. Orange Beach in Alabama, not far from where I had grown up, offered all of those things. Marie-Anne preferred cold-weather vacations: a cruise from Seattle to Alaska; a scenic road trip up New York and into Montreal; Iceland. This discrepancy would come up every time I suggested going on vacation. I would get so flustered by the intense difference of our desires that I would simply abandon the entire topic. We would just carry on, working, doing errands on the weekend, rearranging our deeper irritation instead of kicking it out into the ocean.

I knew the reason behind Marie-Anne's unwillingness to go to a beach. It had to do with hair and skin.

Ever since the cortisol spikes hit, in addition to the weight gain, she had gotten hairier. She told me that it had something to do with increased androgens, some hormone associated with men. The term for the condition was hirsuitism. If she would have let me talk to her doctor I might have gotten more details. But the bottom line was that Marie-Anne had increased amounts of hair under her armpits, on her neck, on her sideburns, and on her chest down to her round belly. In each area the hair had started as a light red shade, eventually turning into a kind of furriness. All of it had driven her insane. And she was constantly running to a salon on JFK to get waxed and cleaned. I always tried to underplay it, telling her that she was only getting psyched out because she was used to having little body hair.

Marie-Anne's skin had also grown thin, susceptible to bruises and slow to heal. But the worst part were the so-called striae—reddish-purple stretch marks on her belly and under her arms. It was like a massive purple cat had scratched her stomach upward from the groin. Or perhaps some insouciant child had done purple finger painting on her jutting stomach and on the fattiness of her back above her hips. The stretch marks were harder to deal with, because they hadn't appeared the first time around when she was initially diagnosed. But this time, during the second expansion, they came. And it crushed her. Going to a beach, in short, was out of the question. I had tried to suggest that maybe she could go fully clothed, or perhaps even consider one of those burkinis produced in West Asia—"for medicinal rather than theological reasons"—but had been shouted down. I was glad to be told off like that because my suggestion hadn't been legitimate. I wouldn't want to be seen at a beach with a tented-up woman. I had only made the suggestion out of the moral obligation of informing a patient about all their options.

With a beach vacation looking unlikely, I briefly harbored the possibility—well, more of a fantasy—of getting myself to a beach alone. It would not be some hedonistic spring break getaway to St. Tropez where I would lay out on a yacht with skimpy European sluts and bountiful Brasilieras, spending the night in foam-filled clubs. It would be quiet. The weather might even be on that cusp between pleasant and blustery. It could even be cloudy, with a chance of rain, so when I did sit down on the beach, I would have to keep gazing toward the clouds and pleading with them to not douse my little moment of freedom. There would be no one serving me from some beachside bar. I would drink what I brought with me. And there would be no one to talk to, save the brief and cordial smiles that the locals walking their dogs give to those tourists who sit around on the sand where their dogs urinate. Then one day, perhaps the second-to-last day of the vacation, the weather would open up, the skies would clear, the sand would heat up, the water would become balmy, the seagulls formerly sitting on the stumps would become airborne and destructive, and the children would emerge onto the sand from whatever underground cavern they hid in during cold days to throw themselves shirtless and belly-first into the immense, onrushing ocean with the same kind of innocent audacity as those migratory birds that announced the end of a winter by hurling themselves into the voracious and wicked northern sky.

It was a beautiful fantasy, but it wasn't one that I could, or would, turn real. That would involve leaving Marie-Anne behind, like she was some kind of leper who had to be excluded from the territory of the healthy. I could not do that to her. Every time my inner eye turned even briefly toward oceanscapes, toward its unitary harmony, to its ability to turn everything into oneness, I yanked my gaze back to Philadelphia, to its smokestacks and underpasses, to its townhomes and trains, to its Gothic cathedrals and stentorian cement. Everything in Philadelphia was pairs, pushing and pulling at each other with all their imperfection, all their dirt.

It was my turn to make the effort in the marriage. The next weekend I took Marie-Anne for an out-of-town date. We rented a car and went to Cape May and strolled through the Bird Observatory. It was mostly shorebirds and songbirds and a lot of American woodcocks. Their distinctive walk inspired Marie-Anne and I to start doing the rumba, swishing our hips just a little, mouthing our own music. Later we tried to find a bald eagle but weren't that lucky. We came back and rented golf clubs and went to a driving range in Cherry Hill. On the way Marie-Anne said she wanted to drive through Camden because she had heard of a neighborhood where a number of local women had gotten into immigration marriages with Muslim sailors who pulled into port and decided they didn't want to go back. We saw a family that fit the description in front of one of the old row houses. The couple made me consider how Candace and I might have looked together. Marie-Anne tried to persuade me to venture farther into Camden and see Walt Whitman's grave, but I threw up my hands.

I made no mention of Candace. It would be hard, but she would have to pass away from my thoughts. It surprised me how easily I could return to the customary after the criminal. I wanted to think that this wasn't because I forgave myself, but because my core was an ethical one and it was easy for it to return to its original status.

The same forgetfulness would also have to be applied to Ali Ansari, though I probably wouldn't cut him out, just reduce our interactions until we were no more. It had been an interesting adventure with him, leading me into the Muslim communities, the Muslim experience. The defensive fundamentalists. The suburban slackers. The reggae mystics. His own activist dandyism. No doubt there was a whole universe of submerged communities among them, just waiting to be discovered. But those would have to be unearthed by someone else, someone like Ali Ansari, who stood to gain something from giving the Muslim experience prominence, who needed to do it as a kind of affirmation of his identity, who was comfortable with the narrowness of tribalism, who was adept at turning it into commodity, into gold. I wasn't that man.

Another week passed. Marie-Anne and I commenced talking about her career. She was eager to unload, particularly about an emotional phone call she had taken in the hallway. She said that Karsten King had been upset that her trips to the Persian Gulf hadn't translated into a sale, even into relationships. MimirCo was beginning to wonder if perhaps there was a gender issue, if perhaps they needed a man to instill confidence in the buyers. Women were still not considered very trustworthy business partners in the Persian Gulf. Marie-Anne, for all her pride, was adrift in a sea where a big swinging dick was a necessary oar.

"Let's take a broader perspective," I said. "Is this something you even want to do? Sales is a dirty business."

"Well," she gathered herself, "I believe in the product. Beyond that, I believe in the salary."

"What's missing? What is it that you need to get over the hump?"

"I need to get MimirCo the Wazirati contract," she said. "They are having all sorts of internal security issues in the Wazirate. But I can only get to the Waziratis if I can reconnect with Mahmoud. He is friends with the Minister of the Interior in the Wazirate."

"Mahmoud of Salato fame? Qasim's buddy?"

"He was my buddy too. Before he up and disappeared."

I hung my head. "He disappeared because of me. You can say it."

She made a dismissive gesture. "These relationships are fluid. We just have to play it right."

"And what does playing involve?"

There was a convention and conference in New York that she had been eyeing. She suggested running into him there. But not too obviously. "You should just discover him somewhere. Warm him up. Reel him in. He doesn't drink, so remember that. You'll have to ply him in another way. And baby," she reached out and pinched my cheek, "no more Islamic faux pas please."

"I think my time with Ali Ansari was useful to correct some of that."

"It would be great if you could pronounce Arabic words right."

I coughed and spat and gurgled something vaguely Germanic. "Like that?"

She laughed and set about making plans. It would be her job, she said, that would free us from our hectic urban lives.

I hugged her hard and thought about how much I loved her. Despite the mistakes I had made, love was intact. With love, we ran into what logicians called the paradox of self-reference: when something was neither true nor false; when judgment became impossible. With love, by having fused yourself with another person, there was nowhere from which you could take perspective of your individual self. Love was the only torturer in the world that took away your personhood by giving you more personhood; namely, the other. This was why, after thousands of years of human progress, the only way to replace love was with more love.

The convention was in a week's time, to be held at the Pierre in Manhattan. I looked forward to getting away from Philadelphia. It was too constricting. Half the time, out of fear of running into George Gabriel, or Ali Ansari, or Farkhunda, or Candace, I didn't even dare leave the apartment. I wanted to be somewhere else. Where I could be anonymous and unknown. There was no place better for that than New York. It was where the world came to remember its irrelevance. To be reconstituted as a nothing, the way the Muslims went to Mecca to be reborn with the same amount of sin they had at the moment of their birth.

We took the slower Amtrak and arrived at the Pierre on a Wednesday afternoon. The subject of the convention was media freedom in Islam. The lobby was full of conference attendees. They ranged from journalists and activists to hordes of bloggers and social-media stars. The thought leaders were there too, both those funded by the think tanks and the unfunded ones who hired out their thoughts and cared little for consistency.

Marie-Anne registered. I walked around the checkerboard floor, and went up and down the emerald stairs, gawking at the tiles in the neoclassical ceilings, checking out the cherrywood elevators. Under the sky-blue dome there was a painting of a pastoral scene, complete with cherubs and Greco-Roman columns. There was a café in the rotunda. I pulled up a chair and picked at crustless sandwiches, cranberry scones with Devonshire cream, and buttery Scottish biscuits. Instead of the Earl Grey I took a red jasmine from Ceylon. The tuxedoed waiters hovered near, refilling the cup, rearranging the biscuits. I nibbled in silence and waited for Marie-Anne to catch up.

She hadn't so much as sat down when I heard a fast click of heels move past us. It was a group of men.

"Crap," Marie-Anne said. "That's Mahmoud!"

"Now what?"

She lowered her voice. "You go to him. I'm going to duck out."

Once Marie-Anne was gone and I had paid the bill, I smoothed my clothes and walked over to the foursome. I waited for a brief lull in the conversation and then put my hand on Mahmoud's shoulder.

I was quite surprised when he stood up and said my name. It was flattering to be recognized.

"And how have you been?" he said, adjusting his skullcap over his flowing locks.

"Your Salato guy never came back."

Mahmoud grinned. He turned to the three men still seated and mouthed Qasim's name. They tittered knowingly.

Mahmoud pointed to an empty chair. "Sit with us, sit with us," he said. Despite the calculating, almost premeditated manner in which Marie-Anne and I had brought about this meeting, when Mahmoud gestured for me to join his group I couldn't help but hum with excitement. He had the avoirdupois of a gatekeeper and I had been let in. I had come a long way since offending Qasim. The officious, vaguely patriarchal authoritativeness exuding from these men distinguished them from the chaos that Ali Ansari and the Gay Commie Muzzies personified.

The three men were Samir, Sajjad, and Saqib. They were all close to forty, with a little gray along the temples, all clean shaven, two of them with platinum wedding bands, and the other a tan line on his finger. They were all American citizens, either by birth or through dual nationality. Samir and Sajjad were from an organization that represented interests of the country of Insanistan. Saqib worked as an engineer for a defense contractor; he didn't say which.

We chatted casually and drank tea. I felt at ease, not the slightest bit tendentious. I mostly talked to Mahmoud. He had grown up in Cleveland; played baseball at Cal State Fullerton; even struck a home run in the College World Series. The Dodgers had expressed interest in him but that was right after the Oklahoma City bombing. When the first fingers of accusation were pointed at Muslims his life changed directions. "After I saw how eager Americans were to blame Muslims for anything that went wrong, I knew I had to go into public service. To make bridges." He pointed to his wardrobe. "Of course, first I had to look the part."

"Bridges are important nowadays," I said.

"More than ever. I just don't want this clash of civilizations to take over the world. It's important for people to see that we, America, are not at war with Islam, but with a certain demonic ideology within Islam, with a perversion of a great religion. America has been good to me—as I suspect it has been to you—and it's important that we let people around the world know about how great we have it here. Relatively speaking, of course."

I smiled into my cup, thinking that it was probably a good thing Ali Ansari wasn't here. He and Mahmoud were very different. Ali Ansari was a passionate man. He believed in the cultivation of his tribe over everything else, even if everything else came crumbling down after. Mahmoud was a sober man, a serious man, a man who believed in certain principles of civilization, culture, and progress, and sought to effectuate them through institutions and governance. Ali Ansari would thrive in anarchy. Mahmoud wouldn't let things fall apart around him.

"The confrontation between the civilized West versus this demon Islam out there is actually a war, a war of ideas," he continued. "In this war we represent an ally of the civilized West called moderate Islam. We intercede. *Ahl-ul-wast.* Arabic for 'people of the middle.' We're like that tea. Not too hot and not too cold."

"Being Goldilocks isn't very sexy though," I said.

"Maybe," the man named Saqib spoke up. "But she ate the tastiest food, sat in the coziest chair, and slept in the best bed." He spread his arms to gesture at the Pierre.

The conversation carried on. I limited my participation to listening. It became evident that Saqib, Samir, and Sajjad were with Mahmoud for much the same reason I was—trying to extract some unknown greater benefit. Their flattery came in the form of encouraging him to pontificate about a limitless number of topics and he was eager to oblige. His favorite subject was power and the manner in which people became corrupted by it. His analysis was a mixture of spirituality and political evaluation. "People like Osama bin Laden and Saddam Hussein try to dominate others because they are ultimately incapable of attracting attention through their character," he said in a measured way. "And that is because they are distant from God. If they were closer to God, then they would find God organizing the world in a way that favors them."

"But Osama bin Laden and Saddam Hussain are dead," I said.

Mahmoud laughed. "Well, isn't that just the way God works? He grants victory to those He favors."

"Does that mean God favors us?"

"What else can it mean?"

The gathering broke up a little before sunset. I was about to head back to the room and tell Marie-Anne how I had gotten the ball rolling when Mahmoud came near and put a card in my pocket. He then stood aside and waited for me to pull it out.

I took a look. It showed that he was the Muslim Outreach Coordinator at the State Department.

"Color me impressed," I said.

"If you're not busy you should come with me and I can introduce you to some people. It's just a little mixer. Do you want to go tell your wife that you'll be late getting back?"

"You know Marie-Anne is here?"

"I know every name that registers," he said.

I wasn't certain how he would perceive her presence so I didn't say anything further. Instead I followed him out and into a cab.

There was still some light outside when we reached the rooftop Sky Room on West 40th Street overlooking Times Square. We headed to a reserved table where there were a series of fine white sofas and white tables with black trays and tea candles. A group of young people waved at us. Most of them were women. They wore tight jeans or slacks paired with leather riding boots or heels. Some were in hijab. The few men were in shirts with knife-sharp creases or outfits that were premeditatively rumpled. Most had cropped beards.

Their current topic of discussion was whether Islamic explorers had come to the New World prior to Columbus. Everyone had little bits of circumstantial evidence—the name of a slave, the story of a settlement, the tale of a general wading into the water—that they believed was sufficient to establish the truth of their assertion. They simply had no smoking gun. No entry in a royal ledger. No pictures. No drawings. Nothing tangible, just conjecture. I let them talk without interruption.

As introductions occurred I learned that none of the people had a specific profession. Some referred to themselves as pundits, others as commentators, others as activists, and yet others as social-outreach alchemists. They considered themselves writers or intellectuals, though they hadn't yet gotten around to the onerous task of publishing. A few of them were putting together an anthology featuring one another's commentary. A majority of them were from state universities and junior colleges and bristled at the "elitism" and "privilege" of those who went to private universities or the Ivy League. They were also resentful of the ones that went off into investment banking or engineering or law in pursuit of "making paper." They believed that life was better spent reducing conflict in the world, reforming the faith of their forefathers, and working for international harmony, all of it done in the name of America.

Mahmoud led me in their midst. "Fend for yourself a moment," he said. "And if I may advise, just don't order any booze."

"Why not? It looks like they have a nice bar."

He wagged a finger. "There are certain protocols to being a moderate Muslim."

I nodded and stopped a waiter, ordering bruschetta and sparkling water. Then I sat down near a group of young people and asked them what they did.

A black-haired girl with blond highlights smiled. "Just trying to make sure the average American Muslim is heard," she said. Her name was Leila and she was an Afghan-American from Texas. "The world has a lot

of misconceptions about us and we really want to help clear those up."
She came and sat next to me and asked the waiter for a "virgin something."
She smiled at me and added, "Like me."

"How do you go about clearing misconceptions?" I asked.

"Well, we have a couple of exchange programs," she explained. "We
go abroad and talk to Muslim communities in other countries and tell
them how integrated and assimilated the Muslims in America are. How
we don't suffer Islamophobia here. Well, there is some, but it's negligible."

"How do you determine what's negligible?"

"Well, like, the Japanese got put into camps," she said. "So compared
to that, we are free. We can think and do whatever we want."

"But you work for the State Department."

"No," she laughed. "We work *with* the State Department. Our minds
are our own."

"Freelance public relations?"

"Exactly. I make contacts. Honestly, if Mahmoud brought you here
then he thinks you could mesh well. You should join. And it pays well."

"How well?"

"Like thousands of dollars just to go on one trip," she said.

"Well, I'm definitely considering it, Leila." I pressed her hand with
both of mine, looking into her stark green eyes. She couldn't have been
more than twenty. Her neck, her breasts, her stomach seemed light and
tight, as if the littlest touch would cause her body to thrum like a string.
But more arresting was the force field of her character, her presence. I
was drawn to it. I wanted to part it with conversation and let it enfold me.

Leila became my temporary handler and led me into a number of
conversations, one of which was about the moral emptiness of American
foreign policy and how only the involvement of the Muslim mind could
tilt it back to righteousness and justice.

In that group I met a young, Mohawked twenty-something with
countless piercings and tattoos of crescents in the color of Persian tile.

Her name was The Ism. She was accompanied by Saqib, who put an arm around her waist. The Ism was a film director with various documentaries about religious subcultures under her belt, and now she wanted to make a feature-length film that would help Muslims gain some love and respect.

"I am motivated by our common humanity as descendants of dust."

"Dust?"

"She means God," Saqib said.

"Why not just say that?"

"She finds God too ineffable to refer to directly so she compares Him to something that is just as pervasive."

The Ism was in the middle of shooting a superhero chronicle and had come to Mahmoud to help her secure a final round of funding, which he had delivered promptly by connecting her with his friends in Hollywood. The film was called *The Last Jinnmaster.* It featured a pair of analysts from the Pentagon who are fighting crazed villains in a country called Estan. After the fantastical villains from Estan—who wear beards resembling turbans—destroy a series of all-girls schools, the Pentagon analysts seek the help of a mysterious Estani leader living in the Poconos. This man is The Last Jinnmaster. He is an exile from Estan and has the ability to control the Islamic supernatural. The Pentagon officials convince him to loan his jinns to them, to assist them in the great war on Estani terror. The Jinnmaster is reluctant at first; but after being reminded of all the things America has given him he agrees to loan his minions to the Pentagon. In alliance with American soldiers and drones, the jinns are able to rescue "all those poor little Estani girls that just want to go to school." In the end the jinns are given congressional medals and the villainous senator who didn't previously respect anything Estani is put in the position of pinning the medals upon the Jinnmaster and his jinn.

Mahmoud came back to check on me just as I was about to offer The Ism some promotional assistance. He made sure I ordered a couple of entrées and even let me sneak a Long Island iced tea in the coatroom. The act of deception created camaraderie between us. He brought me around to all the other mavens I hadn't gotten a chance to talk to and they reminisced about conferences they'd attended together and future trips they would take, all paid for by companies that did business in Muslim-majority countries, particularly the ones ringing the invaded ones. They all wanted to know when I would start working with them.

I considered my possible future colleagues. They seemed happy and joyous and oblivious, without the resentment that wracked Ali Ansari, without the caution that animated people like Brother Hatim, without the melancholy that preyed on people like Farkhunda. These people were optimists. They had a community that subscribed to the generally accepted definitions of success. They were approved by the Secretary of State. With them I would be considered nothing less than a brand ambassador of America. And this time around, my boss would be someone who actually valued my identity, considered it essential, understood it. Wasn't this life, promoting international harmony and other feel-good things, preferable to wandering about North Philadelphia with angst-ridden grifters, pornographers, backsliders? That life didn't seem suited to someone of my age; someone of my cleanliness. This new opportunity could even give Marie-Anne everything she sought. The contacts with the Wazirate. Respect at MimirCo. We might even buy the condo.

I went over and put an arm around Mahmoud's shoulders. I told him I wanted to help him win the War of Ideas.

Marie-Anne squealed so loud that one of the maids notified the manager and we received a phone call to make sure everything was all right.

"I can't believe it, I can't believe it!" She kept touching the blue folder marked with the gold State Department seal that Mahmoud had given me at the end of the night. She put on the DVD of events that former outreach contractors had done. And she smiled at the all-important

210 * Native Believer

direct-deposit form. In her excitement she didn't even ask if I had gotten a chance to push her and MimirCo.

"So what does all this mean?"

"It means the US taxpayer wants to send your husband as a Messenger of America."

"To do what?"

"Basically, they need me to tell people to hate us less."

I read through the details in the folder. My first trip would be to Madrid. I would be part of a six-person team, including Leila, and we would meet with elementary and junior high school students and talk to them about diversity in America. Other events included speaking with members of Muslim communities, most of whom were recent immigrants to Spain and held a contemptuous view of the United States due to our country's association with war and such.

Marie-Anne was thrilled at the speed with which I'd turned myself into a sort of private, mercenary diplomat.

"I bet there will be tons of eager little Muslim girls at these meet-and-greets," she said and put her hand on my chest. "Don't get tempted."

"I've met some of them already," I replied and let her fondle between my legs.

"Are they pretty?"

"They are," I said, closing my eyes, sighing. "And very young."

Marie-Anne's hand made a fist, like she was squeezing a wet towel. "How young? Skinny? Are they skinny?"

"Almost illegal young. And they are skinny. Anorexic skinny. Like they eat everything and never go to the gym but never gain an ounce of fat."

We started touching the tips of our tongues together. She tasted of champagne. Her thighs clamped on either side of my leg. She grinded herself and massaged me at the same time. "Is there one you like?"

"There's one who likes me," I said. "And she'll be sleeping just next door to me the whole trip."

Marie-Anne sighed, tearing into my neck with her teeth. "Tell me about her. Describe her. Is she little? Does she act like a doll?"

"So tiny. A little doll."

Between gasps and moans and squints and sighs I described Leila's body, moving from her hair to her neck to her flat breasts in the silk blouse. I talked about her docility, her virginity, how the waiter probably wanted to hold her hair and yank her neck. I talked about the darkness of her skin.

Marie-Anne gushed on my thigh. I reached down and extracted my cock from her hand. I was in the gap between her thighs, but not inside.

"Yes," she said, eyes closed, thinking about the scene with me and Leila. "She doesn't know what to do. She's stupid. I'll finger her. Just drive her into the wall. Just pull her hair back and pound that little . . . that dirty, dusky, little bitch."

"You'll throw your hand on her mouth, slap her face—"

That was enough to make Marie-Anne's shoulders drop. Her body clenched twice, like she was being shot in the spine, and her thighs shook until she was heaving and crying. She wanted to say something but there was only drool and lust in her mouth. She reached for my wrist and dragged it up her pale body and started sucking on it. My stomach tightened and my groin raised up. I ejaculated into the air until it felt like my cock would turn into a string. The two of us fell over after the confetti, mumbling and moaning, mouthing invisible words to each other.

Over the next few minutes we caught our breath. Marie-Anne squeezed herself into a ball and tucked herself into my side like she had never before. She felt embarrassed by the fantasy and tried to play it off by making flattering comments about the beauty of Muslim girls. To try to distract her, I reached over and began kissing her mouth, stifling everything.

212 * Native Believer

She kissed me back and during the kisses she fell asleep. I stayed up and watched the light falling on Marie-Anne's skin. For a very brief moment the ache of being a man with no children didn't rear its head. Marie-Anne's presence was enough. But I was aware that loneliness would return, as it always did, reminding me that upon the waterway of Time I could neither look behind me nor ahead. I had to live in this moment, in the present, to be satisfied only with myself. I had no legacy. One day the steam in my riverboat would evaporate and the story being told onboard would just sink into the sediment. It wouldn't be carried forward. Within a short time no one would even be aware that once upon a time in Philadelphia there was a man who had confronted some of the pressing quandaries of his age. They wouldn't even know what those quandaries were. I thought of the great explorers who had discovered the New World, including Amerigo Vespucci. If he hadn't left his maps behind, would we even call this strip of land by his name? We wouldn't. He would be exactly like all those Islamic explorers who'd been coming to these shores for hundreds of years before him. Forgotten. All because they didn't leave drawings behind. The production of a map was the difference between an explorer and a wanderer.

I was still awake, Marie-Anne snoring lightly beside me, when I got a message from Candace. I opened it in bed. It was a picture, the kind to make me regard my phone with wide eyes, with the brightness full, with my back up against the headboard, with the reading light on. Candace wore a stylish see-through face veil, a *niqab*, with heavy eyeliner, golden eye shadow, and eyebrows perfectly shaped. The hand tucked under the chin had the same color nail polish as the eye shadow. There was a slight depression where the mouth was, the cloth sucked into the shapely lips.

Until now I had maintained a firm silence with Candace. The lack of contact was strategic. If ever I was going to tell Marie-Anne and seek her forgiveness, the singularity of the act would have to be an essential part of my explanation.

This picture, however, broke through my planning and made me speak. If I wasn't a rational man I would've said that Candace had the power of revelation, to bring from some higher plane of information little metaphorical bits of discursive knowledge, to leave me splintered and scattered upon the floor from the impact.

Candace's appeal had less to do with language and more to do with womanhood. She had appropriated one of the world's great symbols of female traditionalism, and by heightening its effect through colors and sensuality, she'd put herself forward even more in opposition to Marie-Anne than before. Did I want the conventional American woman in her corporate clothes with her assertive and assured but otherwise plain and conventional way of dealing with the world? Or did I want this American performer with the askance eyes, someone comfortable with, even desirous of, donning the symbols of female subjugation, before whom I might be able to assert the privileges of masculinity as a matter of right? Marie-Anne and I had lost sight of, become confused about, the geographies of gender. Candace, on the other hand, postulated clarity.

You look . . .

I was always curious, she wrote before I finished my reply. *How would you name your kid?*

I erased what I had written and froze. The night I had been with Candace, right when I had been at her threshold, without any protection between us, she had whispered to me that she wasn't on birth control. It was this knowledge that had propelled me, driven me, to complete the act, to not let myself withdraw due to some pang of conscience related to Marie-Anne and marriage. Perhaps to Candace, telling me that information had only been a casual reminder, a bit of sexual etiquette. But for me it had been a momentous possibility. It was the pursuit of posterity that separated the significant from the insignificant. The English people had been nothing until one among them showed them that legacy and inheritance and heritage trumped everything, even the edicts of God Almighty.

I started over. *Why do you ask?*

She didn't answer.

Hey. Why are you asking that?

No answer.

Hello?

I shouldn't have sent the picture. Please delete it.

With great reluctance I put the phone away; but I didn't delete the picture. I thought if I kept it, somehow the likelihood of picking up the thread of conversation might be easier.

With Candace's cryptic confession rebounding around the room, I couldn't go to sleep. Marie-Anne had her back to me on the bed. With my thoughts adrift, I took the State Department folder on my lap and flipped through the information, using the light over my right shoulder, trying to distract myself with the future after the past ceased to maintain consistency. The pages discussed the inception of the Muslim outreach; how we were a kind of civilian diplomatic corps intended to augment the work that the professional diplomats did; how there was a great deal of hunger in the world to hear from America's minorities.

When I grew sleepy I closed the folder. I was about to put it away but I couldn't help noticing the way the golden insignia shone in the light. This was what it meant to have charisma, I thought, when an inanimate thing had the ability to capture all the light in a room. At first I was struck by how compulsively I fixated upon the eagle. I tried to remind myself that it was just a bird on a cardboard folder. Then it occurred to me that I was being utterly unfair to this symbol, this icon, which gave an assurance and a warning that in this world, over which there was spread an eternal sky, there was a power that owned the entirety of the air. Not since God had there been an entity that had so completely owned the firmament.

The folder was pressed against my chest, the eagle close to my heart. I thought back to the early days with Ali Ansari, particularly after hearing him going on about foreign policy. I had been so indescribably afraid. It wasn't a specific fear, of the sort that actual criminals might feel. It had been the fear of the unknown, the fear of the possible, which meant a fear of everything. Frequently I had thought: What if there was a recording device in the vicinity of Ali Ansari? What if there was an FBI informant in our midst? What if Ali Ansari was that informant? What if I got caught up in some investigation? I didn't think that I would get taken to Guantanamo; but I also knew that merely being accused of a crime would be enough to destroy my life. Now I didn't have a reason to be afraid. Now I had armor. Now I was under the shadow of the eagle. It was the feeling of safety, of having immunity, of being protected. I didn't have to fear unseen authorities anymore. I *was* the authority. I could fly, free, anywhere. Armed with the most piercing gaze.

I went to sleep a little less troubled. Let Candace shroud herself with mystery; in time I would find a way to see into her as well.

The next day Mahmoud invited Marie-Anne and me for lunch at Pershing Square, a café located outside Grand Central, underneath Park Avenue. It was a hot and brilliant day and the restaurant had set tables out on the side street. Where we sat we were covered by a sliver of the shade from the cigarette box–shaped skyscraper of 120 Park Avenue (formerly Philip Morris International). In its lobby the Whitney Museum was having a traveling exhibition and there was a good deal of foot traffic on the pavement.

Marie-Anne looked beautiful in a white chiffon blouse with silver-belted black slacks that widened at the ankles and showed only the tips of her closed-toed heels. Her hair was pulled back in a hard ponytail, accentuating the line left in her jaw.

Conversation was as easy as the cool drinks. It was made even easier by the fact that all three of us had been at the same seminar in the morning, one focused on the liberation of Muslim women. The four American NGO workers had all presented different case studies about how to support Muslim women such that they weren't reliant on patriarchal superstructures or held down by religious restrictions. Marie-Anne had been particularly interested in the idea of giving microloans to Muslim women.

"But my concern," she said while forking her salad, "is that the women won't pay back the loans and then the financial institutions that underwrite them will go bankrupt."

Mahmoud dismissed the concern: "Repayment rates are very high."

"But what exactly is the financial institution's return?"

"The purpose of the loan isn't to get a return. The purpose is to give a woman an opportunity to think highly of us."

I sat up. "That seems kind of crass . . ."

Mahmoud wasn't having it. "Look, we're all friends here. Let's appreciate that charity is just a pretext. We need the women on our side. It's the only way to win hearts and minds. And giving loans is the most humane way of accomplishing this. Would you rather that we go the French way in Algeria? Go and rip off their veils and clothes and order them to become Western? Because that will just earn us enemies. That's not the American way. Money talks better than force. It's not bribery if you call it liberation."

"Does this actually work?"

"You give people freedom and they come over to your side. Why do you think when the British were building their empire they went around the world and freed everyone's slaves? It wasn't because they cared about black people. It was because it reduced the number of people who might fight against them. When I give a microloan to a Muslim woman today, it's no different than when some British admiral raised a flag in Western Asia and announced that any slave who touched the mast would become free, irrespective of whether his master allowed it or not. We are getting their weakest on our side."

Marie-Anne turned to me with a smile on her lips; stone in her eyes. It was meant to convey that I was being too skeptical and should tone down my rhetoric. I shut up and looked in the direction of the exhibition.

She faced Mahmoud. "That's how you know you're on the right side," she said. "If what you do is increasing the number of free people in the world. Why shouldn't we give unto others what our founders gave to us?"

"To the pursuit of happiness." Mahmoud raised his glass. "May every Muslim in the world have access to it."

Marie-Anne clinked back. "And also, too, to the rule of law," she added. "Which can only be brought about through effective law enforcement and surveillance."

Mahmoud chuckled. He put an elbow in my side and pointed at Marie-Anne. "Please tell me that I didn't just fall into a MimirCo commercial."

We all laughed. Marie-Anne patted him on the thigh and straightened his skullcup. "You didn't fall into a commercial, because when you watch a commercial you still have an option. Here you are bound to commit, like you got my husband to commit to your little venture."

"Fair enough," Mahmoud said. "But as an employee of the State Department, I can't do anything that's unsanctioned."

"You're just building bridges," Marie-Anne replied. "The bridges will remember you when your government gig comes to an end."

I observed her. Just a few years ago she had been an impatient novelist and short-story writer, desperate to be published, throwing herself at the mercies of tenured university professors and washed-up hacks who advertised their self-published books on social media. And the only opportunities that had presented themselves had been inseparable from her having to become some hack's secretary and mistress. Yet here she was now, in a far more lucrative field, making deals happen without having to whore her body out. I felt proud of her. Who would have thought that the business of war would be more feminist than the business of art?

Marie-Anne and Mahmoud discussed how MimirCo ought to go about getting the Wazirati contract. Mahmoud was frank with her: The Wazirati royal in charge of the Ministry of the Interior was facing unrest in a number of his city-state's coastal villages, where due to the tribal nature of the families it was impossible for him to send physical spies. He needed eyes there and it didn't matter if they were mechanical.

This news was met with urgency on Marie-Anne's part. She started shooting messages off to her superiors.

Finding the conversation progressing this quickly and smoothly allowed me to relax. I put my hands behind my head and sunned myself like a lion. In the wild Serengeti of the world my lioness was on the hunt.

Midnight train back to Philadelphia. We had gone up coach; came back first class. The little cities of New Jersey sliced past us, enclaves for close-knit communities of immigrants to begin the slow and steady climb from anonymity to respectability. A teenager had been pushed onto the tracks near Edison and there was a four-hour wait. The EMT pulled up on a street not far from where we sat. I could see an old Indian woman in a sari trying to speak to the policemen. Marie-Anne called MimirCo during the delay, updating them further about the Wazirati connection. They were excited to send her to the Persian Gulf and asked how she had pulled off making the arrangement. She looked at me and smiled. She didn't tell them the details. She just said she had been sitting on the jack of clubs.

The next few days Marie-Anne bubbled with a kind of lightness I hadn't seen in a long time. She purchased a few bottles of Chianti Classico and we hung out on the rooftop of the building or went down to the river and secretly drank from a bottle in her purse.

The only thing that prevented me from fully engaging with Marie-Anne's celebration were thoughts of Candace. I had to find out how she was doing. I had to find a way to talk to her. Four weeks was enough time to miss a period. A cross to appear on a white stripe. An appointment to be scheduled with a gynecologist. I imagined a life percolating inside Candace. Any iota of me, no matter how small, had to be cultivated, had to be allowed to prosper. It didn't matter where or through whom my blood became a part of the land. There had to be someone in this vast country who could look back upon his generations and give me the pleasure of recognition. It didn't have to be a shiny mirror as long as it had the power of reflection. To grow old in a country that reviled me was only acceptable if there was someone who came after and pitied me.

For the next two days I plugged away via text messages and voice mails. E-mail had long ago ceased to be a useful method of reaching a person; but I tried flooding that account as well. One-word messages.

Why.

Aren't.

You.

Answering.

When personal contact became fruitless, I tried looking her up through the Al Jazeera website, but there was no record of her anywhere. I even tried the age-old trick of first-name-dot-last-name-at-domain-name. It came back *Mailer Daemon.*

In the middle of the Candace-induced mania I received a message from Mahmoud. He sent over the e-mail confirmations, another set of governmental direct-deposit forms, and the briefing for our time in Madrid. We were to leave in three days. I also received a separate message from Leila who said she had gotten herself teamed up with me on purpose.

The deadline torqued me into more fervent action. The only thing left to do was to drag myself over to Candace's apartment and sit in wait. With Marie-Anne in town it wasn't the easiest thing to get away, because she wanted to invite herself wherever I went. The only effective excuse involved making up an errand for Richard Konigsberg. He and I hadn't been in touch since his departure; but Marie-Anne didn't know that.

It seemed inappropriate to wander through North Philly. I decided to take a taxi directly to her apartment. Passing through like a tourist, I reminded myself that I was never meant to trapeze through the area like a native son. I had neither contributed to its character nor had a part to play in its resurrection. I had been foolish for glibly assuming it would impart enlightenment to me, infuse me with vitality. I was not meant to lead a small life, hunkered in the shadow of abandoned mansions, telling myself I was content between sky and cement. I was meant to ripple outward to the great centers of power, places like New York and Washington, and lay my hands upon the stones of strength. And I certainly would not leave any child of mine languishing in this district. I would not turn out like Richard Konigsberg, one day discovering that my child had existed without my knowledge.

I arrived at Candace's apartment building early in the morning and banged at the door repeatedly, fruitlessly, throughout the day. No one came in or out. In the afternoon, her neighbor who used to blast music lowered the volume on the stereo and parted her door a little to yell at me, telling me not to ruin her high. "Besides," she said, "you can't get into an apartment no one lives at." The neighbor's disclosure was perplexing and shocking and immediately caused me to double back and conjure the directions from the night we'd spent together. Had I come to the wrong apartment? I ran down to the front door and carried out a hurried archaeology of memory. Here was the hole where Candace had said rats came from. Here was the handrail which she had taken for support and I had pressed up behind her to kiss her neck. Here was the elevator in which she had pushed the second-floor button with her buttocks. It had all been real. It had all happened. It wasn't the hallucination of a drunk man. It wasn't the yearning of a man who had failed at impregnating life so much that he had taken to impregnating fantasies. I searched for the picture of Candace I had saved. I found it. I scrolled back to the pictures we had taken with Ali Ansari the night we visited him. Those were still there as well. I was not a madman. I existed—if not wholly, then at least in close proximity to the real.

I returned to the apartment the next day and carried out a repeat performance. The same lady from next door cracked the door and gave me the same comment as the day before, except this time she threw a shoe at me. Since I was leaving the country in the very near future and didn't have time to stalk around North Philly any longer, I texted Ali Ansari for help.

Need you to find a girl. She might be pregnant.

Farkhunda? came the reliably immediate answer.

No. The one you met at your apartment.

The mixed convert?

Yeah.

You knocked her up? Guess I don't blame you. She had a nice ass.

Hope you remember it well enough to spot it in North Philly.

He asked for her number and place of work and told me he would get on it. *What do you want me to do if I find her?*

I don't know, I said. *Wait for further instructions.*

I was grateful that he didn't ask for any more details. He didn't judge what I had done. He simply praised me when I did something great and extricated me when I fell into something reprehensible.

In short, a true friend.

Chapter Eight

L eila sat next to me on the flight and I was glad because she talked so much that it was hard to get lost thinking about the mystery of Candace.

Leila had been to Madrid before. It was the place where her transformative moment occurred, where she started thinking of herself as a moderate Muslim.

After the flight Leila and I settled into our hotel and met with the State Department liaison who Mahmoud had appointed for us. Our first meeting in Madrid was with a community centered around the Saudi mosque. Our liaison described it as Wahhabi, but emphasized that it was a gift given out of generosity. He insisted there was "no ulterior motivator." He told us that the massive white walls of the mosque were meant to remind the Spaniards that though Islam had been driven out once, it had come back by the grace of God. He was accompanied by a slick and smiling Saudi cohort. They spoke flawless English and led us through a tour of the immense grounds, including the prayer halls, the cafés, the gym, and an amphitheater capable of holding more than a thousand people. "We just had Amr Khaled here," the guide said proudly, referring to a famous evangelist. "Filled all of it." After a short siesta in the café, where newly arrived Moroccans served us tea and biscuits, we walked through the well-endowed library full of texts in Spanish and Arabic. The standard collections of *hadith*—Bukhari and Muslim—were arranged neatly on the shelves and there were numerous manuals about prayer and ablution.

I picked up a copy of the Koran. The Saudi guide came over and told me the translation was by Muhammad Asad. He looked at me like I was expected to know the name. I told him I didn't. He smiled and said that Asad was one of the most famous converts of the twentieth century. "Almost as important to us as Malcolm X." Asad had been born Leopold Weiss in a Jewish family in Austria and had converted to Islam when he fell in love with the Saudi rulers and the freewheeling libertarian life they led in the desert. It baffled me to think that one of the inheritors of Austrian history—with its Bach, its Mozart, its Wittgenstein—would feel inclined to tie himself to the sands of Arabia, where even the greatest man of literature was one who was celebrated for his illiteracy.

We continued the tour. There was a religious high school in the mosque, catering to the children of Muslim diplomats. Girls, all with their heads covered in white hijabs, sat on one side, and the boys were on the other. Leila and I sat in between them, along with our liaison, and the students heard us talk about life as Muslims in America. Leila's delivery was polished. She talked about Afghan food marts and Afghan weddings and how she had come to hear about the tragedy of the fallen towers and the fear and anxiety she felt "until I heard the President of the United States tell everyone that Islam was a religion of peace."

My own delivery lacked much in the way of substance. It meandered through my childhood growing up in the South and my eventual life with Marie-Anne. I absolved my life of its warts and villainy. I didn't mention the story about residual supremacism. I made no mention of the panic Brother Hatim felt regarding his fundamentalism. I said nothing about people like Ali Ansari. I hadn't been brought here to give a bad impression.

One afternoon Leila and I wandered to the Prado. Guards, sentries, guides, clad in their dead-blue blazers and knee-length skirts, stalked the halls like silent wraiths. The majority of them were aged, infirm, with bloated ankles, using the numerous rocking chairs provided to them out of the kindness of the administration. I found myself transfixed in front of a painting called *The Bearded Woman*, by Ribera. It was a bearded man in a red robe, breast out, feeding a baby, with another man in black standing behind. But the man with the breast was not a man. The painting was of a woman called Magdalena Ventura, who had decided to grow a beard at the age of thirty-three. I noted that in a few days I would be turning the same age.

We came out into the afternoon. It was a surprisingly intense sun, with hammers for rays; but they fell upon me soft, like the keys of a piano in a light jazz piece. The drone of the people in the squares was like the hum of another instrument. Leila's clicking heels provided the percussion. We headed toward the Atocha memorial, erected on the site of a train bombing.

We entered the monument from the bottom—from underground, through a subway door—and then passed the names of all the victims of the attacks. Then the subway door sealed shut and we entered a dark and empty chamber with a huge hole in the ceiling. There was a hollow tower extending up into the place where the explosives had shot out into the street above. Inscribed inside the tower were messages of condolence.

This was where Leila's transformative moment had occurred.

"It was a couple of years ago," she said. "I was here during a college trip. One day I came here. Walking distance from the Goya in the Prado and Picasso in the Reina Sofía. I just thought to myself, those artists depicted all that violence and yet there is still more violence in the world." Her face took on a pained expression. "It was so crazy to sit there, you know? I realized it had been Muslims not much younger than me, acting in the name of my faith, who had carried out the attacks. All I could think about was how Muslims once brought Alhambra to Spain and now gave this." She had become a reformist as a response. She needed to believe that there were Muslim peacemakers, because to not be a reformist would mean that she would have to be terrified of being a Muslim.

I envied Leila in that moment. She had, from the very start of her adult life, known that she was nothing but a Muslim and found a space to live in, thrive in. I, on the other hand, had grown up under the mis-apprehension that I wasn't similarly circumscribed. I had lived under a lie. Why had I not seen my chains earlier? I might have worn them like bangles like she did.

The whole thing reminded me of a novel I had read once, written by a Russian émigré. At the start of it a man called Cincinattus C. is arrested for an inchoate crime and taken to prison. Except for being ac-cused of "gnostical turpitude" the man is never given a reason for his ar-rest. The reader is left to ponder what kind of crime gnostical turpitude really was. Cincinattus stays in the farcical prison, under the aegis of a cruel warden, for a very long time, until the moment of his execution is imminent. Suddenly the entire edifice of the prison withers and fades from his view. Cincinattus had willed it away.

Residual supremacism was nearly as obtuse. What George Gabriel had been hinting at was the notion that underneath the cultured exterior, underneath the man who knew Chagall and spoke highly of Nietzsche and Goethe, there was a latent man, a zealot, one who drew direction from the supremacist message of the Koran, aspiring to ultimately over-turn the existing bookshelf and seek out domination in the name of Allah. I had been identified as an agent of Islamic expansion, the fear of which was woven into every Westerner, who had known a thousand years of Islamic assault, from Spain to Russia, from late Rome to early America. This fear transformed and cohered into a different form after the shadows struck New York. No longer was it a fear of an empire of faith lorded over by a sultan, armed to the hilt, strapped with swords, but robotic sleeper cells waiting to be activated by some dark man in a dark cave. But either way the fear was the same as it had always been: Islam sought ascendance and Muslims made that ascendance happen.

The trouble with this narrative was that it didn't apply to me. There had been a misunderstanding. I harbored nothing toward Islam, or toward any other idea in the world that might assert itself as a competitor to America. I didn't recite *la ilaha illallah*, neither out loud nor in any recess in my heart. For me there was no deity but America, and this was all there was to it.

But that's the thing about misunderstandings. Unless you have the power to take control of the one who has misunderstood, you have to participate in the misapprehension. You have to enter the prison that someone else has constructed for you, and you have to live there with all the patient forbearance of Cincinnatus C., without any guarantee that the prison might wither and break.

Later in the week Leila and I went to visit a far less stellar mosque, in inner-city Madrid. It was located on a block where the shops belonged to newly arrived immigrants from North Africa and where many of the signs were in Arabic. The imam here was a portly man named Qahtani, who seemed always to be surrounded by college-aged men and women. When Leila and I arrived outside the mosque, an old jobless laborer from Algeria began grilling me. He spoke Arabic and assumed I did too. I simply made a thumbs-up sign and said, "USA!" He made a thumbs-down and disappeared.

The mosque was three stories, with a large courtyard downstairs, a large prayer hall on the second level, and a third level where the administrative offices, conference rooms, and women's section were located. The old building had the smell and disposition of a place held together through will and hard work. The shelves for the shoes were old and creaky. The bathrooms were tired, damp, with leaky faucets. The carpet in the prayer room had worn ages ago. There was no library so much as a series of shelves in various rooms.

The imam led us to a small room where Leila and I waited for the youth to arrive. The room was full of junk, old sofas, broken chairs. Once we were alone Leila started snooping around, digging into a box containing trashed books. She laid them out before me. Most of them were theological manuals about ablution, prayers for the bathroom, and the like.

"Goddamn!" she said, raising a small green book over her head.

"What?"

"Look at the name."

It read, *Jihad fi Sabilillah*.

"What is that?"

"A pamphlet," she said. "It was written by these assholes—Qutb, al-Banna, and Maududi. Mahmoud considers them the trinity of evil. This book created all the bin Laden and Zawahiri types in this world."

"Well, good thing it's in the trash then."

Leila tucked it into her purse. "That could just be for show. I better take it with me. Mahmoud might want to see what kind of literature lives at this mosque."

"But if it's in the trash, maybe they really aren't interested in it."

"At one point they owned a copy. That is troubling."

"You're probably overthinking it."

"I know Muslims well. I've been one all my life. We become quite good at putting on a show."

We sorted through the rest of the books. They were old guides about the virtues of patience; manuals about Islamic ethics; and commentaries on the Koran. Leila dismissed them and sat back down to wait for the youth.

"I'm a little worried now," she said.

"Why?"

"This seems like a fundamentalist place. And I'm a Shia. If these guys turn out to be crazies, they're going to come after me for not wearing a hijab, for not being a Sunni."

I wanted to tell her that she was panicking for no reason. But her increasing paranoia seemed to cut into my own sense of security as well. By the time the young people had loaded into the room—men on one side and women on the other—I was also looking at them with suspicion. Maybe they were exactly as Leila had alleged. Maybe they were all immoderate and maniacal.

The discussion, though, revealed anything but. The youth were engaged and informed and wanted to know about the internecine and granular theological debates that Muslims in America were having. About women becoming prayer leaders, about the inclusion of homosexuals, about excommunicating the extremists. These were things that Leila was better suited to handle. I let her talk and turned to play with the two-year-old son of a cheerful man in a leather jacket. I barely said a word throughout the presentation.

After the event was over, the men in the room came toward me to ask about my career and other hobbies. They were, almost all of them, in technical and engineering fields, with a few working as businessmen or entrepreneurs.

"I assume things must have been very difficult for you after the towers fell," the man with the son said to me. "Being a Muslim here, it became an insult."

I looked around to see where our State Department liaison was. I didn't see him. I pulled the Spaniard closer to me. "Same with us. Same thing happened. They insult us for being Muslim. I was fired for being a Muslim."

They seemed intrigued; my confession was something they hadn't expected to hear.

Leila overheard my comment and came rushing over. She gave me a severe look for veering so far from script. "But you see, what the Muslims in America did is that we started to get involved in the politics and the media of our country. So we couldn't be excluded. We are not marginalized in any way."

The mention of media struck a nerve with the men.

"No one in the media wants to hear from us," said a black-eyed Syrian-Spaniard with an Italian wife in a paisley scarf. "There are no Muslim columnists in any papers."

"The Left and the Right," said an immigrant from Jordan. "They just want to beat up on Muslims. We are responsible for all the job losses. We are responsible for all the crime. We are responsible for violence and death."

"Have you tried writing to the newspapers to complain?"

"We write all the time but they don't publish us. And the reporters don't care."

A frustrated lull hung over the room. The ever-cheerful Leila tried to use words like *bridge-building* and *peace initiatives* and *networking methods*, but no one stirred. I offered no meaningful assistance.

Eventually the little group drifted apart. Leila was pulled back toward the women. The guys, growing disenchanted by the meeting, invited me out to watch a match between Real Madrid and FC Barcelona. The only place to go were the pubs. A couple of the establishments didn't let us in because they were aware that Muslims wouldn't purchase alcohol. It was almost halftime when a pub finally let us in. Even there the bartender and the patrons gave us dirty looks and had us sit far away from everyone else. We ordered fries and soda. I picked up the tab for all of us. I left a 100 percent tip; it was to bribe respect.

I ended up spending a couple more days in Spain, mostly just touring the museums or having listless conversations with Leila about what she wanted to do with her life. Her ultimate goal was to be a feminist human rights lawyer who served on war-crimes tribunals and on the side ran an Islamic reform think tank. Mahmoud had agreed to mentor her until she achieved her ends. Placing her in the State Department program was meant to bolster her credentials. She planned on putting a few years in, and then transitioning into an aide role for a senator, where she hoped to offer commentary on foreign policy and the Islamist threat. Then she would hit the lecture circuit and live her life fighting radicalization and fundamentalism.

I had no such long-terms plans. I simply wanted to return to Philadelphia five thousand dollars richer and get back to sorting out my little vicissitudes.

Chapter Nine

Marie-Anne had been sent to Las Vegas to meet with some of the soldiers who operated the drones out of Nellis. After that she needed to go to the Persian Gulf. I missed her; I had wanted to tell her all about my trip. I also hoped that if she saw that I had a solid gig going, she might become inclined to talk about starting a family. The possibility that Candace might be having my child didn't make me less inclined to seek the same with Marie-Anne. If anything, it compelled me more, not only to cover up the crime I had perpetrated, but to remind myself that I was serious in my recommitment to Marie-Anne.

I took the alone time to spruce up the condo, to make it more of a home for her. I went and bought a couple of aloe plants to deal with the summer humidity. I got the air-conditioning vent and met with a real estate agent to find out about the financing that we would need in order to purchase the apartment. Later I went to seek out a bespoke tailor on Market Street and had myself measured for a pair of suits. I also got an estimate done for new kitchen counters. There was money in my hand and it had to be spent.

All this time I also kept in touch with Ali Ansari. He told me about the difficult time he'd had in tracking Candace. Not only was she not at her apartment but she also hadn't been to work. He had made some inquiries with her colleagues at her job and they said she had taken personal days and gone home, without any explanation. She had no family or apparent friends in the area and Ali said that the trail had gone cold.

I told him it would be a good idea for us to meet. I recommended getting together that night at my apartment. But he said he was traveling back from New York and suggested meeting up the next day, at the deli near the Divine Lorraine.

"What took you to New York?" I asked, unaccustomed to him leaving Philadelphia, wondering if perhaps it was something Candace-related.

"Will update you."

The next day I got to the deli a little before Ali. The sun was out, with egg-shaped clouds passing before it, a smokestack trying hard to touch the sky with its whorls. The owner stood at the door in his stained yellow wifebeater with his hand on his hip and a remote control pointed at the high-definition TV hanging on the wall. A number of young men chatted with one another about a soccer match. I had never much gotten into soccer. It was a game of perpetual motion, a sport for those who wanted to act more and reason less; we preferred our sports with starts and stops, with pauses affording the athlete time to come up with a plan for attack, the way the ultrarational like to play.

There was a smaller TV in the corner of the deli, dusty and unused. I went and sat before it. I looked around for the young attendant who used to work here. Chris had been his name. Not seeing him, I gestured for the old man to come over.

"You a spy?" He wiped his hands on his smock.

"Excuse me?"

"I never see you before," he said, loud enough for some of the younger men to glance over.

I felt a pulse of panic go up my thighs. I thought of Leila sneaking that manual out of the trash in Madrid. I thought of all the time I'd spent around people close to the State Department. Was there some unstated war between the moderate Muslims and whatever strain this old man was affiliated with?

"I think you misunderstand me," I offered.

"No," he wagged his rag, "I know exactly who you are. Only two falafel places in city. Me and Hisham in West Philly. He send you here to watch me, yes? You are caught, no need to lie."

I assured him that I was not committing culinary espionage and wasn't even aware of Hisham's existence. This made the old man quite happy. "And even if I knew him," I added, "I'd be on *your* team because you are from my neighborhood."

"Good," he said. "This is why I like Philadelphia. So very neighborly. What you will order?"

I ordered a burger and watched Al Jazeera. I wanted to add bacon but knew better than to ask. A bit of instrumental music, interspersed with the pleasing sound of an announcer, came on the set. Globes and parabolic maps and gold-flecked leaves flew around on the screen and revealed a young female anchor with a Turkish name sitting confidently in her chair. She sprayed out a sentence in near-perfect Victorian English.

The old man saw my interest and got out of the way.

The anchor was interviewing a Malaysian geographer. He wanted to take the opportunity of the unveiling of the newly erected clock tower in Mecca—which he called "the Big Bin"—to make the world drop Greenwich standard time and replace it with Mecca standard time. His first argument vis-à-vis the Big Ben in England was simply, "Our clock is bigger."

The anchor didn't seem to find this convincing. "The other clock is older . . ."

"Fine, fine," the man said, stroking his goatee. "But Greenwich time is a colonial relic. We could accept their time before but we won't accept their time now. We are almost first world ourselves."

"But aren't there pragmatic reasons to stick with Greenwich?"

"Like what?"

"Well, the international date line," said the anchor, "as it currently

234 * Native Believer

stands, is exactly 180 degrees to Greenwich, which makes the line fall somewhere in the middle of a giant ocean—and that is convenient because it prevents conflict and confusion. If you were to make Mecca the meridian, the date line would end up running right through the West Coast of North America, so even though it would be Wednesday in New York, it would already be Thursday in San Francisco."

The geographer chortled and got excited. "So what? You make it seem as if it's important for New York and San Francisco to have a consistent clock. Maybe when America was powerful such things were true. But now? Bankrupt countries don't have a right to a schedule that makes sense."

"Maybe," the anchor replied. "But you haven't really given any clear reason why Mecca should be the meridian."

"It is very simple," the geographer said with narrowed eyes. "If you were to move far away from the earth, and look down at it with a telescope, you will see that Mecca falls at the exact center of the earth, and in the exact center of Mecca you will find the holiest place of Islam—"

"I'm going to stop you right there," shrieked the anchor, adjusting her hijab. "Your comment would only make sense if the world was flat. But if the world, as has been known for some time, is round, then its exact center can't be on the surface. It must be deep in the middle of it. At least that is what my physics teacher taught me. I think we're going to end our—"

"No, wait, wait," pleaded the geographer. "Fine, so you do not accept religious argument, I understand. But what about history? Long ago, long before Islam even, Arabs used to worship time. They used to call it *dahr*. They even had a goddess in its honor."

"You are on stronger footing with that," the anchor commented. "Except this was two thousand years ago."

"Yes," said the geographer, now visibly irritated. "But if after thousands of years the Jews can claim Israel, then after many more thousands of years the Arab can claim time, no?"

The anchor rolled her eyes and continued arguing. I zoned out and turned my gaze outside. A couple of youths passed by, flipping a football to each other.

Ali Ansari arrived during a commercial break. He carried a pair of heavy bags with him, one of which obviously contained camera equipment. He rummaged through his pockets, but was short on change. In his hurry he dropped a ring on the ground. I picked it up and handed it back to him. Then I ordered a second burger for me and one for him.

"Been awhile, buddy," he said, tucking the ring back in his pocket.

"I know," I said, regarding his scruffy face. "I've been out of the country. For work."

"I didn't know you got a job. Here I thought you were an autonomous dude."

"I'm a freelancer," I said.

"Do you get paid?"

"I do."

"Then you are a hireling."

"Aren't we all?" I pointed at the heavy bags next to him. "Are the cameras for your cash cow?"

He shook his head and slit both his throat and groin. He had dismantled the pornographic enterprise. Gone so far as to formally dissolve Talibang Productions, so that it no longer existed even on paper. It seemed sudden to me; but for him it had been a long time coming. It boiled down to no longer wanting to turn the Muslim into a performer for the Western gaze. Using the example of black men in porn had been a bad one. They weren't to be emulated. They were workers who were exploited: exploited for their bodies; exploited for the color of their skin; exploited for the poverty that made them take injections and consent to surgery and performing in a risky and perverse environment for next to nothing for their labor. There had to be another way to become known.

Besides, Ali Ansari had other, more pressing projects. He had finished his wrestler documentary, the one about Martin Mirandella, and it had turned out better than expected. Last week he had found out that his documentary about the blacklisted wrestler had won the Haddon Prize, worth fifty thousand dollars, and would be screening at Sundance and the Toronto International Film Festival. The award committee was impressed by the manner in which he had teased out a tension in contemporary America, where even non-Muslims could be affected by the prejudice that Muslims faced.

I asked him what he was going to do with the money.

He smiled and said that he had already reinvested it, this time in underwriting a guerrilla concert and documentary about the Gay Commie Muzzies. "That's why I've been in New York so often."

"What does *guerrilla concert* actually mean?" I asked, removing a pickle from the burger.

Ali Ansari smiled. He said it meant sneaking into the building site at the Freedom Tower in New York and holding an hour-long show, as well as a reading of the Koran, all of which would be broadcast on the Internet using miniature cameras. They were doing it because they wanted to flip off all those people who'd said that building a mosque so close to Ground Zero should be prohibited.

It struck me as the kind of thing Candace might have come up with. Then again, she and Ali Ansari had similar ways of looking at the world.

"That's bold," I said.

"It is," he agreed. "But the time is right."

Our eyes turned to the screen. The news program came back. Next up was a sober discussion about debt capital markets in the Gulf. It was followed by a short conversation with an Wazirati government official who made a plea to all the foreign and domestic companies doing business in the region to follow the labor laws that the government legislated. Some of the companies bringing laborers into the Gulf were sticking them in obscene housing projects where the sewage was leaking into their rooms and down the middle of the street.

"Marie-Anne is out there right now," I said.

"In the middle of the action?"

"Basically."

"So things are working out for both of us," he said.

We had discussed everything by now, except for the question of Candace. Perhaps to put off avoiding the conversation even longer, Ali went to get us mint tea. When he came back he started talking about the people we used to hang out with. I let him talk because I was curious to hear what had happened to that little community. Tot and some of the Gay Commie Muzzies had gang-banged Farkhunda and prompted her to leave the group and become a hard-core feminist; Saba had taken off the hijab and become a modesty fashion designer; Hatim had moved to San Diego to become a bodybuilder. The fallout from Farkhunda's departure created an irreparable split in the Gay Commie Muzzies. The group siding with Farkhunda left and joined the Fatwawhores. Tot's segment decided to get jobs and joined the Bawa Muhaiyaddeen Fellowship.

"That leaves only one order of business," I said.

Ali nodded. "Trail's gone cold. Nothing on social media. Unless you want to get the authorities involved, I think you're going to have to forget about her."

"Damnit."

"You really don't know if she's pregnant or not?"

"I don't know anything," I replied. "We haven't been in touch since she sent me a picture of herself and ghosted."

"What if she is?"

It was a question of heritage, wasn't it? We new Americans—the ones who didn't have the heft of generations behind us, who didn't have great-grandfathers who had run ranches, or laid train tracks, or built dams, or died for this country in wars, or even thirsted their way through droughts and dust bowls—had only one way of mooring ourselves to the country. Through reproduction. To hasten the process of generation-building as much as possible. So if Candace was pregnant with my child, even if the child was illegitimate, I would want her to go through with it, and I would keep her secret and keep her provided for, and one day Marie-Anne would just have to understand how important all this was to me. We all had to make sacrifices for me to be fully American.

I conveyed all this to Ali in broken sentences. He mulled it over for a moment.

"If this whole thing is about children, aren't you better off having children with your wife? She's white and everything."

"She won't have them."

"She won't have them? Or won't have them with you?"

I pressed my finger on the edge of a knife. It was too late to reel back the discussion. "I want to say it's the former. But it could be the latter."

"Well," he said after a drawn-out pause, "what if she doesn't want to have children with you because of who you are? Maybe she fears that her children will be stained by your existence. They would have a name like yours. And even if they didn't, they would still resemble you. It isn't a hospitable country for people who look like us. And it won't be that much better for children who are only half sand-nigger."

"I haven't wanted to think like that."

"It's not pleasant."

"You're saying my wife is racist."

"I'm not saying that," he replied. "She did marry you, after all. But you guys were young when you married. You were driven by passion. Even her parental disapproval didn't make her pause. But you guys are old now. Cautious. She's had years to work through the passion. Maybe when she thinks of you in a cold and rational manner she sees all the struggles you've had and just doesn't feel comfortable passing them on to her children. This is why, I think, I'll probably end up marrying a Muslim girl. She will know exactly what she's getting into with me. Even a convert has a better idea than a non-Muslim."

I tried to play his comments off with a joke, saying I never thought I'd hear Ali Ansari—porn magnate, player, dandy—talk about marriage. But that was just the surface conversation. The inner one was directed toward home. Could it be that all this time, while I thought that Marie-Anne was cursed from the inside, she thought I was cursed from the outside? If her mother, despite all her work on behalf of civil rights in South Carolina, could find reasons to object to me, why couldn't Marie-Anne, despite having married me, develop reasons to be wary of me? Was that why I wouldn't produce a successor to put into America?

"What about Candace?"

Ali heard my inner cry. He came and sat next to me. "You're going to have to forget her." His face was composed, almost stern. It wasn't advice; it was admonishment.

"Why?"

"Because she deserves better. She deserves someone who doesn't need validation from the Old South to feel American. Someone that knows how to be a new American, this dirty and muddy mix that America is today. With presidents who are East African and celebrities who aren't WASPS. This new America isn't for you. Maybe it was because of where you grew up, but you can't separate being American from being white. I thought you might be able to change. That was why I introduced you to GCM and told Farkhunda to suck your cock. But you can't change. You can't embrace your dispossession. The love of the plantation is too deep in you. You need to focus on Marie-Anne and forget about Candace. Don't turn her into your little concubine. Let her go find someone who is comfortable in the fields. This is the age of the field Negro. You just stay in the house."

I tucked my hands in my lap and nodded. Ali helped me delete the texts. He also pressured me to delete her phone number, as well as the picture she had sent. Afterward, we replayed the video of him threatening to kill George Gabriel and had a little chuckle over it. He asked me to delete it too. I told him I would; but not yet. I couldn't let go of all my good memories in one session.

As we headed out of the restaurant I asked Ali if he needed money for the cab ride home. He declined, saying that he was going to get picked up.

I was too melancholy to wait around to see how he got home.

With Marie-Anne out of the country, I made a harder turn toward work. I sent Mahmoud a series of messages and waited for an answer. It took some time before I got a callback. He said he was in Philadelphia for a meeting. "Come and eat some steak with me," he invited. "On me."

I headed out on foot. It was fall, nearly winter. Something portended a hard frost. I looked out at the junipers and maples and oaks and firs. They twisted and touched each other all year long. But while the evergreens stayed clothed and warm the whole time, the seasonal trees had their clothes torn off and were made to suffer a frozen death. When you observed nature comparatively like that, you got a different message than the greeting-card one about the circle of life. You got one about the permanent superiority of one group over another.

We had decided to meet up at a steakhouse in Center City. I knew Mahmoud only had an issue with my eating habits in front of other Muslims. Since none were around I went ahead and ordered pulled pork and wine. I smiled at his disinterest. We were beginning to develop workplace customs. This was the kind of relationship I had wanted with George Gabriel.

The meal was mostly Mahmoud talking. He didn't have a moment to just genuflect, to relax, to give in to the lethargy and boredom that might bedraggle others. This was really the first time I had been alone with him, and I tried to make an effort to get to know him. Family? Children? Permanent residence? He was agnostic about all those things.

Like bees around a hive, his thoughts, his comments, always seemed to circle back to the question of how to most effectively present the case for America to the world at large, particularly to the Muslims who didn't seem to buy into it. "They must be made to see," he liked to say, "what we already know about ourselves." He treated this project like it was a mission, like a celibate man who has been trained his whole life to do a singular thing, as if the slightest mismanagement would bring cataclysms raining down. I wanted to know what motivated him. Was it like me, a generalized adoration of the founding principles of the Republic, or was it something else, perhaps some irascible character flaw, such as the need to be liked, or perhaps some hidden scarring that he kept bottled? But he gave nothing away. He was as tight as his black skullcap.

After the meal we went for a walk in the direction of the Federal Courthouse, circling around Independence Hall and the Liberty Bell, toward the National Public Radio building. I looked in the direction where Candace had projected the verse from the Koran. I didn't bother telling Mahmoud about the performance and my subsequent response to it; he didn't need proof of my loyalties.

We sat on a bench and stared through the windows where a radio host was chatting with a guest. It was like a silent film. Depending on the kind of music added to the background, the host and the guest could be made into anything. Perhaps that was how it was for most of us. We were noiseless things defined mostly by what played behind us, and we had never figured out how to make our own music.

Something about witnessing the silent interview caused Mahmoud to start speaking about himself. He said he came from inside Islam. But unlike those who came from Islam and wanted to restore it to prominence, he regarded it as something that had prominence once, but couldn't be allowed to have prominence again. His reasons were complicated. He asked me to follow his train of logic.

"If you consider the last fifteen hundred years of Islam, do you know what you see? You see that for a majority of the time Islam was imperial, dominant, superior, in control. The Golden Age. But you know what I see when I hear the Golden Age stuff? I hear a lie. Islam wasn't supposed to be about a caliph, about influence. It was a thing made up by an orphan to bring some sense to the world, to reject the greedy capitalism that he was surrounded by, to free the slaves, to focus on an invisible deity in the sky in an effort to distance himself from the crass materialism of the living, breathing idols draped in gold. At least that's what it started out as. That was early Muhammad. But then later Muhammad, as well as his followers, all jumped the shark. They lost sight of what was beautiful about their message. They decided to become caravan raiders and invaders. And from their betrayal of themselves an entire jihad state emerged out of Arabia. It created corporations. It enslaved nations. It turned itself into an idol. It became what it wasn't supposed to be. The Golden Calf. The America of its time. So what I want is to take the Muslims back to that feeling of despair and dispossession that Muhammad must have felt to first come up with this thing called Islam. Take everything from them. Render them orphans. My hope is that if the Muslims get to start from scratch all over again, they might not become the greedy monsters they became last time."

"Tough love then."

"The toughest. But it is love. All I know is that I want to make sure Islam never again becomes anything other than a movement of the spirit. No Islamic bombs and no Islamic finance and no Islamic fashion and no Islamic world. Just the believer and her God. I can give that to the Muslim through America, the überinfidel, whose job it is to regulate the believer."

"Doesn't that make *you* an infidel?"

"Sometimes the true believer has to become an infidel."

"Well then," I said, "I hope I can help you get to where you desire."

"Tell me about the trip to Madrid."

"It was excellent. I clicked with the students."

"I heard you told them how you got fired from your job."

"I got carried away."

"Not at all," he said, plugging his ears for a moment as a pair of bikers roared past, American flags foisted on their antennae. "It is exactly the kind of confession that gives you legitimacy."

"How do you mean?"

"You told them that you were discriminated out of a job. And yet there you were, standing in front of them, talking about how well America treats its Muslims. It's a very convincing presentation. I would want you to play that up in the future."

"In the future?"

He wanted to send me out again. There was Canada and Ireland and Austria and Malaysia and Indonesia. All those spots were open. Quick five-day jaunts. He would even link them together so I could hit them all at once. Leila could go with me. We made a good team. I was relaxed; she was intense.

"I could use the money," I said. "Marie-Anne and I are still trying to make the down payment on our condo."

"The place I saw near the art museum?" he asked. "Lovely place. You spruce it up and it would be heaven."

"No need for heaven," I said. "Just something that will make people jealous."

He clapped me on the back. That's what he liked about me: I offered no flights of fancy. No idealism. I was a merchant and merchants made good followers.

"Let's just say I gravitate to authority."

"Yes," he said, "I've met your wife." He stood up and shook my hand, the other arm gesturing toward a cab. "I'll send you the paperwork as soon as I get back to New York."

I dropped him off at his hotel and went to buy new luggage.

* * *

Three days later I was on a plane. I could only smile at my position. This was the life of a jetsetter, I thought. Home one day, an interregnum to sort out and pay the bills, and then back in the skies again, accruing miles, living in high-end hotels, impervious to the trepidations that haunted when you were on land. There was a glamour to all of it. Not referring to the hustle-bustle and the physical toll of the travel. But the ability to look superciliously upon those who never got to leave their stations. The sense of pride a race car driver had over a man riding a rocking horse in his living room.

I looked down at the bounteous and blue water below. The world spread out before me like a personal playground. And to make it interesting—I glanced at Leila sleeping—I had a pretty little girl with me who many people confused for my girlfriend. It didn't seem it could get any better. Suddenly I no longer missed Plutus, where my life was tied to my desk, where all the glory was given away to our clients. At Plutus people spent their entire careers trying to find ways to set themselves apart from the crowd, to be recognized as having a distinct skill set. With this touring gig I had made that move without even needing to try. I was glad that there was a War of Ideas in which I could fight. It was a safe war, but one which still rained glory.

The five-country tour started in Canada. We met with a group of hand-selected Muslim students from the University of Toronto and York University who grilled us about American foreign policy, including torture and extraordinary rendition. We took them out to a hookah bar and told them how our foreign policy wasn't exactly what we wanted it to be but how in the course of a war certain sacrifices and judgment calls had to be made.

Next up were Ireland and Vienna, where the students were not as polished as the Canadians, most of them very recent immigrants from North Africa, Pakistan, and Turkey, and they were more interested in what life was like growing up in the States, whether we obsessed over Muslim sports figures like they did, and whether we had any doubts about our status as American. I flatly told them I loved being an American and felt not the slightest hesitation in saying it.

In Malaysia and Indonesia we went to Kuala Lumpur and Jakarta and met with three different groups of thirty-odd students and gave presentations at high schools. Most of the questions were about pop culture and the place of the American Muslim in that environment. This was where I shone. I told them about a filmmaker friend who was radically challenging racial stereotypes through his movies and about Muslim guerrilla reggae groups who were demonstrating that there was a place for everyone in the American cultural scene. I ignored the part about losing touch with these people. It was a presentation, not a confession. At the end of the trip I organized a makeshift spoken-word competition with Indonesian youths performing works written in English. Their poems had a Shakespearean tenor to them. He was the only Western poet besides Tupac and Biggie who they could name.

In every city I told the story about my firing. I talked about how my boss had seen the Koran on my shelf, placed higher than Nietzsche, and had discriminated against me as a result. I told them that even though in the beginning I had considered George Gabriel's actions a slap in the face of my heritage, I had eventually come to realize that he wasn't to blame. He was just unaware of what Muslims brought to America. I wasn't resentful, I said, because I was a realist. If the blame rested anywhere, I explained, it rested with the men with Muslim names, acting under the aegis of Allah, who had created a schism between Islam and America by resorting to violence. They were responsible for the bad taste in the mouths of people like George Gabriel. "But there doesn't have to be a schism," I said with great passion in my voice. "And I am evidence of that." In this manner I proffered myself as evidence of the possibility of bridge building, of the fact that if there was anyone to be resented, it was the terrorists and extremists of Islam, not the average American. Mahmoud had been right: my ability to make myself the Muslim everyman worked wonders with the crowds. By the time we reached Indonesia I was talking about the firing as part of my introductory spiel. My commentary seemed to evoke in the people we met a mystique in favor of American power. It must be a great entity indeed if even those who were wronged by it could become inclined to offer it forgiveness.

There was a kind of deception in being a moderate Muslim. It was less a philosophy and more of a position, a persuasion tactic. The trick was to lead the Muslims to believe that I was with them, from among them, that our connection was Islam, all the while putting before them a likable, even lovable vision of America, the same America that regarded them as infidels to the Enlightenment, as those who didn't believe in our project, as those whom we needed to save. The triangulation came easier to me than to Leila, who was still quite young and needed to be able to believe that she was engaged in a reconciliation of civilizational proportions.

I had no similar misgivings. I was, simply put, an evangelist, channeling my strengths—in this case my appearance and my connection to Islam—as a way of proselytizing. I was an extension of the high priesthood that was formed in Washington, and which spread upon the world like a storm. The only way to assure the permanence of the Republic was by spreading its theology far and wide. It wasn't anything devious we were doing. Every religion had a right to promulgate itself, to bring new members into its fold, to give its priests the opportunity to reach out to the skeptics, the disbelievers.

The question of what I am, it seemed, had been conclusively answered. For the first time I wasn't ashamed of saying my eight-lettered name.

CHAPTER TEN

During those five weeks, Marie-Anne was on her own world trip. In the Wazirate, for a possible sales pitch, and then to Doha, to sit down with an Al Jazeera broadcaster in studio. I thought it was bold of her to start doing media. She said the publicity would help her networking if she publicly discussed what MimirCo did.

We kept in touch as best we could. Her trip to "the Arabian Gulf"—as she had started calling it to appease her hosts—would take longer than expected because Mahmoud had arranged for a couple of extra meetings for her, one in Saudi Arabia and the other in the UAE, in addition to the one with the Waziratis.

I also kept in touch with Mahmoud, via e-mail, telling him about how well my trip had gone. The aim was to find out if there were any more paid junkets. He said there weren't any immediate trips scheduled, but I was on the top of his list of people he would call up once there were. He also mentioned that he was in stuck in DC for a while because he was trying to create a Deputy of Muslim Outreach position. "But don't tell anyone about that," he said.

From the way he worded the e-mail, along with the compliments he had given me when he had been in Philadelphia, I was confident that he was creating the position for me. I let myself imagine what it would be like to get the offer. Maybe Marie-Anne and I would be able to move to Virginia. She would be close to MimirCo and I would get to dress up every day and go to Foggy Bottom, hobnobbing with diplomats, with ambassadors. I pictured the cuff links I might buy. In addition, I would have a massive flag pin, and it would be affixed on my chest every day. Eventually it would seep into me, permanently embossed upon the walls of my heart, so that even the angels wouldn't mistake me for who I wasn't.

The same morning as the e-mail from Mahmoud I got a message from Marie-Anne. It came with a lot of exclamation marks. Her appearance on Al Jazeera was confirmed at last and they were going to put her on live that evening.

On the appointed hour I took myself to the deli near Divine Lorraine. The place was mostly empty, just the old man who had accused me of being a spy from West Philadelphia. I sat down at the bar and ordered my usual chicken burger and proceeded to wait for the segment.

It was the same news program, with the same anchor that Ali Ansari and I had watched last time we'd been here. After a couple of unrelated segments the anchor brought out her main guests.

There was Marie-Anne, dressed in a loose pink tunic with a light scarf thrown around her neck. Her red hair shone in the studio light; her skin, heavily touched up, seemed a little murky, almost gray. The anchor greeted her by restating her qualifications and affiliations.

"I'm happy to be here," Marie-Anne replied.

"Tell me what you think about that expert," I said to the old man.

"The white woman?" He seemed to put the emphasis on *woman* and only gave a brief glance. "Why?"

"She may have something interesting to say."

We turned back to listen. The anchor asked Marie-Anne a series of questions that revealed some of the campaigns she'd worked on. It quickly became apparent that Marie-Anne's team had sifted a great deal of the video that led US troops to the doorstep of various militant groups around the world. Marie-Anne took the compliment in the anchor's voice and tried to spread the congratulations to all the other people on the program. I was quite surprised by how candidly Marie-Anne spoke. She had never shared so much about the program with me.

The show faded out to advertisements.

Upon returning, the anchor introduced a pair of new studio guests. One of them was an old bearded man in traditional tribal clothing, sitting morosely with his arms folded. The other man was someone I recognized: it was Sajjad from the Pierre.

As the camera focused in on the anchor's face, I saw a certain rapid blinking of her eyelashes and a twitch in her forehead. It suggested an imminent explosion. I started worrying about what Marie-Anne might have to face.

The attack didn't take long to arrive.

"Ladies and gentlemen, we return to our program. We are here today with a private contractor working with an aerial intelligence-gathering program," she said while pointing to Marie-Anne, "and we are now joined by Sajjad Shahryar, an Insanistani columnist and former member of the parliament, who has been advising the Pentagon on its plans to arm its surveillance robots. We also have in our studio Rahim Farid, a resident of the Insanistani tribal belt, who spent his entire life savings to come to Doha and talk about the killing of his son by a missile shot by an unmanned surveillance craft. We'll turn to you," the anchor looked at Marie-Anne, "and ask you what your response would be to someone like Mr. Farid here. Why would you feel the need to arm your robots with missiles?"

The first real fight Marie-Anne and I ever had occurred over Scrabble. We had played a long game and our scores were both in the high 300s. Marie-Anne was ahead. I only had one letter left: Z. She had just finished making the word *EROS*, leaving open a triple-letter score just above the *E*. I stuck the *Z* in the open space and won by one point. It left her horrified. She kept shaking her head saying that the correct spelling was *zeroes*. She was so adamant about rejecting my version of the spelling that she laid down an official challenge. We went and consulted the Merriam-Webster, as well as the American Heritage, and found that both spellings were acceptable. This made her cry. Her black mascara ran from the corner of her eyes and trailed along the outside of her face and met at the chin, giving her face a circular black outline. All night she cried, shocked that she had been beaten, shocked that I exceeded her in English. By morning time we had coined a new verb. *Zeroed:* the state of being defeated unexpectedly.

Zeroed was the expression on her face right now. As the tribal man looked at her with congealed, cataract-laden eyes, swimming in tears, Marie-Anne stumbled and stuttered. Her face was blank. She had nothing to say. She was lost.

It was Sajjad who had to step forward to save her. He made a long statement about the regrettable things that happened in wars, offered a brief apology to the old man, and reminded the anchorwoman that using drone technology to hunt terrorists was sparing countless lives and preventing violence from escalating. "I don't think we want a situation in Insanistan where we have American soldiers in a face-to-face position with our citizens," he finished.

The newscaster was adamant: "But no one has even determined if such action is even legal. And isn't it unethical besides that? This man lost his son . . ."

The intercession by Sajjad allowed Marie-Anne to recover from the ambush. She took a deep breath and clenched her fists. "There are gray areas in war," she said. "The question of armed drones is one of them, and people who know law should answer it. But just because its legality is not yet settled doesn't mean that it is unethical."

"Aren't you simply saying that because your technology is ahead of the law you are free to do with it what you like? Even kill this man's innocent son?"

The argument pressed forward, without balance, without rhythm, like a ping-pong match played on a triptych. Marie-Anne was more or less in agreement with Sajjad who, it was revealed, supported increasing the number of drones even more, "because it will reduce the financial cost of the war." The old man who came to Doha to have his say tried to piece together a sentence in English, but Sajjad struck him down in another language.

The anchor, left by herself, tried another tactic, arguing that before sending a missile to execute someone, it might be wise to have a trial to prove guilt.

Marie-Anne jumped back in. "We aren't dealing with people here—we are dealing with terrorists!" she shouted.

The final enunciation was evidently so painful for her that she decided to walk off the set. As she moved away against the protestations of the anchor, she tried to strip the microphone from her body; but it stayed on and continued relaying her muttering. I heard the words "hairy" and "thin-skinned" and "leper" before the wire on the microphone snapped and the camera and the sound connected back to the anchor.

The old man working the deli walked to the TV, his rag-wrapped fingers having intercourse with the glass in his hand. The TV showed a close-up of Marie-Anne. He reached out with the rag hand and touched the pulsating veins in her forehead. "That's a crazy bitch."

"Watch your mouth," I replied. "That's my wife."

He looked at me with disbelief. Like he wanted to punch me. Having seen Marie-Anne flayed publicly, even embarrassed, I was already feeling vulnerable, and I was in no mood for a confrontation. I just wanted to get out of the deli, away from this man's excoriating stare. I got up and leapt to the exit. My sudden move excited the owner and he followed me outside. To avoid any further conversation I ran into the bar next door. He stopped outside the entrance, probably reticent to enter an establishment with alcohol. I could see him through the glass. He was drenched in light from the lamppost above. He cupped his face against the door, dragging his grizzled gray hair on the surface, fogging the glass with his breath. Even though I was just inches from him, because of the darkness that surrounded me, the burning old man was unable to see me.

I walked to a stool and decided to wait him out. I should have never gone into the deli and aimed for camaraderie. Moderate Muslims, who were just playing the part of believers, couldn't be friends with other Muslims. We could only report on them. The rest of the time we were better off in bars like this, separated from them, maintaining a safe and cautious distance from our marks.

When I came out of the bar, the deli was closed, the old man was gone, and I was properly drunk. Marie-Anne's words rang in my mind. *Hairy, thin-skinned lepers.* I knew that if I turned on Fairmount, keeping the penitentiary on my right, I could follow it all the way to Pennsylvania and make it home in about fifteen minutes. But the other part of me, the vulnerable part, the part that had witnessed Marie-Anne dismiss a man whose son had been obliterated, wanted to go and hide. Without thinking, I started hustling down Broad Street, toward city hall.

That night I roamed around Philly in a much larger circuit. I wanted to see everything in the city. To delve into it. To experience its mysteries and hold its secrets in my heart and find joy in my discoveries. That was, ultimately, what it meant to have a home, to be familiar with everything in the space, familiar to the point of hatred, and yet still be surprised by what you might discover.

I headed farther east on Girard than I had ever gone. Once I reached Northern Liberties I went north toward Fishtown, parallel to I-95, its underside booming and rattling with each vehicle. There were only warehouses here, some stockyards, some parking lots full of bulldozers. I heard a barge creaking in the Delaware River. It carried the stench of trash. I saw in the distance, next to an abandoned warehouse, a dumpster lit on fire. There were maybe five or six people standing near it, rocking on the balls of their feet. A couple were close to the fire; the rest maintained an agreeable distance. I headed in their direction, to see into their eyes, to see their faces behind their hair, to see into their hearts. But they didn't acknowledge me. They didn't give me their face for an entry point into their person.

Just as I was about to turn back to make my way home, it occurred to me that I wasn't too far from where Front Street ran into Cecil B. Moore. I could take Cecil all the way toward the other side of Philadelphia and emerge near Diamond Street, where Ali Ansari lived. I had never before cut through the entirety of Philadelphia horizontally like this, and doing it in a vulnerable state, with the possibility that anything might go wrong, only compelled me more.

The one interesting thing I saw on the way occurred near Temple University. I glimpsed the glow of red light falling upon a wall. There was a long, faded mural here. The picture was of a tree. A simple, faded blue tree. Big, tall, majestic, and otherwise without adornments. But it wasn't wholly lifeless. Beaming onto the surface of the wall was an entire panoply of red lights. Lasers. It was the same technology Ken Lulu had used to project the Arabic words onto Constitution Hall. Except this time, instead of words, each little light made the shape of a distinct bird. Many of the birds found in Philadelphia were there. A pair of large sandpipers, different types of rails, as well as gulls, warblers, meadowlarks, thrushes, woodpeckers, crows, sparrows, terns, and ducks. They were depicted hopping around on the tree, a little artificially created avian society. I stopped and joined the admiring audience. One of the men standing there told me it was a new urban arts program that the city had started.

I arrived at Ali's doorstep drenched in sweat. I gazed up at the sky, the clouds reformulating above. I sat on the steps and put my hands on the cement. A sense of connubial stasis passed between me and the city. I gently caressed the cement, trying to locate in its lines and patterns the faces of all the people I knew. The people I loved and the ones I sought escape from.

Suddenly I felt a warm hand reach out for my shoulder.

I turned abruptly, about to push the agent, when I realized that the person facing me was Candace.

She was in a tracksuit, with a big blue jacket, a black scarf tied around her head, and a jeweled pin in an eyebrow. She had her hands on her hips, giving support to her back.

"You should stay south of Girard," she said.

I reached for her, something between a kiss and an embrace. I got neither. She backed away and pulled at my arm to grapple with my turgid hand. "Where have you b-been?" I stuttered. "I looked so hard."

"You looked? Or you sent someone?"

I stared at her with all the bereavement I could muster. "What was I supposed to do?"

A man's voice came from behind me: "Hey, glory hole passing for a human, I'll tell you what to do. Leave my wife alone, stop wandering around these parts, and go back to your hairy, thin-skinned leper."

It was Ali Ansari. He was dressed in his favorite coat, but instead of slacks he wore jeans folded up to show his ankles. He had added a beige skullcap and black plastic frames. An Islamic rosary was in his fist. His scruff had become a beard. His eyes had the rotating intensity of camera lenses. The ring he had dropped at the deli was on his left hand.

It all made sense. Ali's abandonment of Talibang could have only occurred through Candace's guidance. Her disappearance could have only taken place through his complicity. Their courtship must have been a conspiracy they carried out against me. Sheikh Shakil must have been the officiant at a wedding held at Masjid ud-Dukhan. The meeting at the deli must have been Ali's way of getting me out of Candace's life. She must have been the person who picked him up. In a way, it was all very inevitable. People like Ali Ansari and Candace always found each other, even if they were temporarily distracted by technocrats like myself.

I focused on Candace's belly. She was just about the size that it was conceivable the pregnancy could have been my doing. I would have given anything to peer into the amniotic sac to find out if that was my progeny, conceived in this soil, to be born in this soil, to be raised as a future master of this soil.

Without thinking, I reached for Candace's stomach. If only I could touch the womb, I might be able to sense the identity of the father. It would be like in the films, when the journeymen reach the orb and it lights up only for the rightful recipient of the magical power. My hands opened, my fingers throbbed, my eyes widened.

But I was not able to touch. Not even to get near. Ali Ansari got in my way. He punched me in the mouth and split my lip. I looked at him with my hand to my mouth, as if I would yank at his beard, snatch at his skullcap, break his rosary. But in the end I had to watch the two of them leave together, arms around each other's waists, taking their family into their home.

Left alone in the street, I ran to the nearest gas station and stemmed my blood. There were no paper towels and I had to use my undershirt. I came out to Broad Street near the law school and hailed the first cab headed toward the art museum.

At home, having patched up my wound a little, I jumped on the Internet. I researched every method for how I could determine the identity of Candace's baby. It didn't take long to realize that all of the legal methods of determining the child's paternity were closed. Once Ali and Candace got married, the law made a presumption that he was the child's father. I read something about assertions and rebuttable presumptions by another party, but that seemed like the kind of bureaucratic mess that I couldn't carry out without Marie-Anne's knowledge. It was also likely to be very expensive. There were the personal methods, obviously, like go-

ing to the hospital when the child was born and somehow getting away
with a piece of the child's DNA. Or I could send an infiltrator. Maybe
someone like Leila. The other possibility involved bribing someone to
get into the medical records at the Children's Hospital of Philadelphia.
There were darker options too, those involving intimidation or black-
mail. Options that might prompt a direct confession. None of those were
things I had much familiarity with.

With the permutations and schemes dying out from lack of possibility, I went over to the window and peered outside, toward North Philly.
It mustered nothing more than a glow. No grandiose homes, no fountains spouting silver, no stepping-stones to the stars. Just fungal pools
and unctuous hovels. Just stripped sedans and broken vacuum cleaners.
A depression sloping toward an abyss. But to me it was a treasure chest.
A jar of wine. A skein of water. A womb. I saw the indistinct face of an
heir, an inheritor, a vice-regent fluttering somewhere past Girard College.
Out of my grasp. Beyond my reach.

It was Ali Ansari who had taken that from me.

With a hard yank I shut the blinds. They jammed at an angle and
sliced at my wrist.

CHAPTER ELEVEN

M arie-Anne returned three days later. My torn lip had healed. She came out of customs in a state of euphoria. The cause of joy was a commission check worth twenty thousand dollars delivered to her from MimirCo in Doha. It had wiped away the memory of the Al Jazeera fiasco. She put it in her palm and slid it toward the ceiling of the cab. It floated into my lap. The question of how we would use the money was foremost on her mind. She asked me what I thought about using for the down payment on the condo. On top of what she brought home, I had eight thousand saved up. I told her I was ready to make that call.

"We are really doing it, aren't we?" she said. "Faster than we ever expected. I mean, wasn't it just last year that we were worried what we were going to do after you lost your job?"

Marie-Anne's cheerfulness increased as we arrived home. The guys from maintenance had come into the apartment while we'd been out. Marie-Anne had secretly purchased the cast-iron stove that I had coveted and gotten it installed while I'd been at the airport. We stood next to each other, staring at the stove's reflective surface.

"I think we should have a party."

"Shouldn't we celebrate on our own?"

"We owe our success to a lot of people," she replied. "We should take a moment to thank them."

"Fine then," I said. "But this time you do the preparations."

Marie-Anne took to the hosting like she was planning a wedding. She created an online document and worked her way through the checklist. She had the ability to maintain sustained concentration even toward minutiae. I, on the other hand, required epic or grand aims in order to produce that kind of focus. The difference between us was one of vision. She had a preexisting conception of what she wanted to accomplish, presumably learned from her mother's lifetime of socialization, whereas my organization always had something of the artificial to it. I imitated things I had seen in magazines or in films. I developed the nagging suspicion that had she been the one to organize the party for Plutus, she wouldn't have made the mistake of leaving out items that might prove controversial. My only request this time was that the wine had to be Cheval Blanc. All the great years.

Early the next morning Marie-Anne and I decided to go for a walk toward Manayunk. The river was empty and frozen. The municipal department hadn't yet sifted the snow off the pavement and we had to trudge along holding each other's hand. It was heavy going and we barely made it to Boathouse Row. With a little more gumption we pressed on, toward the underpass bridge. We were surprised to find the area populated by a group of homeless men. They had brought the numerous trash cans from the park to one place and lit them all. Most of the cans had died but a couple were still going strong. Their faces glowed red from the fire. We ignored them and moved ahead into a clearing where some earlier adventurer had swept the snow off a bench facing the river.

"I still can't believe you were on TV."

"Too bad it went so terribly."

"I liked it," I said. "Except the bit at the end. Where you called people hairy, thin-skinned lepers."

"You heard that?"

"Your microphone was on."

She sighed, pulled me under a tree, and made me look at her. In the middle of the park she opened up her jacket and unbuttoned her shirt and turned her naked torso to me, presenting the streaks of purple on her chest, the cat scratches of illness on her belly, the excessive hair all over.

"Take a long look at yourself, then take a long look at me, and tell me who is the hairy, thin-skinned leper."

Tears filled my eyes. I should have known her muttering was directed at herself; I should have known she was berating her body like she always did. She cried too. The last time we had both cried together was even before we had stopped sleeping together. It was the night we had come back from the doctor the first time. Except then she and I held each other and cried as one, in bed, putting our lips like bandages upon each other's eyelids. Now we were more than a foot apart, the blood from the eyes staining our faces, using the back of our hands to smear our skin.

I reached out and touched Marie-Anne's hand. It was shaking in the cold. I buttoned up her jacket and tied her scarf around her head.

That whole day we held each other. There was nothing more to it than the reestablishment of tactility, touch. We didn't say a word. The aim was only to show Marie-Anne that she hadn't been shunted from the territory of the healthy. That even if the rest of the world found her a sad hog of a woman, I wouldn't treat her like that. I had the past on my side. I had seen her as she had been before the transformation. If she sometimes forgot what she had been, I would be right there to remind her, to make rhyming verbal remembrances to be tucked away in her purse, her luggage.

Ever since she put on weight, became disfigured, she had started thinking of herself as a monster. This made her want to take revenge against all those who were able to remain beautiful—namely, all the petite and sprightly women who we came across. That was why Marie-

Anne had been so intent on her ownership fantasies. By being able to render the Candaces and the Leilas of the world subservient to her, by imaginarily feeding on their blood, by owning them in their most vulnerable posture, by crushing them under her bigness, Marie-Anne had been able to destroy some of their beauty. And because I hadn't known better, rather than putting a stop to it all, I had encouraged it, had actively participated in the vampirism.

"Who do you think is the most beautiful person?" I asked Marie-Anne after a snack of hazelnut spread and bread.

"In the world?"

"Yes, objectively."

"I don't know. You tell me."

"I hate to say it," I replied. "But I think it's your mother. I never saw a more beautiful woman in my life."

"She always was. Is it wrong to say that sometimes I miss her just because I feel like I am denied being able to look at her?"

"We can't help what we find beautiful," I said and stroked Marie-Anne's rounded-moon face.

I guided her to the living room and we slid down to the carpet, leaning against the sofa. I searched for the film with Isabelle Adjani and found it after a moment. I took it out of the case and slid it in. I didn't show Marie-Anne the inside of the cover where her father's inscription was written. I simply let the film get started. She watched with great curiosity in her eyes.

The opening scene showed Adjani arriving in Halifax by boat, in pursuit of the man who she loved, for whom she would eventually suffer madness. As the atmospheric darkness from the film washed over, both Marie-Anne and I became somber, our laughter bowing out from the room. I kept staring at Marie-Anne's face, to gauge it for reaction, to be astonished by the way she was mesmerized. She was aware that she was quite drunk, so she was a little skeptical of what she was seeing.

"Is that . . . ?" she pointed. "Who is that?"

"That is Isabelle Adjani."

"It's not my mom?"

"No," I said. "It's Isabelle Adjani."

Her big, lightly rippling eyes went soft. Deep inside it seemed like there was a pile of petals in them. "That's definitely the most beautiful person in the world."

We watched the film together with a kind of college-era intimacy, drifting away from the scenes to kiss, touch, fondle, and grope each other. We remembered the film again and tried to seem informed about everything from Victor Hugo to *Les Mis* to Napoleon, only to realize we had no idea what was happening on screen. But somehow we kept blubbering to each other, a man and a woman after so long getting to be a boy and a girl.

A little while later Marie-Anne decided she didn't want to watch any more. Her arms shook from the effort required to stand, but with some help from me she was able to get up. She took a deep breath and gathered herself and then, with an invitational finger, told me to follow her to the bedroom.

Inside she started to undo her clothes a little and asked me to tell her where she would meet Isabelle Adjani. She was ready, as always, to turn me into her ideal self.

"You won't meet her," I replied.

"I won't?"

"No," I said. "You will become her."

"Me?"

"Yes," I said. "And I will be with her."

"But why?"

"Because you've forgotten what it feels like to be beautiful. Maybe by immersion you can remember."

She said she was scared. I told her not to be. And so that day when

I took off Marie-Anne's clothes she wasn't aghast by her body because she was Adjani and flawless. And when I kissed her softly she wasn't ashamed to kiss back because she was Adjani and sensual. And when she yielded her being to me she wasn't afraid because she was Adjani and there was nothing to fear. We weren't the first people in the world to beat back the tyrannies of disease by imagining ourselves as more beautiful than we were, and we wouldn't be the last.

That night we went to Bishop's Collar for a drink. I remembered to take the multicolored pen to give back to the rude bartender. Before turning away I informed him that the woman he had mistaken for my mother was actually my wife. The bartender was so surprised by my statement that he straightened up and extended his hand. "I never caught your name."

"They call me M."

"Just M.?"

"Yeah."

"What does it stand for?"

"Whatever you want," I said. "M. is for man. M. is for menace. M. could be my name. M. is for madness. M. starts the name of my wife."

The bartender grumbled, crinkled his noise, and took to attending other patrons.

When I came back Marie-Anne wore a smile. She held my stool as I jumped on it, my feet dangling.

"You're so good to me."

"I don't know what you mean."

"You seem to think that when you walk a few feet away from me I can't hear you anymore. But I'm like a bird. I see and hear everything you do." She raised her chin in the bartender's direction.

After two Long Island iced teas each, which Marie-Anne pointed out was reminiscent of our honeymoon, we teetered our way home. It was hard to remember, in our mind-altered state, exactly what path we took back, whether up Pennsylvania, or through the alley next to Figs restaurant. But I remembered clearly what happened when we got inside.

Marie-Anne kept hold of my arm and took me to the bathroom. She had me sit down on the edge of the tub and lifted up the toilet seat. With a nervous nod she walked toward the medicine cabinet and took out the bottles of vitamins that had, at last, ended up in their appropriate place. She unscrewed their tops and one by one started plunking the pills into the toilet. Every time I asked why she was throwing perfectly good vitamins away, she shushed me and returned to the project.

Once finished with the bottle she opened the cover of the toilet and pulled out two more bottles that she had hidden, dumping the contents away with each hand, a fistful at a time. With a deep breath she sat down on the toilet seat and turned my way.

"Those aren't vitamins. They are steroid pills. I've been artificially spiking my cortisol levels."

"I don't understand."

The condition Marie-Anne actually had was called Munchausen syndrome, something she had been carrying around since she was a child. It caused her to fake injuries and illnesses in order to garner sympathy. It wasn't genetic, it was psychiatric. Often the victim of Munchausen became extremely adept at mimicking the most far-fetched of diseases. This was the case with Marie-Anne and the cortisol imbalance. She had engineered it. All of it. The hirsuitism; the painful periods; the weight gain.

"It started when I was five," she sobbed. "I went to the bathroom and cut myself. I remember it was with my Minnie Mouse scissors. That was how I got my mom's attention. When I was injured was the only time she would really talk to me kindly. You know how kids are. I just kept doing it. Anytime she was mad, anytime she was busy with her friends, anytime she made up new rules, I gave myself something. A cut. A fall. A twist of the ankle. I even let a boy slap me once so I could go home with a bloody lip. By college I figured out I had a problem. The counselors put me in therapy. My way of controlling it was by writing stories. Something therapeutic about making up other things besides illness. That's when I met you. That's why I turned to you—because you encouraged me to write. My mom wasn't enough to make me stop from hurting myself. Only you were."

I reached out for her. "But you relapsed. You relapsed hard. Why?"

"I relapsed when I found out I couldn't have children. Three years ago. I went to the doctor and learned I was broken. *Inexplicable infertility,* they called it. I should have told you. I should have let you hate me. I should have let you leave me. Instead I manipulated you for love. For pity."

She was a crying mess. I stood up and gathered her. The shower curtain got pulled into the embrace. We stayed silent for a long time. The drops of the water ran down the curtain and onto the floor by way of the bones of our feet.

My mind reeled at the vicious circularity of it all. The vitamins to conceal the cortisol. The Munchausen to conceal the infertility. One lie built on another, an orchestra of dissimulation. The world regarded me and saw a practitioner of subterfuge. In fact, it was my wife who was dormant, latent, mysterious. All my opportunities to abscond were gone. All the opportunities to create a new life were gone.

Marie-Anne was the one to whom I belonged and to whom I returned.

The party was to be held at Figs. The small restaurant tucked into Meredith Street on the other side of the art museum annex. We rented out an entire section. Marie-Anne wanted take over the whole establishment, but the hostess insisted on keeping a few tables open for walk-in customers.

The day of the party came quickly. Marie-Anne had charted the weather well in advance and picked an exquisite day. Not a cloud in the sky. Moderate temperatures and, because she had paid the security guards to serve as valets, there were no parking troubles. But at the last moment, heavy clouds moved in and a steady snow started accumulating.

Marie-Anne wore tan leggings with a beige dress and a sapphire rope necklace with a matching bracelet around her left wrist. I remembered the necklace. We had bought it a few years ago, but she had never worn it before because she'd been afraid it would get damaged or lost. Now she was more confident about our earning potential.

Saqib and Leila and The Ism were the first to arrive. Leila brought two other activist friends with whom she was launching a feminist think tank. They wore designer hats and red-soled boots.

Mahmoud was not far behind them. He wore a brown skullcap with a flag pin on the side. He came alone, gave me a big hug, and slipped my retention letter in my pocket. I patted it and smiled. The rest of the evening we made conspiratorial faces at each other, waiting for the best moment to surprise Marie-Anne with the news.

Marie-Anne's teammates were next in. Mike Wu and P.P. Sharma needled each other about finally getting into Marie-Anne's "private places," and Amos Jones came with a redheaded girlfriend who seemed to know of Marie-Anne from the stories Amos had shared. Karsten King, the former marine, was next with his wife, Rebecca, an adjunct professor who traveled through Muslim countries to report on the mistreatment of women under Islamic law. She'd come down from Boston where she was teaching a university course called "Giving Voice to the Voiceless." She joked that if Karsten taught a course it would be called "Giving Eyes to the Eyeless." He replied that his course would be called "Giving Spine to the Spineless." Marie-Anne said she didn't care what it was called as long as it ended with, "Giving Bonuses to the Bonusless."

I studied the room. The laughter tended to rise and fall in a collective manner, a democratic din, two cups of rice boiling permanently in an open pot, always a stew, never a spill. It struck me how revealing the little gathering was. In this get-together one could find both the handshake and the fist of American dominance. The convex and the concave. The pulley and the winch. The wine and the iron. The American eagle gave love as it took life, it smiled as it drove the stake, it invoked law as it invaded, it screamed "We are humane!" as it muffled the cries of the murdered with bombs. Sajjad and Leila and Mahmoud and Rebecca King and I had one role: to soften and to cajole, to claim friendship and give out gifts. Marie-Anne and Mike Wu and P.P. Sharma and Amos Jones and Karsten King had another role: to flatten and to crush, to accuse and give out death. It was the beautiful symmetry of a system that aimed at nothing less than permanence.

Were I another kind of man, a man who had cultivated freedom in his soul instead of all the dandyism of the early twenty-first century, I might have recognized the things I was feeling and swept my hand all around me and found there lurking, in ghostly proximity, the souls of all those who wanted revenge, who wanted apology, who wanted acknowledgment, and extended them my assistance, possibly smuggled them into the empire and let them let loose their own songs of war. Perhaps their elegiac meditations could help me utter a single phrase of rebuke: *I am aware of what is happening and I do not accept it.* But that man, the one against the empire, I was not. I was a man of the empire. Wasn't that how Ali Ansari had defined me? This man, when enervated, when given a spoonful of consciousness, didn't rise up from the bed with a fist in the air, trying to be Spartacus for the victims. He was a master, instead, of self-deception. Every heightening of his conscience, every little burst of revolt, he only knew how to interpret as a sort of misanthropy, as a sort of mistake. When all the prayers of the violated gathered in him, rather than say anything in their favor, he kept silent. It was the civilized thing to do.

The waiter brought me a glass of Cheval Blanc. I stood apart from everyone in a corner of the room, taking drink after drink, sloshing the wine. I needed to tear through multiple bottles, to prove that the ownership was real, to believe in my ascension.

Suddenly my eyes turned to the general dining area. On a solitary table with a pink rose centerpiece sat a singular man hunched forward, popping nuts into his mouth. I didn't have to stare very hard to recognize him. It was George Gabriel.

I immediately slunk behind a nearby pillar. Marie-Anne passed by and paused to see what I was looking at. I took her hand.

"What's he doing here?"

"I invited him," she said.

"You should have cleared it with me."

"No. Let him see how great we're doing."

There was a chandelier right above him. George was reflected in every piece of glass. A thousand little versions of him. Just sitting there. Now drinking wine. Now fixing his tie. Now wiping his face with a napkin. I took a glance at Marie-Anne and then walked over to him.

"Hello, George," I said, putting my glass down near his hand, confining him a little.

"Hello there." He glanced up without a hint of surprise, as if he had known I'd had him under surveillance. "And hello to you, Marie-Anne."

"Hi, George," she whispered. "How is everything?"

"Everything is as it should be," he said. "Dinesh couldn't make it. And my wife is out of the country. I'm here by myself."

"Why don't you come over where the rest of us are?" I found myself saying.

"You're over there?" He leaned to check out our side of the restaurant. "I thought it would just be us. That's what I thought."

"Just some friends. People from DC and Virginia. Some of the younger ones are from my new venture."

"That is good. That is good." George nodded, then stood up and adjusted his blazer, dropping a couple of twenty-dollar bills for his check. "I appreciate it. I appreciate the invite. It isn't what I expected."

Rather than asking me a follow-up, George turned toward Marie-Anne. "You are still working with MimirCo? I read about their activities recently. I remembered your relation to them from your party."

She blushed and wavered a little. "That's right."

George lifted up his right hand and, using his middle finger extended fully and index finger bent in half, pointed at me. "I never thought you would approve of criminality."

"I'm sorry? What criminality?"

"War crimes," he said. "The angel-of-death game that MimirCo plays. It is outside the scope of international law. Is that what you are here to celebrate?"

"We are celebrating," I said, "but not what you are suggesting. We are celebrating having the means to buy our apartment. The same place where you disrespected us before."

"I'm glad," he said. "But how will you live in a house paid for by the blood of the innocent?"

I raised my voice. "It isn't like that."

Marie-Anne put a steadying hand on my arm. But the sound of my voice was such that some of our friends in the other room heard it and came over, standing behind us now, forming a protective circle, turning their judgmental eyes in George Gabriel's direction. They didn't need to know who he was. As long as he aroused enmity in us, they considered him presumptively diseased.

I drew comfort from the circumference. One by one I introduced each of my friends. Name, title, status. Name, title, status. Name, title, status.

They came forward and took George Gabriel's hand. He gave a nervous laugh and glanced toward the exit. I turned to Marie-Anne. She had plotted this moment. She had set him up for his demise and made certain I would be there to witness it. When George Gabriel's authority and moral certitude would be defeated. When his wing-wide shoulders would break. When he would crumple to the ground in a clatter of spine. It was the reward she had set up for me for my loyalty.

I drew closer. My body glowed like the executioner's knife. When there was nothing left I would put my hand on the small of his back and lead him to the exit, and on the way I would tell him that if he ever wanted to advance in Plutus, like his predecessor Tony Blanchard had, he should feel free to give me a call and I would hook him up with contracts in the Imperial City.

But I didn't get to balance the equation of life with my vengeance.

Once George Gabriel finished greeting everyone he looked upon us as if we were a collective, a herd of gazelles merged into one another, his gaze a swift-moving cloud passing over us. His voice tore like a storm: "American jihadists. You're all American jihadists."

With that pronouncement he buttoned his blazer, turned on a heel, and made his way toward the exit. He flipped the curtain and disappeared from sight, the beads clattering against each other.

The scene George Gabriel left behind wasn't exactly one of devastation. Most of the group was far too polished, far too experienced with the varieties of human opinion, to take George Gabriel's evaluation as worthy of irritation. Mahmoud quickly made a comment about the blinkered worldview of certain secular humanists. Their inability to see that without the revitalizing work that the clash of civilizations represented, Western culture would make a fatalistic turn toward immolation, unable to shed from its bodice the fat of decadence and cowardice. He offered the example of the Ottoman Empire. The songs of their civilization were sung with the mouths of their muskets. But when the mystically inclined among them convinced those in power that it wasn't geographic expansion but the pursuit of spiritual health that defined superiority, they took a fatal turn toward their demise. Karsten King agreed with

270 * Native Believer

Mahmoud and they quickly raised their glasses to toast all the worms, urchins, sloths, squids, bugs, and other spineless creatures with whom people like George Gabriel deserved to live. Laughter released the tension. The party returned to its earlier equilibrium. Marie-Anne released my arm and went back to drink. She was content with making him run. It was sufficient for her that he had been revealed to be a coward.

Every part of me wanted to follow Marie-Anne back to the party and to indulge in the mockery that came so easily to them. But I couldn't let go of the edict George Gabriel had passed. How dare he think himself capable of telling me who or what I was. Had I not expanded since the last time I met him? Perhaps the first time he'd passed judgment on me I had no defense—because those condemned to Islam can't really stand up for themselves—but this time around it wasn't Islam that George had insulted. It was my Americanism. This thing couldn't be touched. It was incomparable. It occupied a metaphysically exalted position, not afforded to any other concept in the world. Once you were American—truly, fully—you got to throw around yourself the cloak of perfect rationality, drape yourself in the colors of universalism, surround yourself with certitude. Once you became American, anyone who diminished America was presumptively wrong, presumptively wicked, presumptively lesser. I couldn't have punched George Gabriel in the mouth for insulting Islam, because people would have called me a savage, declared me a terrorist. But if I scalped him, if I tore George Gabriel's skin for insulting the honor of America, the onus would be upon him to show why he had provoked the master; he would be the one who would have to prove that he wasn't an apostate. The revelation coursed through me as if I'd been embraced by a president who had come down from the pantheon that originated in Philadelphia.

I picked up a poker from the fireplace, its handle embossed with the name of the restaurant and its head marked with a sharpened cross, and I ran after George Gabriel. There he was, under the smoky halogen lamps in the forgettable night, a shuffling monster, casting three shadows simultaneously, one of which walked upright and moved forward toward the river, while the other two lengthened and shortened, lengthened and shortened. Snowflakes tried to land upon him and failed.

I followed him until he was on the pedestrian bridge on Spring Garden Street, the river a frozen battle underneath, the cars like cracking whips on I-76, the sky caving upon us. I said nothing when I drove the fire poker through him. Two-handed, with torque and twist. The human body is pierced by iron almost as easily as by words. George Gabriel's mouth opened in a screamless scream. I took him into my arms and put my lips over his lips and let his words dribble into my mouth. Then I let him fall into the Schuylkill, wounded, and sent the poker with him. Down went the gnarled knight of derision. Never again to rise. Never to stand as an impediment in the expansion of this man known as M.

The authorities did not doubt me when I told them what Ali Ansari had done. Not after they saw the video I showed them.

After a while, even Candace believed me.

Acknowledgments

The author would like to thank the following people, in precise order of their significance in the author's life, for their support and love. This list, based on social media interactions, e-mail metadata, phone metadata, and personal interaction with the author, should be considered the definitive ranking of everyone in the author's life.

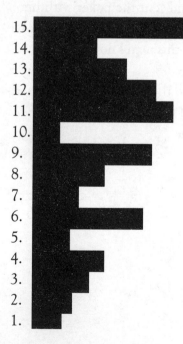

[Portions denied are S-FRD and thus outside of ISCAP jurisdiction.]